ABOUT THE BOOK

From the Amazon and Barnes & Noble Bestselling Author of the Coast Guard RECON Series

While in Italy for a forensic accounting project, Madison Montgomery discovers she is being followed through the streets of Florence by a Russian who seems to have ties with the local Polizia. But why is he following her? Absolutely nothing is making sense to Monty, other than she is scared to death.

Executive protection expert, Jacob Boxer, is in Florence when one of Callahan Security's biggest clients, Jameson Drake, calls in a favor. His lead accountant is in trouble and needs protection. Unfortunately, no one seems sure from who or what. When he gets to know Madison, Jake loses the fight to hold fast to the cardinal rule of personal security: never bed the client. While their pleasure-filled night was worth breaking the rules for, Madison's situation goes from bad to worse when they learn not only does someone want to frame her for theft, they want her dead.

Being on the wrong side of both the Russian and Italian mafias could be a death sentence. On the run through Tuscany and the streets of Florence, every turn takes Monty and Jake farther from safety and closer to disaster.

Catch and Release
Copyright © 2022 Lori Matthews
eBook License Notes:

You may not use, reproduce or transmit in any manner, any part of this book without written permission, except in the case of brief quotations used in critical articles and reviews, or in accordance with federal Fair Use laws. All rights are reserved.

This eBook is licensed for your personal enjoyment only; it may not be resold or given away to other people. If you would like to share this book with another person, please purchase an additional copy for each recipient. If you're reading this book and did not purchase it, or it was not purchased for your use only, please return to your eBook retailer and purchase your own copy. Thank you for respecting the hard work of this author.

Disclaimer: This is a work of fiction. Names, characters, places, and incidents are products of the author's imagination, or the author has used them fictitiously.

*This one is for Stacey and Kimberley.
Thanks for always listening.*

ACKNOWLEDGMENTS

Once again, I couldn't have written this book without the help of my whole community. I would be lost without them. My deepest gratitude goes out to my editors, Corinne DeMaagd and Heidi Senesac. They are truly amazing and make me look so much better than I am. Thanks also goes out to my cover artist, Llewellen Designs for making my story come alive: my Facebook guru, Amanda Robinson, my Review Crew who are kind enough to post reviews for my books, my beta reader, Jenn Herman. Big hugs to my personal cheer squad which I could not survive without: Janna MacGregor, Suzanne Burke, Stacey Wilk, Kimberley Ash and Tiara Inserto. My husband and my children who make my hair turn gray but also make me laugh. And to you, the reader. Your emails and posts mean the world to me. The fact that you read my stories is the greatest gift ever. Thank you.

CHAPTER ONE

Madison Montgomery stopped and pressed herself flat against the stone wall. She listened, but the footsteps stopped as well. She waited. Nothing. The sound of far-off traffic reached her ears, but she could barely hear it over her own harsh breathing. Maybe she was imagining things. Who would follow her? She shouldered her bag and crossed a narrow cobblestone street from one lane to the next.

The sun was just setting, but it was dark in the lane. The old Florentine buildings blocked the light so effectively she was having trouble seeing. She moved as quickly as she dared but running on cobblestones in high-heeled boots was not something she wanted to try unless absolutely necessary.

The darkness got thicker the deeper she moved into the small lane. Was that the sound of footsteps again?

Not for the first time, she regretted taking this assignment from Jameson Drake. If she'd just said no, she could have been back in her cozy New York apartment on the Upper West Side. But she wasn't good at saying no, at least not to Drake.

A pebble rolled along the street, but she hadn't kicked anything. She stopped again. The person following her wasn't as quick this time, and a few more steps echoed off the buildings before silence fell. There was only another twenty feet before she rounded the corner into an even narrower lane that the smallest cars couldn't go down. She didn't have a choice. She couldn't go back. She went forward and turned onto the tiny lane. Screw it. She broke out into a run. Her shoulder bag banged against her as her boots clomped over the cobblestones. She raced down the lane, fear chasing her every step.

She burst from the lane into the piazza, startling a few passersby so she immediately resumed a more sedate pace. She kept her head down and stood close to a large group of tourists that were gathered in the piazza. They were taking pictures and listening to a guide who held a white flag with an *Adventure Travel* logo.

Glancing back over her shoulder, Madison glimpsed a man emerging from the lane she had just exited. She left the tour group and quickly joined a queue of customers waiting outside one of the restaurants. Hiding behind a group of American tourists, she watched as the man searched the square for her. He was tall, over six feet, and lean. His face was pockmarked, and he looked to be in his late forties. Russian or Ukrainian or possibly some other former Eastern Bloc country. Probably Russian. He just had that look.

Why the hell would some Russian be following her? She moved forward with the crowd. They were only two groups away from the seating hostess. The smell of tomato sauce and cheese wafted over. Her stomach churned. If the guy didn't move soon, he would see her when she didn't enter the restaurant. Madison bit her lip and watched as the man moved toward the middle of the square. Once there, he turned in a slow circle.

She stepped behind the group so they were between her and the man. She waited, minutes ticking by. When the line moved, she hazarded a quick glance. The man was gone. Madison peered around the square. Where did he go? In the far corner of the piazza, he was just disappearing down another narrow lane.

Madison's shoulders sagged in relief. She stepped around the Americans and hurried along the perimeter of the square until she came to another street. This one was bigger and two over from the smaller lane the Russian had gone down.

She kept pace with the crowd, shuffling along with another group of tourists, this group Asian. Luckily, she had dark hair and blended with the rest of them. It was only a five-minute walk to her place from here, but she didn't want to increase her pace and stick out in any way. A shiver danced across her skin. She wanted to go home. Back to the relative safety of New York. No one ever followed her *there*.

Florence had seemed like just what she had needed to get her out of her funk. She normally loved to travel with her job but, lately, it was all getting on her nerves. Florence, however, was one of her favorite cities, and who didn't like pasta?

When Drake had asked her to take the assignment, she'd accepted. Getting the opportunity to have an up-close look at the account logs of a fashion company was good for her, since her ultimate goal was to get into the fashion business herself.

Madison loved numbers, and forensic accounting was usually so interesting. She liked the investigative edge it brought to regular accounting. Doing it in the fashion world in Italy seemed like a dream come true. Now it was just a nightmare.

She needed to call Drake and tell him of her suspicions. But what did she suspect? She wasn't sure. Madison shook her head. She knew the spreadsheets looked good. Too good maybe? The numbers just didn't feel right, and she trusted her instincts. They hadn't let her down yet.

She turned the last corner onto her street and came to an abrupt halt. The Russian was standing in front of her Airbnb, talking to Mrs. Rover, the British woman who looked after the building. She spun around and went back around the corner. Leaning on the adjacent building, she struggled to pull oxygen into her lungs. What the hell was going on?

She adjusted her bag one more time, from one shoulder to the other, wondering why it felt so heavy. She had her laptop and her wallet and keys, but she always carried that stuff. The clutch. The damned clutch purse that Giovanni had given her. It wasn't even her taste. It was black with rhinestones and huge rivets. Not her style at all. It was also frickin' heavy. She'd planned on giving it back to him first thing in the morning. Now she wondered if she'd get the chance.

She peeked back around the corner. The Russian was still speaking with her landlady, only now the *Polizia* were beside him. The officer said something, and the Russian pointed. Then he turned and pointed to another officer that was back by the car. While the man was nearly facing her direction, she pulled out her phone and opened her camera. As he gestured for him to follow the other officer into her building, she snapped a picture. The Russian was a cop?

She watched as the cops entered her building. They must be going to search her apartment, but why? What were they looking for? What could they possibly want from her?

She eased back around the corner and leaned against the wall. She should just walk over there and ask what was going on. That was what a reasonable person would do, and she had always considered herself reasonable above all else. But she was in a foreign country, and she didn't speak the language. Worse yet, she was unfamiliar with the legal system in Italy. Did she have the same rights as she would at home?

She ran a shaky hand through her shoulder-length hair. This was all so surreal. She closed the camera app and started to make a call, but then stopped. Should she really call Drake? He'd helped her so much already. She didn't want him to think she couldn't take care of herself.

Then another thought hit her. Could the people after her be tracking her? She half-choked on a laugh. If they *were* tracking her, she wouldn't still be standing a few hundred feet down the street from the people that wanted to speak to her. She touched the screen on her phone as she turned and walked away from her street. She put the phone to her ear and said a silent prayer.

She had the distinct feeling she was going to need all the help she could get.

CHAPTER TWO

Jacob Boxer threw his blazer across the back of the chair, dropped his cell on the coffee table, and sat down on the nearby couch. It had been a long day of trying to remain calm while his asshole client ignored or challenged everything he'd said. Just once, he would like to have an easy client. One that didn't think they knew better than he did. At least he finished the job without hitting anyone, including the joker who'd hired him. He deserved a medal and maybe a raise or a better job. Jake frowned. There was no better job, at least not for him. This is what he knew how to do, this and nothing else.

He kicked off his shoes. After unbuttoning his left sleeve, he started rolling it up. He noticed a small coffee stain on the cuff. Suits weren't his thing, but he wore them to work. In the beginning, he'd found that hard, but now he was used to it and actually enjoyed owning some good quality suits. He must look good in them if the admiring glances he got from women were anything to go by, but the dry-cleaning bills were steep, and sometimes he longed for the days when he'd worn a khaki T-shirt and camouflage cargo pants as his daily uniform.

He yawned. He wanted to jump in the shower and then crash for the next twelve hours, but he hadn't eaten since breakfast, and it was almost nine. He'd ordered right after returning to his suite and the hotel kitchen had promised to send him up some food pronto.

He finished the first sleeve and started on the second. He didn't want to miss the room service guy, and there was no way he'd be comfortable with someone entering the room while he was in the shower. It didn't matter that this hotel was one of Jameson Drake's finest. Jake was not going to be unarmed and undressed with strangers in the room. Call it a holdover from his days in the military, but being vulnerable was not something he would ever do willingly.

He leaned back into the couch cushions and put his feet up on the coffee table. He grabbed his cell again and scrolled quickly through his emails. Nothing pressing from work. One from his mom. He hesitated, trying to decide if he was up to opening it. It was going to be some sad tale about why they needed more money. He loved his family but not one of them could manage their funds. His dad had worked in a manufacturing plant for years making metal brackets but finally his body gave up on him and the disability check somehow always fell short.

It wasn't their fault really. It was just…draining and not just financially. They had never wanted much in life and they were content with what they had for the most part. They just didn't understand why he wanted more. Why couldn't he go work at any of the factories in town like his brother? Why did he have to join the Navy? Once he got out of the SEALs, it was the same old song and dance. *Why not get a job at the factory like your brother and your cousins?* His parents loved him. They just never understood him. They didn't like that he was doing something different but they sure liked the money it brought in.

That wasn't really fair. They didn't ask for a lot, but what galled him was the money he sent monthly to them they gave to his brother and then they were short. That pissed him off to no end. His brother was young and had choices. He could choose a different job or career path. Hell, he could just work hard and ask to get promoted but he refused. He liked his job as a welder. It didn't require much and he left when his shift was over. Even that would be okay if he just didn't spend a hell of a lot more than he made. He was always hitting up their parents so his mother would email *Jake* and make some excuse as to why they needed more money.

He put his cell back down on the table without bothering to read the email. He was just too damn tired to deal.

Closing his eyes, he took a deep breath and let it out. Bone weary, that's what he was. He hadn't had a vacation in years. Well, at least it seemed like years. He'd had a quick week off last year to see his family, but that was it and that wasn't restful. It had taken everything he had not to fight with his brother. He needed a month at the beach with sunshine and rum drinks. Preferably with some lovely female company as well.

Jake must have dozed off because he started and jumped to his feet, disoriented when his cell phone rang. He reached down and grabbed his cell. "Boxer," he snapped.

"Did I wake you?" asked his boss and best friend.

"Nah, I was just resting my eyes. I'm finished with Lancing. What a complete asshole."

Mitch Callahan chuckled. "Yeah, he's some piece of work, but his money is green and he's friends with a couple of our major clients, so we had to fit him in as a favor."

"Drake likes him? I find that surprising," Jake grunted as he sat back down and put his feet back on the coffee table. He leaned against the cushions once again.

"No. It's not Drake. He can't stand Lancing. Thinks the guy is a total moron. One of the other ones, Ramirez."

"The Brazilian guy?"

"Yeah. They're racing buddies. They race Porsche Cup cars together. Listen, you got anything planned for tonight?"

Jake swore silently. Mitch was about to give him another job, and all he wanted was to sleep. "I'm exhausted. I was just about to eat and then crash for a good twelve hours."

"Look, I know you've been working long hours, but Drake called and needs a favor."

Jake groaned. "Can't you call one of the other guys? Someone must be free. You just hired a new crew. They can't all be out on assignment."

"Actually, they are, but that's not why I'm calling you. One of his accountants is in some kind of—"

"Numbers aren't my thing, bro," Jake broke in.

Mitch laughed. "I know. Believe me, if it was an accounting problem, you'd be the last guy I'd call. No, looks like the accountant got involved in something, and now the cops want to speak with her, or at least she thinks—"

"I'm not a lawyer," Jake ground out. Mitch's numbers jab had hit a little too close to home. Jake hated working with numbers, but that didn't mean he couldn't do it. "I can't help with that."

"Let me finish. She called Drake and said some Russian-looking guy was following her. I guess she evaded him, but when she got back to her place, he was ordering the cops inside. He wasn't wearing a uniform, though, and she thought the whole thing was weird. She doesn't want to speak to anyone until she knows what's going on."

"Still sounds like she needs a lawyer."

"Maybe, but she snapped a picture of the guy and sent it to Drake. Drake sent it over. The guy following her *is* Russian, and he's not a cop. He's former Special Forces. GRU."

Jake dropped his feet off the table and sat up. "What is a former Russian military intelligence spec op guy doing following some accountant? What the hell is she working on for Drake?"

Mitch sighed. "He had her investigating the books of some fashion house he's thinking of investing in."

"What do the Russians have to do with it?"

"Nothing as far as we know. The guy is *former* GRU, so maybe he's freelance now."

"How can a freelance former GRU guy be ordering cops around on U.S. soil? In what world does that exist?" Jake demanded. "What the fuck?"

"Um, that's the reason I'm calling. The cops aren't American. She's in Florence. As a matter of fact, she's in the lobby of your hotel, waiting to meet with you."

CHAPTER THREE

Jake let out a string of curses. "Mitch, I'm exhausted. I need some downtime."

"I know, buddy. I get it. If there was anyone else close by, even a few hours by plane, I would call them, but no one else is available." He paused. "Drake says the woman is really freaked out."

"If a former GRU guy was after me, I'd be freaked out, too."

"She doesn't know that part. We're still running him through our systems. We should have a name and some background on him shortly."

"Then how do you know he's former GRU?"

"Dragan recognized him."

"Fuck." If he had crossed paths with Dragan, then the guy was a badass for sure. Dragan had done some wild shit in his day, and the men he had come up against were the scum of the earth. Jake gave a big sigh. "Fine, I'll meet with her." He stood up.

"Thanks. I owe you one."

"You do, Mitch. You really do."

"We need to talk when you get back to New York. There are some changes coming, and we need to discuss your…" Mitch paused, and

Jake heard muffled voices. Mitch came back to the call. "I'll reach out as I get details on the Russian," and then he was gone.

Changes. We need to discuss your… What? Job? Aspirations? Lack of respect for your boss? Jesus, way to leave a guy hanging. Jake's heartbeat ticked up and his gut knotted. This job was all he had. He needed a break, but he didn't mean a permanent one.

He sat down and put his shoes back on. No time to worry about that shit now. He stood up and grabbed his suit jacket. He hadn't taken his holster off, so he put the jacket on to cover his gun. Jake walked over to the hotel room door and opened it, almost crashing into the room service waiter. "Shit. Sorry," he mumbled as he moved back and held the door open for the waiter to bring in the cart.

"You ordered dinner, sir?" the waiter said in a thick Italian accent.

"Yes, sorry. Just leave it by the coffee table." Jake pointed to the seating area.

"Very good, sir. Do you want me to set it up for you?" The waiter wheeled the cart laden with silver trays inside the room.

As the waiter passed, the smells of dinner hit his nose. Jake's stomach growled, and he sighed again. He really wanted to eat. "No that's okay. I'll manage."

The waiter nodded, rolled the cart over next to the coffee table, and then returned with the bill. Jake signed it and left a nice tip.

"Thank you, sir. *Buona sera.*"

Jake nodded and then closed the door. He walked back over to the cart and lifted the lids. Steak with fries and a nice green salad. He had thought about pasta but he'd been eating too much of that in recent days.

The smell of the steak made his stomach growl again. He replaced the lids. If he started eating, he wouldn't stop. The scotch he ordered was there as well. He picked it up, peeled the plastic off the glass, and took a healthy gulp. He set it down again. Drinking on an empty stomach wasn't the best idea, but he wasn't letting good scotch go to waste. Jake turned and went back to the door. He opened it more cautiously this time and then left the room, making sure the door was locked behind him.

From his room, the elevator was diagonally across a good size mezzanine. The hotel was located on a hill on the outskirts of Florence. All the rooms were on the outside of the building to provide the best views of the park-like setting the hotel was situated in and the city of Florence below.

Jake was on the second floor so he passed the elevator and headed down the stairs. On the ground floor, he entered the foyer area by the elevators but saw no one. He turned to his right and walked into a larger central space. There were two businessmen at the registration desk, but no woman. He went into the last room, which was part of the dining area, but it was empty. He took a tour of the whole bottom floor, but nothing. Where the hell was this woman?

"Are you looking for me?" a voice said behind him.

He whirled around and stared. He wasn't sure what he'd been expecting, but she wasn't it. The woman was short, no more than five feet five inches in the high-heeled boots she was wearing. Her dark hair had a curl to it, and she had big, hazel eyes. She was wearing a black blazer over a white blouse and a black and white checked patterned skirt that ended above her knees. Her tall black boots came almost to the hem of the skirt. She clutched a large black bag hanging off her shoulder.

"You're Mr. Boxer, yes?" she asked tentatively.

"Ah, yes, I am." Mitch had told him she was an accountant, and Jake had assumed it was an older woman who looked, well, average. This woman was stunning and young. She stood, staring at him. He hesitated only a moment before he asked, "Sorry, where did you come from?"

She pointed to a wall. There was a barely distinguishable door there.

"Right." He was more tired than he thought. He'd missed it completely. "Let's go take a seat in the restaurant, and you can tell me what's going on." He led her toward the dining room and stopped at the hostess stand. Once the hostess assured him that sitting in the bar area was fine, they moved over to sit at a small table in the corner.

There was one chair with its back to the door and a bench seat on the other side of the table. No one was nearby so they wouldn't be overheard. He pulled out the chair for her, but she sat down on the bench seat. Jake blinked. He would not sit with his back to a doorway. Ever. So she was just going to have to wedge herself into the corner. She was a tiny thing so it shouldn't be hard.

Jake waited until she sat and at least appeared to be somewhat comfortable and then sat down beside her.

She turned and stared at him. "Why are you sitting here?"

"The same reason you are. I never sit where I can't see the entire room. If you want to move, go ahead. Otherwise, we're going to be cozy here together." He secured her gaze with his own. He wanted her to know he wasn't joking, but neither was he coming on to her. His gut tightened. There was real fear in her eyes. It ratcheted his protective instincts into overdrive.

Madison shook her head. "I'll stay here."

Jake just nodded. The waitress came by and asked about drinks. She was young with a wide smile and lots of teeth. It made him think of a shark. They both declined drinks and she went off in search of other prey.

"Okay then," he said, "let's start with your name."

"My name is Madison Montgomery. Most people call me Monty."

"Okay, Madison, tell me what exactly is going on."

She frowned at his use of her first name, but she'd have to get used to it. He just couldn't call her Monty. He knew a guy named Monty, and he was a slimeball who sold used cars in New Jersey.

Madison licked her lips before she blurted out her story in a rush, "I was followed by a Russian-looking guy and then he turned up at my apartment with the *Polizia*."

Jake took a deep breath and let it out slowly. "Let's try this step by step. When did you notice that you were being followed?"

"Earlier this evening."

"Is this the first time you noticed someone following you?"

"Yes," she breathed. But then she tilted her head. "Do you think he's been following me for a while?"

"I have no idea. I got a phone call maybe twenty minutes ago about you, so it's not like I have any details." He tried to keep impatience out of his voice. "Why don't you start at what you think is the beginning?"

She turned and looked at her hands on the table. Then she looked back at him. "I really have no idea where the beginning is." She shrugged.

Jake studied her face. She was older than he'd first thought. Her size made her look young, but there were a few fine laugh lines starting around her eyes, and her brow had a permanent furrow. He judged her to be in her early to mid-thirties. "Okay, then start when you arrived in Italy. I understand you are doing some work for Drake?"

She nodded. "Yes, he asked me to lead a team to investigate a fashion house he's thinking of investing in. Valentina Veridani."

"I thought Milan was the capital for fashion in Italy. Why are you in Florence?"

Her eyebrows went up. "You follow Italian fashion?"

"No, I don't follow fashion," he growled, "but I know the basics." This was shaping up to be a long fucking night.

"Oh, well most of the large fashion houses like Ferragamo, Gucci, and Cavalli all started here in Florence. They are still headquartered here today. Prada and Chanel both have large offices here as well. Milan took over in the seventies as the fashion capital so that's what you hear about, but Florence was the place for fashion until then. Florence still has distinction when it comes to the industry, and Valentina Veridani wanted to pay homage to her city's fashion roots so she started her brand here."

Madison's face lit up when she lectured him on the fashion industry. She obviously enjoyed that world. It explained why she was so well put together. She stood out in a crowd as having style. Some people were like that. Jake was not one of them. Jeans and T-shirts were his go-to. Although, he still believed every man should have a good suit or two in his closet. And some nice shoes. Good shoes were so important in his line of work. He was on his feet all the time. If his shoes sucked, his feet hurt. Being in pain was not fun, and it was a distraction.

"So where is the rest of your team?" Jake asked.

"They went back at the end of last week. The majority of the work was finished. There were a few loose ends that I wanted to tie up, so I stayed and booked a flight home for Sunday."

"The loose ends were going to take a whole week?" Somehow, he didn't think so. Maybe she was involved in something else, and this was why the Russian was following her.

She looked annoyed. "No, I was going to take most of the week off and see some more of Florence before I left. Drake okayed it."

Jake held up his hands as if to ward off an attack. "I'm just asking."

She sighed. "Anyway, I went back to the Veridani offices yesterday morning and tried to address said loose ends. I asked some questions of Veridani's accountants about a couple of items. They answered them. I called a couple of different vendors about a few things and a couple of charities that Veridani donates to. That was it. It wasn't a busy day or anything. But…" Her voice petered out.

He cocked an eyebrow. "But what?"

Madison fidgeted with a napkin that had been on the table. "No buts. I don't know… It was just normal. There're always a few things left outstanding that need to be tied up. I chatted with people. One of the people I worked closely with, Paloma, showed me the jewelry that Valentina Veridani created. They have it in the office on display. It was all just regular. Although"—she cocked her head again—"I did have to go into the office last night to fix something for Paloma. Someone had reset the parameters of a report and she thought she'd lost some data, but it was no big deal."

"I see." Actually, he didn't. Not at all. It was all industry talk, accounting jargon. All he really understood was that, for her, it seemed routine. He tried again. "Is there anything you did here in Florence that might attract police attention?"

"What? No! I only ever left my apartment to go to work and maybe out for dinner. Sometimes, not even that since we worked practically around the clock this time. Drake wants to make a decision before fiscal year-end for one of his businesses, which is different from calendar year-end. There was no time to sightsee, or to go out for dinner and drinks, or get into trouble. Most of the team complained about it."

Jake frowned. "So no personal time then. Was there anything about this job that stands out to you as different from any other?"

"Not really. It was pretty straightforward… which, I guess, in a way, was weird. The financials of companies can be very convoluted, but their accounts were clean and organized, which made for a nice change."

"So the company's books are in good order and you tied up all the loose ends. Nothing else stands out to you about your time at Veridani or your interactions there?"

Madison shook her head. "I'm still waiting to hear back from a couple people, but that's it on the business front."

"What about personally? Any personal interactions that stand out to you?"

She immediately shifted in her seat and started fidgeting with the napkin again, a sure sign of a problem. Jake ground his teeth. If this turned into the Russian being an ex-boyfriend that she wanted to make jealous or some shit, he was going to have it out with Mitch. But when he glanced at her again, the way she was fidgeting, watching the door, her fear was real. He was sure of it.

His protective instincts pushed to the surface. Madison looked so small, fragile somehow, and her fear was palpable. He tried to rein in his instincts. Maybe they were in overdrive because he was so tired. He glanced sideways at Madison. Then again, maybe not.

The waitress came by and asked if they wanted anything. "Scotch on the rocks," Jake said and then turned to Madison.

"I'll have the same," she said.

Jake kept his face neutral, but he had pictured Madison as a wine drinker. Maybe she was under normal circumstances. "You were going to tell me about your personal interactions."

She glanced up at him. "Right. Well, I got a call from Giovanni Veridani, he's one of Valentina's brothers. He and Marcello, her other brother, took over the brand when she died unexpectedly of a heart attack.

"Anyway, he asked me to have a late lunch with him today. I tried to get out of it, but he wouldn't take no for an answer. He said he had something he wanted to share with me. I thought he meant about business. It wasn't like we exchanged more than a few pleasantries before then. He'd immediately handed me off to his assistant, Paloma. I finally acquiesced and met him at a little restaurant a short distance from the Piazza Della Signoria, you know, in the middle of

Florence. It was empty, and I think they opened it just for him. Or us, I guess."

Jake had a bad feeling. He didn't like where this was going. The waitress returned with their scotches at that moment and set them down on the table. She smiled and asked if they wanted anything else. At the negative headshakes, she left. Jake picked up his scotch and said "cheers" and then took a large swallow. Madison also took a big swig from her own glass. Jake could feel the burn all the way to his belly. He glanced over at the woman sitting next to him. She didn't flinch when she drank. He liked that.

Madison continued. "We started off okay, but then he got a little too friendly, touching my hand and trying to be flirty. It made me really uncomfortable. I tried to steer the conversation to business topics, but he wasn't having it.

"He tried to give me a clutch purse, but I turned it down. I can't accept anything like that. It could be considered a bribe. I explained that to him, but he said it didn't matter since the audit was essentially over. I told him I just wasn't comfortable with accepting anything and that the lunch had been a bad idea."

She took another slug of her drink before continuing. "He got upset, almost angry, really. He told me I had insulted him by not accepting his gift and I wasn't behaving in a respectful manner. He stood up and stormed out, leaving the clutch on the table. The whole thing was bizarre.

"Up until that point, Giovanni had behaved perfectly. His brother Marcello was the one who was flirtier at the office. That's why I thought lunch would be fine. If it had been Marcello, I would've totally avoided it."

Jake gripped his glass so hard his knuckles turned white. Men who took advantage of women were assholes. Men who tried to intimidate women so they could take advantage were animals and should be put down like any other rabid beast.

He cleared his throat. "I'm sorry you had to go through that. It must have been…upsetting." Scary as hell, he imagined, but he didn't want to put words in her mouth or make her think any more about the situation than she already had. "Then what happened?"

"Well, I grabbed the clutch and left the restaurant. I decided there was no point in saying anything to Drake. It was over and done with. I decided to drop the clutch purse back at Veridani's front desk first thing in the morning. I was on my own time so I walked around Florence. I did some sightseeing and grabbed a nice dinner.

"I was heading back to my apartment when I noticed—no, that's not right. I *felt* like I was being followed. I kept turning around to see if someone was there, but I didn't see anyone. It wasn't until I pretended to stop and look in a shop window that I caught him in the reflection. He was watching me but pretending he wasn't."

Jake was impressed. "Where did you learn that bit of trade craft?"

"From the movies. I was shocked it worked, but I was more freaked out that some Russian guy was following me."

"How do you know he was Russian?" Jake asked before he took another sip of his drink.

"I don't. It's just a guess. A friend of mine used to drag me to Brighton Beach in Brooklyn to drink vodka and eat caviar. You know, the place that's called 'Little Odessa' because of the tight-knit Russian community. They have a certain look."

"Yeah, there is with the Brighton Beach crowd," Jake agreed while nodding. It was not the most savory of neighborhoods. Lots of organized crime hung out there. Madison Montgomery was full of surprises, and not one of them had turned out to be good.

"Anyway, I zigzagged down a lot of alleys and streets until I finally had to break out into a run and hide in plain sight in a piazza to lose him. Then, when I turned the corner onto my street, he was there, and he had *Polizia*, uniformed officers, with him. He was speaking to my landlady. I went back around the corner and called Drake. I have no idea what's going on." Her voice shook a bit. She grimaced after she took another swallow of her drink.

"The man *is* Russian as you guessed, but I can't tell you anything more as yet. We're working on it." He decided to keep to himself the fact that the man tailing her was former GRU. Her hand holding the glass shook a bit, and her eyes darted around the room. No need to freak her out even more until he had something concrete.

"One thing," Jake said, "why do you have an apartment here if you work for Drake in New York? Did you have that before the job for Drake? Do you come to Florence often?"

"What? No. No. I'm a freelancer, and Drake hires me for certain jobs because he knows I have no political gain from any of his deals and because I'm really good at what I do. He's not so sure about some of the people in his office. There's so much politics in a big company. He likes me to come in sometimes because he knows I will be unbiased.

"Jobs like this one can take a while. Most people don't like to be away from home for longer periods. I often have to be on site for a month or sometimes longer. I don't mind the travel but I don't like staying in hotels long term, even nice ones like this."

She glanced around the bar. "This is one of Drake's, isn't it?" At Jake's nod she continued, "I prefer to rent a place, you know, like an Airbnb or something if I'll be in a place for a while. I love to discover neighborhoods and cities like a local rather than a tourist, plus I find hotels too impersonal and noisy with all the comings and goings. I don't like to be around all the tourists."

Jake liked her confidence. She knew her worth, and he admired that. "Makes sense, I guess. Do you have any clue why the police might want to search your room?"

"None. I just can't fathom what they might want."

"And you didn't want to speak to them?" he asked.

"Would you? The guy followed me all around town. If he wanted to speak to me about anything legitimate, why not just pull up beside me in a police car and flash a badge?"

The lady had a point. There was definitely something off about the whole situation, but he was too in the dark to know what at the moment. He needed information and sleep to figure all this out, and not necessarily in that order. "Okay, well, let's head upstairs."

"Excuse me?" Madison reared back. "What do you mean head upstairs?"

Jake clenched his jaw and took a breath. "You can't wander around all night. You need a place to stay where you will be safe. If, indeed, the cops are after you, they will be smart enough to check the hotels, most likely starting with the ones that Drake owns since they probably know he's your boss. If you check in, you will have to give them your real name and your passport, making it easy for the cops to find you.

"We can call Drake and get him to smooth the way around that, but that takes time, and it involves more people. As it is, the waitress here has seen you. And maybe the doorman." When he raised an eyebrow, she confirmed with a nod.

"So, the best thing to do is to have you come up to my room. It buys us a bit of time, and I can keep you safe. The cops won't find you unless they actually show your picture around. I think they'll start with your phone and wait 'til morning before they start some sort of all-out search, if they even do. It's not like you murdered someone or stole something valuable so it should be low priority. In the meantime, we can get more information so we have a better idea of what we're dealing with."

He sensed her unease, and he didn't blame her. "Listen, the room is a suite. You can take the bedroom and lock the door. I'll sleep on the couch."

She still hesitated, shaking her head no, waving a hand as if to ward off his suggestion.

"I have to be honest with you, Madison. I am coming off a job that had me running for the last thirty-six hours straight. I need sleep if I'm going to be effective, and we need more information. We can't really do anything until we know what the hell is going on."

Madison nodded slowly. "I guess that will work. For now." She hoisted her bag over her shoulder.

Jake stood up and slid out from behind the table. Madison followed suit. He caught the waitress's eye, and she came forward with the bill. He handed her cash with his best sexy smile, the one women seemed to love, no matter what nationality. It was enough to cover the bill and leave her a generous tip. She glanced at Madison and then smiled back at him.

Jake leaned toward her and spoke in a soft voice, "If anyone asks, you haven't seen this woman. I was here by myself."

The waitress's gaze met his. "Of course, *Signore. Buona sera.*"

Not for a minute did he think she would lie for him, but it was worth a shot. He escorted Madison from the bar area and back up the stairs instead of the elevator. Even though Madison wore heels, she didn't complain. From the first day he stayed at the hotel, he'd known the best ways in and out of the building and had an escape plan figured out. It was standard practice.

He said a silent prayer they wouldn't have to use it.

CHAPTER FOUR

Her protector took the stairs two at a time. The big man had long legs, so it was a struggle for her short ones to keep up. Her feet were already killing her from the running in her heels she'd done earlier. They were made to be fashionable, not for exercise, and it would take her feet days to recover.

Her bag banged against her ribs. It seemed like it weighed a ton, and her shoulder was hurting. All in all, she was a bit of a hot mess at the moment. Not something she liked being. She couldn't remember the last time she was this discombobulated.

Madison sighed and continued to follow her companion across the large mezzanine toward a set of double doors. The landing itself was like the rest of the hotel, ornate and beautiful. There were frescoes on the ceiling and marble on the floors. The balcony that overlooked the small lobby downstairs was framed by green velvet drapes, and busts of famous Florentines were on either side. The main light over the space came in the form of a massive crystal chandelier. It was stunning. *Well it would be. Drake owned it.* Jameson Drake only owned and dealt with the best.

She glanced at the man beside her as he opened the door to his room. Did that go for him as well? Jake Boxer. What kind of a name was that? He was probably about six feet tall, which gave him about a foot on her when she was in sock feet. He was well-built. Broad shoulders tapered into narrow hips. His dark brown hair was thick with a bit of wave to it, and a rugged jawline added a hint of danger, but it was his eyes that struck her. They were tired but still watchful. He didn't miss much. They were also a piercing shade of blue. Drake said she could trust Jake with her life. He'd done so on many occasions. It was just hard for her to trust anyone at the moment. The day had been so strange, so surreal. But she had to admit just being around him made her feel slightly better. She had no doubts that he could protect her if she let him.

"There," Jake said as he stepped out of the way and ushered her into the suite. Inside was more of the same. There was a beautiful fresco on the ceiling and two floor-to-ceiling doors that led to a balcony framed by more velvet curtains. These were red. There was a red velvet sofa directly in front of her along with two matching chairs and an ottoman in the middle. A television hung between the windows across from the sofa. A cart loaded with silver room service trays was parked by the coffee table. Nothing looked touched, the lids still in place. The cutlery was still wrapped in the napkin. Was that why he was so gruff? He hadn't eaten? It would be cold by now for sure. That wasn't going to make him happier.

"The bedroom is there"—he pointed to the right—"and the bathroom is opposite." Both had double doors.

She excused herself and went to the bathroom. It, too, was all marble with a massive soaking tub and a separate shower. What she wouldn't give to get into a hot tub now and soak for the next hour. She glanced at her watch. It was close to midnight. She'd have to settle for a quick wash with a face cloth. She didn't even have clothes to change into. She glanced at herself in the gold-framed mirror. Her eyes looked large even to her, and the fine lines at the corners were more pronounced. Her mother would tell her, "Stop frowning. It gives you wrinkles." Not much she could do about it at the moment. She was terrified, and it was written all over her face.

Madison. No one called her Madison except her family. It was jarring to hear it come out of Jake's mouth. She'd been Monty for as long as she could remember. It started at school with her volleyball team and then carried over to university and onward. She never really liked Monty, but it wasn't a big deal. Being called Madison all the time was just…strange. She sighed and reached for the white fluffy washcloth.

Five minutes later, she felt slightly better. Her face and hands were washed and teeth brushed as well as she could do with her finger. She felt slightly guilty about searching the toiletry bag she'd found there for toothpaste, but she figured Jake would appreciate her minty breath more than he'd mind her going through his stuff. She ran her hands through her wavy hair and tried to put it into some semblance of order. It wasn't fabulous, but she felt better than when she'd walked in.

Now she needed to chat with Mr. Boxer about her name and their plans for tomorrow. She couldn't go to sleep without some kind of game plan.

Squaring her shoulders, she entered the living room in time to see Jake put the lid back on one of the plates on the table. He was wiping his mouth with a napkin so he must have eaten something.

She stayed a distance away from him, feeling like an intruder. "Sorry I interrupted your dinner."

"I'm used to it," he said without looking up. "Why don't you go get some rest? I already took out the stuff I need for the night. The bedroom is all yours." He grabbed his clothing off the sofa and headed past her into the bathroom. She heard the door click behind him.

"Well, that went well," she mumbled. She debated standing there until he came out again, but after the water in the shower came on, she gave up and entered the bedroom.

It was beautiful. The bed was solid mahogany with lots of soft pillows and a down duvet. The walls were adorned with art that matched the ceiling frescoes, and the marble floors were covered by thick rugs. The turn-down service must have come earlier because the covers were folded back and there were slippers beside the bed.

Madison grinned. The slippers were huge. She had size five feet. There was no way she could walk in them. Her size was another reason she didn't stay in hotels long-term. The robes and slippers never fit, and she always found it slightly depressing.

She sat on the bed. She lifted her foot and started tugging on her boot. Her feet must have swelled inside because it was a serious struggle. She pulled and yanked and flexed her foot back and forth before it finally slid off. She dropped it on the floor and immediately massaged her foot.

"Owww," she groaned. She had blisters.

She reached down and grabbed the other boot. She tugged and twisted, but no luck. She tried flexing her foot, but the boot wouldn't budge. She just couldn't get it off. She stared at the unyielding footwear. It wasn't like she could go to sleep with the boot on, could she? If she slept on her side and kept that boot outside the covers, maybe it would be okay. She could put the robe from the closet over her exposed leg.

Madison snorted. Now she was just being ridiculous. She stood up, limped over to the bedroom door, and straightened her shoulders as she opened it. Jake was standing in the middle of the room wearing nothing but a pair of black boxer briefs.

"Oh, uh... Sorry," she stammered. She wasn't sure where to look so she looked down, which was a mistake because her gaze naturally focused in on his crotch. With a sharp intake of breath, she looked up at him as heat filled her cheeks. "I, uh, need some help taking off my boot." She held up her foot.

He sighed.

"My foot swelled. I had to run from the Russian guy on cobblestones. These boots are not made for that type of thing." She put her hands on her hips. "Obviously, had I known the type of day I was going to have, I would have picked different footwear."

"Obviously," Jake sighed loudly. "Come here then."

She kept her eyes above his waist and limped across the room. The boots added four inches to her height, so her limp was pronounced. Judging by the smirk on his face, Jake was trying not to laugh. Feeling like an idiot, she glanced down again, which was another mistake. He kept himself in great shape if his chest and six-pack were anything to go by. Heat crept up her cheeks again. Those thoughts weren't helping the situation. She stopped next to the sofa.

"Take a seat." He sat down on the ottoman across from her where she sat on the sofa. He reached out and raised her booted leg. He placed one hand on the back of her heel and the other hand on the toe. "Now wiggle your foot as I pull."

She tried to do as he said, but it wasn't working. He twisted the leather a bit, but that didn't help either. He paused in his efforts and looked up at her. "I can cut it off."

"No! I love these! They're my favorite pair," she all but wailed.

He gripped the boot harder and gave it a yank, pulling Madison right off the sofa, where he caught her in his lap. She was so shocked, reactively, she threw her arms around his neck. The heat from his bare legs penetrated her skirt as their gazes locked.

His eyes darkened. "Sorry," he said in a rough voice.

"Uh, that's, I mean… It's okay." She cleared her throat, and her hands brushed his chest as she dropped them from his neck. A small burst of electricity danced across her skin, which motivated her to scoot back on the sofa.

He hadn't taken his eyes off her, and the pulse in his neck thrummed a steady rhythm. What was he thinking? Because she was thinking all kinds of things that weren't helpful. The heat was back in her cheeks but also spreading in her lady parts, so she looked down at her foot.

She cleared her throat again. "Can we try one more time? If it doesn't work, then you can…cut it off." It pained her to even say the words. These were her favorite boots. The leather was soft, and there was a stretchy bit of fabric along the sides so even when her calves had gotten a bit bigger, they still fit.

Wordlessly, he picked up her foot. This time he peeled the top part down and along her calf. The heat from his fingers felt so good on her leg she shivered.

When he couldn't get the boot any farther down her leg, he put one hand on the stacked heel and his other hand on the back of her leg. He gave a tug and twisted the footwear at the same time but held her in place so she didn't fall into his lap again. The boot came off in his hand.

"Here." He offered it to her, then stood.

"Thanks," she murmured as she stood up next to him. Her head barely reached the middle of his chest. She turned and quickly moved back across the room to the bedroom door. Over her shoulder, she said, "Sleep well and…thanks."

He was staring at her and just nodded. She opened the door and disappeared into the safety of her room closing the door behind her. She leaned against it. Having him close by was going to wreak havoc with her system. So much for a nice quiet vacation in Florence.

There was something about Jake Boxer, something she was sure would make sleep difficult to come by and once she did sleep, would invade her dreams. No doubt about it: That man was far too attractive for her own good.

CHAPTER FIVE

Jake plopped down on the sofa and let out a long, groaning breath. Jesus, Madison Montgomery was going to make his life difficult. She looked so freaking adorable with just the one boot on, limping along, and then when she landed in his lap, it had been all he could do to keep from becoming noticeably hard. He'd had to think of horrible things to stop his hard-on from growing. Damn good thing she was embarrassed and kept her eyes above his crotch. The pink hue to her cheeks was super cute, though. He smiled.

He laid down on the sofa and covered himself with an extra duvet he'd dug out of the closet. He glanced at his watch. Just after midnight. Eight hours. He'd settle for eight solid hours of shut-eye. Yawning, he rolled onto his side and drifted off to sleep.

Jake woke immediately when his cell buzzed. A message. He glanced at his screen. Polizia *in the building*. He was on his feet and moving. "Madison?" he called in a hushed voice as he opened the bedroom door. "Madison!" he called again, louder this time.

When she sat up in bed, the blankets fell to her lap, exposing her white lacy bra. "What? What's going on?" She looked around as if trying to figure out where she was.

"The cops are in the hotel. We gotta go. Get dressed." He turned and went back to the living room where he pulled on a pair of jeans and a navy sweater. It was spring in Florence, but the nights were still cool. He hated being cold.

Grabbing his sneakers, he shouted, "Madison, are you ready?" He pulled on the shoes and then snatched his phone from the coffee table. He texted the night manager. *Let me know when they leave the lobby.*

She appeared in the doorway in her skirt and blouse. Her blazer and boots were in her hands along with her shoulder bag. "Almost ready."

"Leave your boots," he commanded.

"What?" She'd been pulling on her blazer, but she stopped.

Jake rose from the couch while pulling on his shoulder holster and then drew on a light jacket. "You can't run in them. Your feet already hurt and are swollen. It'll take too long to get them on, and then you won't be able to move in them. You're better off in your bare feet. It'll hurt, but you'll be able to move."

Madison stood there staring at him, mouth hanging open. "But—"

"We don't have time to argue about this. Grab your bag and let's go." He turned and started toward the door, then stopped. "Do you want to talk to the cops? I can call Drake and get you a lawyer. It might be better than going on the run. Then we'll know what all this is about."

She bit her lip. "I…just don't know. I haven't done anything. I don't know why they'd want to speak to me. If they'd just shown up and said, 'Hey, we have a few questions. Can you chat for a minute?' then it would be fine, but they had some guy follow me. It's just…weird."

He stared at her for a beat. She was right. If it was some legit issue, a cop would have shown up and asked some questions. A former GRU guy was following her. That wasn't for no reason. Someone was fucking around with Madison Montgomery, and now he was caught up in it. *Shit.* He opened the door a crack and looked out. The mezzanine was clear. He gestured for her to move behind him, and they headed toward the opposite side. He stopped in front of the elevator and hit the down button.

"Why are we taking the elevator? Won't we be trapped?"

He glanced at his phone screen but saw no new texts. "No. They're still in the lobby." At least he hoped they were still in the lobby. He wanted to cross the mezzanine to the balcony and look, but it was too risky.

The elevator doors opened. He moved in and turned around. Madison was still outside the doors. He reached out and grabbed her, pulling her in as he hit the door close button. She flew into the elevator and her head smacked him mid-chest. He looked down at her. She really was tiny. Like a good foot shorter than he was and slender, too, he noticed as he put his hands on her waist to steady her.

"Wait!" she said as the doors closed. "What if they're waiting for us in the lobby?"

He leaned over and hit a button that had a minus one on it. "They *are* waiting in the lobby. If we go to the basement, we can get out. The elevator won't stop in the lobby unless they hit the down button, which is highly unlikely. If we take the stairs, they'll see us. The stairs are open and can be seen from the lobby."

"Oh." She stepped back from him, and he let go of her waist. The elevator was one of those small European ones that only fit three or four people. It was the only one in the hotel as well, so most people took the stairs. It also moved at a glacial pace.

"Listen," Jake said to Madison, "in the future, you need to do whatever I tell you when I say it. Do not question me. Do you understand?" Her brows met in a vee, and she opened her mouth, presumably to argue, but he cut her off. "We do not have time to discuss this. If you want to *not* be arrested, then just do what I say. You can argue the point later. Okay?"

She scowled at him but nodded. The elevator came to a stop, and the doors opened. Jake stepped off and grabbed her hand, pulling her behind him. He went straight ahead and then took a hallway to the left. The signs said this was the way to the spa, but that wasn't the only thing in this direction.

His cell pinged in his pocket. *The Polizia say the lady stole jewelry. They are going to your room.*

Thirty seconds later, he and Madison came to the foot of a stairwell. He turned to her. "Did you steal something?"

"What? No." She shook her head.

"Wait here. I'll make sure it's clear." At her nod, he went up the stairs. Halfway up, the wall turned into glass. He stayed low and surveyed the surroundings.

In front of him, the pool glowed an iridescent green from the underwater lights. The seats and sofas around it were all empty. He moved to the top of the stairs and checked to see if the door was unlocked. He pushed gently, and it opened.

Jake turned and gestured for Madison to come up the stairs. A couple seconds later, she was beside him.

He said in a hushed voice, "We're going out this way. Be as quiet as possible. There's more light than I would like right here, and if anyone is looking, they'll see us."

"Let's hope they're all sleeping," she murmured.

He pushed open the door, and they walked out onto the pool deck. He moved to his left and walked swiftly around the pool. On the backside, there was a hedge with statuary in front of it. It ran the length of the pool and across the end of the deck then turned the corner back toward the bar area where they'd just come from. It was at this corner where there was a slight gap. He moved directly to the opening in the hedges and stopped. There was a three-foot drop off the end of the pool deck onto a dirt path. The hotel was in the middle of a park, so it was all trees for about one hundred yards, and then there was a street just beyond that.

He heard a sound to their left and turned to see more police cars driving up the hotel driveway. Soon the *Polizia* would start to search the grounds as well as the hotel. "I'm going to jump down and then help you, okay?"

"I can jump myself," she said. "It's not that high."

"You can, but your feet are bare, and it will hurt when you land. Don't worry, you're going to have to run through about a hundred yards of woods, so if you need to prove you're tough, you'll get your chance."

She glared at him, but he turned and jumped off the wall. He didn't have time for theatrics. He reached for her and put his hands around her waist again. She stepped off the wall, and he lowered her to the ground. She couldn't have weighed more than one-hundred pounds. She was lighter than some of the equipment he'd carried when he was a SEAL.

"They're going to check the cameras any second now and see where we've gone. We have to move fast. Are you okay to run?"

"I can manage," she declared, and he let it go.

If she started to fall behind, he'd just pick her up and run with her. He sprinted off through the trees. A minute or so later, he heard a muffled yelp behind him. When he looked back, Madison was on her knees on the forest floor. He went back and picked her up. "Are you okay?"

She nodded. "I tripped on a branch."

There was a loud squawk and a sudden burst of rapid-fire Italian. There were sirens in the distance as well.

"Shit, they're by the pool. We gotta hustle." He grabbed her hand and took off at a run. She was struggling a bit and she kept swearing, but she managed to keep up. A minute later, they burst out on the sidewalk. He kept a hold of her hand and headed left toward Florence. Thirty feet down the street, he reached into his pocket and pulled out a set of keys. A small blue car chirped as he hit the unlock button. He opened the door and helped Madison into the passenger seat and then went around and slid in behind the wheel. The sirens were getting louder.

"Head down," he growled as a *Polizia* car shot past, headed up the hill. And then a second one. He waited a beat and then started the car. He pulled out smoothly and steered down the hill. He turned left at the first opportunity he had and wound his way down into Florence using as many back streets as possible.

"Where are we going?" Madison asked.

"I have no idea." That wasn't exactly true, but it was close enough. He couldn't use the safehouse he had set up for his last client because the client had actually used it to hide from some crazy ex-business partner, so it was compromised. But there was another hotel he could use. It was about forty-five minutes away. It wasn't located in the best spot for a quick escape, but it should be safe and had the best pizza he'd ever tasted. He pulled the little car over to the curb and checked his email. Nothing from Mitch. He sent a quick text and waited.

"Why have we stopped?" Madison asked.

Jake looked over at her. They were almost shoulder-to-shoulder in the tiny car. "I'm trying to see if we have any new information on the Russian or what the fuck is going on."

"Oh. Why did you ask me if I stole something?"

"The night manager said the cops were looking for you because you apparently stole some jewelry."

She shook her head vigorously. "But I didn't steal anything."

"Yeah, so you said."

"You don't believe me?" she demanded.

"At this moment, I don't have enough information to think anything. It's all just weird puzzle pieces that don't seem to fit together. That's why we need more information."

He studied her in the watery light of the streetlamps. She was beautiful. Even after running through the trees and falling down, she still made his breath catch in his chest. He turned and faced forward. It was better not to look at her. She was too distracting.

He glanced at his phone screen again, but still nothing. "Okay, we're leaving town. I know a place we can stay. It's going to be about a forty-five-minute drive. Do you get motion sickness?"

"No," she said with a puzzled expression on her face. "Why do you ask?"

"Because it's an interesting drive." He smiled then. This was going to be fun.

CHAPTER SIX

Madison swallowed hard and tried not to show just how ill she felt. When he'd asked if she got motion sickness, she'd thought he'd been joking, but the road to wherever they were going was very twisty, and he was taking it at a good clip. She kept flipping back and forth from being terrified they were going to crash into someone on these narrow roads to being terrified she was going to puke all over herself and Jake. Either way, it was not a fun ride.

They'd been driving for about a half hour when she saw a small open area on the side of the road. "Pull off here!"

Jake glanced at her as if to argue but promptly pulled off. She must have looked as sick as she felt. As soon as he brought the car to a sudden halt, she sprang out onto the gravel, forgetting about her lack of shoes.

"Ouch! Shit! My feet." She swore again as she tried to find a safe place to stand.

Jake came out of the car and around to her side. "Stand still. It will hurt less."

She stopped moving. It still hurt, but he was right; the pain was less. "Sorry, I guess the scotch without snacks wasn't a good idea."

"It's my driving." Jake leaned on the car. "I'm trying to put distance between us and Florence as quickly as possible. There are cameras on many of the main streets so the quicker we're out of town the better. There are less of them outside of the major cities and highways. That means we have to take the old, narrow roads and I'm going faster than…is recommended. I'm sorry you're feeling sick."

"That's okay, I guess." She wanted to yell at him, but he was doing this for her. Because her boss asked him to. Suddenly, a cold sweat broke out across her skin. How was she going to pay for this? Personal security had to cost a fortune. She couldn't let Drake pay for it. She'd taken too much of his money already. She made good money herself working for Drake, but not that kind of income.

Her apartment in New York was a tiny one-bedroom. She had savings and investments, but they were for retirement. If she divested now, she'd have to pay tons of taxes and she'd have no more nest egg. The thought of being broke with nothing to fall back on made her stomach heave, and she coughed.

But broke was better than dead, she reminded herself. Not that they knew for sure someone wanted to kill her. The whole situation was a nightmare. At least she had protection. The Russian would have her by now if not for Jake. He'd saved her ass back at the hotel. She truly appreciated that. He was worth every cent even if she had to go bankrupt to pay his bill.

Jake pushed away from the car and opened the trunk. He dug around in a bag and came out with something in his hand. He closed the trunk and came over to her. "Here." He handed her an apple. "Sometimes having something in your stomach helps. The drive is probably another twenty minutes or so, and the road"—he smiled apologetically—"gets worse."

Madison groaned but sank her teeth into the apple. She'd try anything to not puke in front of Jake. It was mortifying enough to admit she felt sick. "Have you worked for Drake long?"

Jake had gone back to leaning against the little car. "I don't work for Drake. I work for Callahan Security. Drake is just one of our clients."

"Oh. I see." She took another bite of apple.

"How about you?"

"Off and on for about five years, but I've known him for a lot longer. "He…" She hesitated and then shrugged. "He sponsored me."

Jake glanced at his watch and then back at her. "How do you mean?"

"I grew up in the same town as him and his sister. They were quite a few years ahead of me, but I knew of them. Anyway, after high school, I worked for an accountant, Paul Turchetta, in our hometown just doing office work, but Paul encouraged me to do more. After a couple years, I decided to go to college. Drake offered scholarships to people in need. I applied, and he gave me one and then another. He essentially sponsored my entire education and then offered me a job when I finished my degree. I actually turned him down and went to work for an accounting firm. I needed to do something on my own, you know?"

She had no idea why she was telling him all this. Maybe because it was the middle of the night and she was ill on the side of the road in a foreign country and the police were after her because they thought she'd stolen something. Or maybe it was just because she needed to tell someone. She'd always kept it to herself, but she had a feeling this whole adventure might not end well, and she wanted someone to know what Drake had done for her. He had a hard-ass reputation, but he was really a good guy.

Or maybe it was because for some unknown reason, she trusted Jake Boxer implicitly. She knew in her soul he was someone she could rely on which was a damn good thing because right now he was the only thing standing between her and the Russian.

"I got some experience and passed all my exams and then Drake needed someone to fly out and do a quick evaluation of a company he was buying. It would only take a few days he told me, and would I be interested? I said yes and took a couple of days off my regular job. Turns out, I liked traveling and doing forensic accounting. So I quit my day job, and now I freelance for Drake and a few other companies." She sighed to herself. It used to be fun, but she was finding it a bit too much these days. The shine had gone off the job.

"Cool." Jake looked at his watch again. "We need to go."

Madison blinked. Heat bloomed in her cheeks, and she was glad it was dark so he couldn't see how mortified she was. She just shared her shit with a total stranger, and he couldn't care less. *Way to go, Madison.* She tossed the apple core into the woods and then limped her way back to the car. Jake had already climbed into the driver's seat and had the engine running.

Soon after they got back on the road, they started a steep uphill climb. Then the road got really narrow. It was no more than a car width. One side was mountain, and the other side was all trees and a steep drop down into a valley. Then came the switchbacks. They were close together and short, maybe three car lengths before the next one-hundred-and-eighty-degree twist in the road. She was so terrified, all thoughts of getting sick fled. She held the armrest with a death grip, and the next twenty minutes passed in white-knuckle silence for Madison.

It was pitch dark; the moon had disappeared. The little car's headlights barely lit the road. "Where are we? You know where you're going, right?" she asked since they had seemed to finish the switchbacks. The road had straightened out again, but it didn't get any wider, and they were still going uphill.

"We're heading to a small inn just outside of Mugello and yes, I know where I'm going. I've stayed here a few times before. The owner, Graziana, is a friend."

"Does she know we're coming? I mean, we're not just going to drop in on some woman at home in the middle of the night, are we?"

He didn't say anything, which didn't bode well. Great. This was getting worse by the minute.

At that moment, the moon broke free of the clouds, and they came to a roundabout with a monument in the middle of it. Jake went around the monument to the right and went straight into what looked like a long driveway.

"Is this it?" she asked.

"Yes." He made an immediate left and turned into what looked like a parking lot of sorts. There was a building with a large plate-glass window along the front. It appeared to have some sort of equipment in it. Jake parked to the left. There were a few other cars but not many.

"What is this place?" she asked as he turned off the car.

"It's a hotel in an olive grove. They make their own olive oil, and it's delicious." Jake opened the door and got out of the car.

Madison exited as well and then cursed when she stepped on a rock. The air was crisp and smelled of wisteria and roses. She turned to take in her surroundings. Up on the hill to her left were the olive trees. The moonlight danced off the leaves. The hotel was on the right at the far end of the drive. It was bathed in the glow of the moon with only a few small lights illuminating the entryway. The driveway to the hotel was long and trees lined both sides. It was also all gravel. She grimaced. It was going to be a long walk in bare feet.

She heard Jake make a call, but he spoke softly and she couldn't make out anything. Hopefully, the hotel had space. All the adrenaline was gone, and fatigue hit her like a rogue wave. She swayed on her feet. A hot shower and a soft bed. They were the things dreams were made of at the moment.

Jake tucked his cell back in his pocket. "She has a room ready for us." He started out of the parking area toward the driveway. Madison followed until she came to the gravel. She tentatively put one foot on the stones but pulled it back. Way too painful. She looked to her left. A field ran alongside the driveway. Maybe she could walk there. She turned and started across. "Ouch," she yelped. The grass was hard. It wasn't any better than the gravel.

Jake appeared beside her. She looked up. "Sorry, it's just a bit painful. I thought the grass would be better, but not so much."

He looked down at her feet and then at the hotel. He suddenly bent down, placed one arm under her knees and one behind her back, then scooped her up.

"What are you doing?" she demanded.

"Carrying you."

She scowled at him. "Put me down."

"No. You can't walk, and I'm tired. I want to go to bed. This is the fastest way to get us both where we need to be." Jake kept walking down the driveway.

"It's unnecessary and humiliating," she huffed.

A laugh rumbled out of his chest. "It's totally necessary, and humiliating would be if I threw you over my shoulder."

He wouldn't dare, would he? When he glanced at her with a look, she knew instantly he would. Hell, he probably had considered it at first but was being kind.

Madison stopped complaining. It was warm in his embrace and, in truth, her feet were killing her. His heart beat a steady rhythm against her ribcage. He wasn't out of breath at all, she realized. Nor was he struggling with the extra weight, which confirmed her earlier thought. He didn't just look good; he was in great shape. Honestly, she wouldn't mind feeling how great his shape was. Sexy didn't quite cover it. This man was hotter than the sun.

When they came to the stone steps outside of the hotel, he set her down on her feet, and she immediately felt the loss of his body heat. The building itself was stone and was probably built centuries ago. It was several stories high with lovely windows overlooking the olive grove behind them. No doubt the opposite side had a view of the valley. There were a couple of outbuildings as well. More rooms possibly.

The doorway was narrow, but the doors were glass. They opened now, and a woman came out. She had medium-length, straight blond hair and blue eyes. She was dressed in a turtleneck and cotton pants with a soft gray throw wrapped around her shoulders. Her face broke into a smile. "*Buona sera*, Jacob. It's so nice to see you, even at this hour." She came forward and gave him a double-cheeked kiss and a quick hug.

"Graziana, it's good to see you, too. Thank you for being so hospitable."

She stepped back. "Is nothing. We have room."

"This is Madison," Jake said.

Graziana offered her hand. "It is nice to meet you, Madison. Come inside. It's chilly out." She ushered them inside the little lobby.

There was a desk on the right with a soft lamp illuminating the area. A printer and computer on top rested on the far edge next to the wall. A tabby cat was sleeping on top of the printer. It raised its head to take them in and then went back to sleep. From what she could see, there was a seating area directly ahead and then maybe a dining area beyond that. The light didn't penetrate that far. There was a set of stone steps on the left. Three steps then a landing and then the steps twisted toward the back of the hotel and disappeared.

Graziana went around the desk and grabbed an old-fashioned key with a large piece of wood attached. "Here, go right up. We settle everything in the morning. It's so late you must be exhausted." She handed the key to Jake.

"Thanks, Graziana. You are a saint."

She made a quick sign of the cross. "No, no. But I appreciate the thought. Go now. See you in the morning. Breakfast ends at ten-thirty so make sure you are up by then."

"*Grazie*," Madison mumbled before she turned toward the stairs. Jake stepped behind her. She took the stairs slowly. The stone steps felt cool on the bottoms of her sore feet. They reached the top and turned right into a large living area with many chairs and sofas and a huge fireplace. She glanced around and realized that the doors to the bedrooms lined the perimeter around the space. They were tall and skinny, like the entry doors.

Jake stepped around her and led the way across the room to a door in the corner. "This is the owner's suite. When this was a working farm a few hundred years ago, this building was the owner's house. This is where he slept."

Madison was having trouble staying upright. Her feet hurt, and she was so tired she could barely keep her eyes open. She raised her hand to cover a yawn and stepped sideways, hitting a large vase beside her. It wobbled, but she reached out and caught it before it toppled over.

The vase had to be about three feet tall. A floral motif covered the outside and there was an opening at the top big enough to put her hand through. It looked very old.

She breathed a sigh of relief when the vase stopped swaying. It was probably some sort of family heirloom. All she needed was to break it, and then Graziana would probably ask them to leave. Madison yawned again.

Jake finally got the door opened. "Sorry." He held up the key that was several inches long. "The lock is a bit finicky." He stepped back for her to enter.

She slid through the narrow doorway with no problem but glanced back to see that Jake needed to turn sideways. It made her smile. There were so many advantages to being small.

The space was made up of two rooms and a bathroom. They'd entered into a sitting room with a small red sofa and two wing-backed chairs in gold. There were two round wooden tables, both with small lamps on them. Wooden shutters were closed over the window at the far end of the room. Off to the right was a short hallway. The suite had high ceilings with wooden beams.

Madison moved to the hallway where she found the bathroom immediately to her left. The room was narrow but long. There wasn't much space between the sink and the opposite wall. It was the same with the toilet. The shower stall was at the end, and it was the width of the bathroom, which meant it wasn't very big. It went all the way to the ceiling, though, which was some twenty feet up. Jake was going to have a hard time fitting in the shower, for sure. When the thought of him naked crossed her mind, she immediately turned and left the bathroom. Thoughts like that weren't going to help anything. She chalked it up to being overtired and that he'd carried her into the hotel. She could still feel the impression of his arms around her.

The bedroom was much bigger. The soaring ceiling was all done in a dark wood, and the bed looked to be of the same dark wood but had a canopy. There was a red velvet throw over the top of a white down duvet. The bed itself was large. Huge by European standards. They didn't do king-size beds in Europe. Full-size was most common. In some places, they put two twins together to make one large bed. This bed was bigger than that. Perhaps they had a mattress made special to suit the frame. It was monstrous, and she'd never been so glad to see a piece of furniture in her whole life.

Jake came up behind her. "I'll sleep on the side closest to the door. You take the inside." The look he gave her told her he wasn't taking any arguments and, at that moment, she didn't have the energy to bother. He'd been a perfect gentleman so far, which was slightly disappointing if she were honest. She really was tired if that was what she was thinking about, considering the circumstances. Or maybe she was thinking about Jake *because* of the circumstances. Either way, she'd just given herself a headache. The real question was what was she going to sleep in?

"Um, I'm okay with the whole bed thing, but is there a store here or something? I would love to sleep in something other than these clothes." Jake ran his eyes over her from head to toe and back again. She ground her teeth, determined not to blush.

"There's no store. At most, you can buy olive oil, but I have a bag in the trunk of the car. It might have a T-shirt in it. Will that do?"

"Er, yeah. That would be great."

He sighed as he turned and left the room. Guilt washed over her. He was just as tired, if not more so than she was, and she was making him go back to the car. On the other hand, she had no other clothes, and sleeping in just her underwear was out of the question.

She went back to the bathroom and did her best to clean her feet and the rest of her with the soap and towels provided. The hotel was charming, and she would have loved to stay here any other time, but now she worried how much this was going to cost her. Mentally, she started tallying up the charges: two days for security at least, a huge suite in the hotel, the car rental, new clothes…

She shook her head. *Forget it.* There was no point stressing about it now. She might just have to get Drake to pay for it and then keep working for him for a few more years so she had enough money to pay down her debt. Or maybe… She'd just have to figure something out later when she could think more clearly. Now she needed to get off her feet and get some sleep.

She heard the door open. "Jake?"

He popped his head around the corner. "Here." He tossed a T-shirt in her direction.

"Thanks." She caught the shirt and held it up against herself. It was a plain black short-sleeved T-shirt that went down to mid-thigh. "Perfect. Thanks, Jake."

He grunted and disappeared from the doorway.

Great. He was her biggest fan now for sure. She closed the bathroom door and quickly got changed. She grabbed her stuff and went back into the bedroom. "Bathroom is all yours," she said as she glanced around, but Jake wasn't in the bedroom. Just then, he walked back in from the sitting room and stopped short. His gaze traveled up and down her body. A look passed over his face too quickly for her to catch its meaning, and then he turned and left the room again.

"Whatever," she mumbled to herself as she rounded the foot of the bed.

She pulled back the covers and crawled in. The bed was soft and inviting. Her whole body was sore. Now that she was lying there, all the aches and pains were announcing themselves. Running in her high-heeled boots and then barefoot through the forest had left her feet and legs sore, scratched, and bloody, and her heavy bag had crashed against her ribs. She was bruised all along both sides of her body. She took a deep breath, and tears sprang into her eyes.

What the hell had happened? How did she end up here? More importantly, how the hell was she going to get everything sorted out?

CHAPTER SEVEN

Jake took his time in the bathroom. Madison was so tiny and had looked so vulnerable in his big T-shirt. He'd had to walk away to stop himself from giving her a hug, which would have no doubt lead to other things. Her eyes were still huge, and terror and fatigue were written all over her face. Her expression had tugged at his heart-strings. *Dammit!*

He finished up and made his way quietly back to the bedroom. He considered going back to sleep in the living area, but the couch there was small and there was no way he'd fit. He needed sleep if he was going to be any good at protecting Madison. But protecting her from what? Was it the Russian or himself that he was more worried about? He couldn't answer that question at the moment. All he knew was Madison Montgomery lit up his protective instincts like fireworks on the Fourth of July.

He glanced at the bed. Madison was already asleep. Her breathing was deep and even. Good. She needed rest. So did he. He quietly took off his blazer and the gun holster, laying them over the back of a chair. He pulled the gun out of the holster, double checked the chamber was clear and the safety on, then tucked it under his pillow. Quietly, he toed off his shoes and then pushed down his jeans. As carefully as possible, he climbed onto the bed. He didn't want to wake Madison. But she didn't move. Not one bit. Good for her. If only he slept that well.

He closed his eyes and tried to relax. His mind had other ideas though. It bothered him that Mitch hadn't gotten back in touch. Usually, the computer geeks on the third floor at Callahan Security in New York were fast. Lately, though, they'd hired a bunch of new people, so maybe there was a hold up. Callahan Security was expanding by leaps and bounds.

Was that what Mitch had wanted to talk about? Jake wanted something more than what he was doing. He didn't want to be just another security professional. He wanted a career path, a trajectory of some sort. The problem was he just didn't have any other skillset. He had hated school. He was good with paperwork but forget dealing with numbers. Anything that had to do with accounting gave him hives. He was barely able to balance his checkbook. It was one of the reasons that he admired Madison. She actually liked working with numbers and understood how to read a company's financials. That was just impressive as hell.

He sighed as he rolled onto his right side away from Madison. He didn't want to wake her. He got comfortable and closed his eyes, but his brain kept buzzing. Why did the cops want to talk to her and who was this Russian guy? Maybe Dragan was wrong and misidentified the guy.

Damned unlikely. Dragan didn't make mistakes. Not ever. If Dragan said the guy was GRU, then he was. So how did Madison fit into this picture?

Jake worked to relax his body first and then tried some breathing techniques to relax his mind. He needed to sleep if he was going to protect the cute accountant. Madison... There was just no way he would call her Monty. She looked like a Madison, or possibly even a Mads. All tiny and cute with those big hazel eyes and dark wavy hair. Nice curves, too. He smiled as he drifted off to sleep.

Hours later, he woke with a start. He turned and realized Madison wasn't beside him. Rolling out of bed, he stood and moved toward the bathroom, gun in hand. It was instinct that had put it there. He had no memory of grabbing it. Jake stopped at the closed bathroom door and listened. Nothing. "Madison, are you alright?"

A gasp and then a grunt sounded through the door. Jake turned the knob and pushed. The door flew open, and he was inside in seconds.

"Ahh!" Madison screeched as she dove behind the frosted glass shower door. "What's wrong? Why are you in here?" Her head popped out from behind the glass.

"A loud sound woke me. I asked if you were okay, but you didn't respond. I thought you might be in trouble." Jake stood in the doorway, his gun hand aimed at the floor.

"Oh, uh, I knocked the shampoo bottle off the shelf when I was trying to get my towel."

Her freshly scrubbed cheeks were pink, and she was having a hard time meeting his eyes. He looked around for the towel. It was draped over the top of the shower door, but one end had gotten hooked on a wall sconce. His mouth twitched. She'd tried to tug it down, and it had gotten stuck. She was too short to reach the sconce to free the towel.

"Would you like some help?"

She narrowed her eyes at him. "Are you laughing at me?"

He did his best to keep a straight face. "Nope." She looked so adorable with her hair all wet and the scowl in place on her face. He unhooked the stuck end. "Here," he said as he offered it to her.

She shot him another look but took the towel. "Thank you."

"Uh huh." He turned and left the bathroom. His shoulders were shaking with laughter but he did his best to keep it silent. No need to embarrass her more than she already was. He went back into the bedroom and put his gun in the holster. He didn't have any clothes to change into so he pulled on his jeans again. The bag he'd left in the hotel safe last night was a go-bag, so it didn't have much in the way of clothing. One T-shirt, which he'd given to Madison last night, and one pair of black cargo pants. Along with a pile of guns, knives, and the like. Hopefully he wouldn't need any of that stuff, but he always prepared for the worst-case scenario.

He raised his arms above his head and stretched. Then he went over and opened the curtains and the shutters. The view was incredible. The valley below was sparkling in the spring sunshine. This place never failed to make him smile. He'd stayed here three or four times now, and not once did he regret it. His stomach rumbled. Glancing at his watch, he let out a curse. "Madison, we have to move if we're going to eat." He turned back toward the bathroom and stopped dead.

"I know. I'm ready." When she'd come into the room behind him, he hadn't heard a thing, but that wasn't what stopped him in his tracks. She was wearing her blazer and her skirt but nothing else. No shirt.

"Um, you… That is, I think maybe—"

"My blouse is drying. It smelled after yesterday, not to mention it had gotten dirty from our little adventure through the trees. I washed it. Hopefully it will be dry by the time breakfast is over. Are you ready? I'm famished." She looked up at him, her hazel eyes sparkling.

"Uh, yeah. Give me two minutes."

She nodded as he breezed past her and went into the bathroom. Her blouse was on a hanger in front of the window inside the shower. He swallowed. Her blazer had been buttoned, but the vee was low and the swell of her breasts was evident, as was a little bit of white lace. The fact that he could recall this with perfect accuracy after only glimpsing her for a second before averting his eyes was not surprising. Nor was the fact that he could call up exactly what her ass looked like as she'd jumped behind the frosted glass of the shower enclosure earlier. What *was* surprising was the emotion these images stirred in him. A fierce wave of lust swept through him along with a desire to protect Madison from everyone and everything. He closed his eyes. That was not good. Not good at all.

He was as good as his word and, two minutes later, he walked out of the bathroom. "Ready."

Madison came from the bedroom to join him in the living area. "What do I do about shoes?"

Jake looked down at her feet. Her toenails were painted a hot pink.

It made him want to smile. The accountant with hot pink toes. "There's a pair of slippers in the closet."

She sighed and dutifully went back to get them. She pulled them on and then walked, or rather shuffled, into the living room. "They're big. It's going to be hard to walk."

"Do you want me to carry you?" he offered. He had no qualms about doing it. He remembered how perfectly her body fit against his last night, and he wouldn't mind a repeat performance.

"Er, no. That's fine. I will manage with the slippers." Her cheeks flushed a becoming shade of rose.

"Let's go."

She preceded him out the door and down to the dining area. They walked through the inside seating to a balcony that was all set with tables for breakfast. The view was phenomenal, just as he remembered it. He picked a table for them where they could see almost one hundred and eighty degrees of the valley below but he could sit with his back to the building. There was a little village with antique-looking buildings with terracotta roofs. The bucolic setting was surrounded by green fields and olive orchards. It looked like a painting.

"It's stunning," Madison murmured.

He smiled at her. "Agreed. It's just one of the reasons the drive up is so worth it."

"Where exactly are we, anyway?"

"The province of Mugello."

"I thought so by the direction we were going, but I wasn't sure. What's the town called?"

"San Galliano. It's a small town with a few shops and restaurants. Just enough for the locals to get what they need. It's done in the typical Tuscan style with the red clay-roofed buildings that have been around for centuries and lots of individual shops. There are more modern pharmacies and grocery stores, but I always like patronizing the locals."

Jake prompted her with, "Breakfast is a help-yourself affair unless you want to order something special, and then we have to check and see if they'll make it in the kitchen."

Madison smiled. "The European breakfast thing. It took me totally by surprise the first time I came to Europe. I had no idea that they don't go in for big breakfasts so much over here."

"The UK does a good breakfast if you don't mind kidneys and fish and beans. I have always found the Europeans like to pretend they are being healthy so they eat their boiled eggs and bacon with yogurt and bite-size pastries. But I do love their coffee. Big bowls in France and fantastic espresso here."

"I know. It's great. And there is something to be said for not eating a huge stack of pancakes all the time. People here seem to be thinner, and they walk a lot."

Jake shook his head. "Don't kid yourself. They all smoke. Europe needs to catch up to the West when it comes to not lighting up. I'll take pancakes over cigarettes any day of the week."

Madison nodded. "All this talk of food, let's go get some." They both stood, and she immediately stumbled over the slippers.

Jake reached out and caught her arm. "Why don't you let me get you something?"

"If you wouldn't mind, that would be great." She sat back down. "And coffee. Lots of coffee."

Jake grinned as he grabbed the basket and headed to the buffet table inside the dining room. The buffet was laid out against one wall. There was a toaster on the near end next to an egg station. Boiling his own egg was not on the list of things he wanted to do, and he wasn't sure how Madison took hers, so he moved farther down the line. Everything was set out in little jars so it was easy to put them in the basket and carry them to the table.

He grabbed some bacon and scrambled eggs, along with a few cold cuts and some olives. He added some yogurt and what looked like homemade granola. Then he moved down the table toward the coffee machine. The line was long. Graziana approached.

He smiled. "*Buongiorno.*"

"Ah, good morning, Jacob. You made it down for breakfast. That's good."

"Yes, but we're in serious need of coffee. Any chance you could bring a pot to the table for us?"

She smiled and winked. "I'll see what I can do. You go back and sit down. I am sure you are still tired from your adventures."

Jake nodded. "Thank you. We really appreciate it."

She brushed off his words with a smile then headed into the kitchen. He went back outside to the table and started unloading the basket. "I brought a bit of everything because I didn't think to ask you what you wanted."

"I'm sure it's all good." She looked around. "But, um, coffee?"

He laughed. "It's coming. Graziana is bringing us a pot."

"Oh, thank God. I can't think until I have my first cup." She smiled up at him as he placed the last of the glass jars on the table. She grabbed an assortment and dug in. Just then, a pot of coffee was delivered to their table as promised by Graziana. The woman and her staff deserved a giant gratuity. Europeans didn't normally do the tipping thing, but sometimes Jake still left extra money if he felt it was deserved.

Jake ate slowly as he watched Madison enjoy her breakfast. If this was any other time, their meal would almost be like a date but, sadly, they were on the run. And as breakfast wound down and their coffee pot emptied, it was time to face some reality. Jake offered more coffee to Madison, but when she shook her head, poured the dregs of the pot into his own cup.

"Madison," he said in a quiet voice, "we need to figure out what's going on."

She sighed and put down her fork on her now empty plate. "Yes, I guess we do. It was just nice to have a civilized breakfast. I could almost believe I was here on vacation."

"I know we've already talked about it, but have you thought of anything else? Any reason why the police might want to speak to you? The hotel manager in Florence said it was something about a theft. Do you know anything about something being stolen? It has to be pretty serious if they came to the hotel in the middle of the night." He paused and then shook his head once.

"What?"

"I almost wish we'd stayed and found out what this is all about." He frowned. "But it's risky. With no knowledge of what's going on, it leaves us at a distinct disadvantage. I'm just not sure if that disadvantage is worth the stigma of running."

Madison leaned forward. "Do you think it will be worse because we ran?"

Jake shrugged. "If it was just the cops, I'd say yes. This Russian guy throws everything off. He could be nothing, or he could be deadly. He's part of the unknown, and that's a big issue."

CHAPTER EIGHT

Jake excused himself to the bathroom while Madison remained at the table, staring at the view. It really was spectacular. If only they were here on vacation. *They?* She shook her head dismissively. She was still exhausted and freaked out. Obviously, she wasn't thinking clearly. Jake was incredibly sexy and had that whole bad-boy protector thing going on, and he made her feel safe which was so much more important than she'd ever realized but he really wasn't her type.

She liked the academic type; highly educated, intelligent, articulate men who could converse on any number of topics. She loved to learn and wanted someone to learn with. That was her ideal mate. Someone who wanted to keep learning things like she did. It was part of the reason she traveled so much. She was always trying to learn about different cultures. Although, lately, she'd found she'd lost interest in travel and learning. Too much time on the road and not enough time setting down roots. She suddenly realized she was lonely.

Anyway, Jake didn't strike her as someone who spent a lot of time reading to learn new things. She didn't even know if he had gone to university. Of course, none of that mattered because they weren't dating. He was being paid to protect her, or at least would be paid to protect her…eventually. He couldn't be expected to work for free. Madison sighed.

She looked down at her empty coffee cup. She was already much older than everyone else who started in the fashion world. What's a few more years? She bit her lip. It had been her dream since she was a little girl to work in fashion. She had imagined herself as a designer with all the top celebrities wearing her brand, but when she grew up, she realized she needed a real job. Her family didn't have a lot of money, so she needed to do something where she could earn a decent wage.

And she'd loved working at the accounting firm. Numbers made sense to her. They were logical. They didn't care if she had money or not. They would reveal their secrets to her because of her skill. She'd been so thrilled when Drake had offered her the scholarship, but if she were honest, there was a small part deep down that wished fervently she had gone to college for fashion and not accounting.

Now, years later, she was damn good at her job and made good money, but she still dreamed about being in the fashion industry. However, recently her focus had shifted from clothing to purses and bags. Madison realized just how important having the right bag for each occasion was. It just finished off an outfit. The right purse was the icing on the cake. The thing that took an outfit from great to absolutely fabulous.

Designing bags was her passion. She wanted to be the next Louis Vuitton, but for real people. She didn't want her merchandise to be priced so outrageously that only the rich could purchase it. She wanted to create bags that were as useful as they were beautiful, and she wanted to do it for a decent price. She wanted everyone to be able to afford a Madison Montgomery bag.

Madison looked up as Jake approached the table. He came to a halt beside her. "Graziana says there's a few shops in the village at the bottom of the mountain where we can get some new clothes. You ready to go?" he asked.

Madison nodded and stood up. She took a step and promptly tripped over the large slipper, resulting in her barreling into Jake's chest.

"Oof," she grunted as he put his arms around her and held her in place.

"Are you okay?" he asked.

She raised her head. "Um, yeah. Sorry. The slippers…" She lost her voice as she looked up at him.

He really did have the most amazing blue eyes. But, right now, they were laughing at her. She cleared her throat and tried to straighten, but Jake's arms were still around her waist.

"No problem. Would you like me to carry you?" The smile that was in his eyes now reached his lips, and he started to chuckle.

Yes! "No, thank you." She pushed off his chest and took a step to the side to go around him. "I'll be fine." She missed the warmth of his arms immediately.

Heat crawled up her throat to reach her cheeks. Seriously. She hadn't blushed this much in years. What was it about this man that flustered her so? Perhaps it was the two-hundred pounds of solid, sexy-as-hell muscle. She clamped her teeth together and walked back through the lobby.

Madison reached the top of the stairs and headed across the living space toward their room. When she got there, she realized that Jake wasn't behind her. Crap. Where had he gone off to? It didn't matter really. She had the key. Pulling the long, heavy skeleton key out of her pocket, she sighed. She needed to get this behind her so she could move forward with her plans in life and, more importantly, she could be through with Jake Boxer. He was costing her too much, in more ways than one.

Madison unlocked the door and entered the room. She dropped the key in her big bag so she wouldn't forget it later. The maid, or whoever, had already cleaned the room, replaced the towels, and made the bed. They were fast. The food and service had so far been excellent. She really wished she could come back some time and vacation here.

She sat down on the bed and rubbed her feet. They were sore today, and not just the blisters. There were some minor cuts from running through the woods, but also the bottoms of them were slightly swollen. They just weren't used to taking such a beating. She groaned as she switched feet. At least they hadn't cut her boots off.

Maybe they would still be at Drake's hotel. There'd be no reason to get rid of them. She'd call the front desk and ask about them once all of this was over.

The room door opened and closed. "Jake?" Madison called out as her heart rate ticked up.

"Yeah."

"Just making sure it was you."

Jake walked into the bedroom carrying a pair of lime green and neon orange running shoes. "Here," he said as he placed the shoes on the bed beside her.

Madison looked down at them. Way too bright for her taste for sure. "Where did you get those?"

"I asked Graziana, and she looked in the lost and found. You know, stuff guests leave behind."

She looked down at them horrified. There was no way she was putting on someone else's shoes. Just no. Especially not without socks. Yuk. Like no 'effing way. She cleared her throat. "While I appreciate the effort, I'm not exactly…comfortable wearing some stranger's shoes." She glanced up at Jake. Surely, he could understand that, right? The look on his face said otherwise.

He snorted. "You would rather go barefoot than have shoes?"

"Erm, well, those shoes, yes. It's just too gross. I have no idea whose feet those were on. What if they have some sort of fungus or something?" She almost gagged at the thought. "And without socks, whatever was wrong with their feet will spread to mine. I—I just can't."

Jake stared at her and then shrugged. "Okay, cream puff. Whatever you say. Get on your feet then, and let's go into town so we can get you some clothes and a new pair of shoes that no one else has ever worn before." He turned around and took a step toward the door. Then he stopped and turned back. "How do you know no one else has tried on the shoes you're going to buy? Maybe someone with horribly sweaty fungus-infected feet tried on all the small shoes in the store. How do you know that didn't happen?"

"I don't." She swallowed. "Thanks for pointing that out."

Jake shook his head and went through the bedroom door to the outer room. "Are you ready?"

"As I'll ever be," she murmured and then got off the bed. She took a couple of steps and then looked back at the sneakers. Her feet *were* killing her. Maybe it wouldn't be so bad to wear them.

Nope. Nope, it would. She continued walking and went to find Jake. She grabbed her bag on the way through the outer room and then walked out the door. She turned and pulled the door closed. Jake was already making his way across the living space, headed toward the stairs.

Madison started digging in her bag for the key. It shouldn't be too hard to find. The bag was big, but the key was huge by key standards. She dug around some more but couldn't find it. "Fuck," she mumbled to herself as she pawed through her stuff once more. She pulled out the ugly clutch purse that Giovanni had given her. It really was hideous with the studs all over it, and heavy, too. She looked around for somewhere to put it down but nothing was close so she set it on the edge of the large vase.

With more room in her bag, she could see a bit better, so she continued her digging. She shifted her weight and angled her bag to catch the light. It glinted off something silver in the very bottom corner of her purse. "Yes!" she said as she shoved her hand into the bag for the elusive key. Of course, she also chose that moment to straighten, which moved her foot slightly so that it hit the corner of one of the tiles on the floor. At the excruciating pain, she jumped back, hitting the vase and knocking the clutch inside.

Madison stared at the dark hole the clutch had disappeared into. What the fuck was she supposed to do now? She was not going to tell Graziana. That woman was near perfection as a host, and it just made Madison feel like an idiot being here, let alone telling her that she'd lost a clutch purse in one of Graziana's prized vases.

Jake was nowhere around and must have gone downstairs already so she couldn't ask him for help either. She stared at the vase, considering, then shrugged. What the hell, she'd leave it there. Someday someone would look at the vase more closely and find a surprise inside. She didn't feel like she owed Giovanni at all since he had been such an ass to her. She'd tell Drake about it and say she threw it out. He wouldn't care anyway.

Decision made, she dug in her purse again and, this time, successfully pulled out the key. She locked the door and then turned. Her heart clutched in her chest when she spied the Russian standing at the top of the stairs.

CHAPTER NINE

He'd been on his way to bring the car around closer to the hotel entrance so Madison didn't hurt her feet when he'd seen the *Polizia*. His first instinct had been to fight. The cops were not a real threat. One was older, in his late fifties by the look of things with thinning gray hair and a bit of a belly, while the other was young, early twenties, with dark hair. They were both standing there finishing their cigarettes as the Russian chatted on the phone and another young officer searched Jake's car.

Jake had no doubt he could deal with the cops in a timely manner, but the Russian was an unknown quantity. Mr. X., if he really was GRU, would know well how to fight, and Jake had no doubts the man would fight to kill. Jake had no qualms about doing that either, but if he lost, then Madison would be on her own, and he just wasn't having that. No fucking way.

As he walked back into the hotel, he'd called Mitch and told him they were about to be arrested. He'd put his go-bag in the hotel's main safe last night when he went out to get the T-shirt. The last thing he wanted was for some kid to break in and steal a pile of weapons. He had hated leaving it in the car in Florence, but he had parked in a well-lit, busy, low-crime area. It was the best he could do. He needed the weapons in his getaway vehicle in case he needed to escape in a hurry. Logically he probably should have left the bag in the car here as well but he just didn't think the Russian would find them that quickly.

He paused long enough to explain the situation to Graziana, and handed her the gun from his shoulder holster. She nodded and smiled at him, immediately hiding the weapon under her oversize sweater. She hurried into her office where he knew she'd stash the weapon with his other equipment in the hotel safe. Graziana was a gem. A smart woman who'd seen a lot in her day. She asked no questions, and Jake greatly appreciated that.

There was no point in running to get Madison and take off. It wasn't that he couldn't get to her in time, and he was sure he could get them out of the hotel, but then what? There was no way to get off the mountain by car since the cops had parked right by his vehicle, and although they could run down, Madison's feet wouldn't be able to take another run through the woods.

Then he waited for the cops and the Russian to enter. When they did, he took the stairs two at a time, forcing the police officers behind him to do the same if they wanted to keep up.

Once they were all at the top of the stairs, the Russian strode past Jake across the space to Madison and gave her the once over, lingering on the closure of her blazer, as if noting the lack of a blouse. The look on his face made Jake's skin crawl. He couldn't imagine what Madison must be feeling. To her credit, she kept her face blank and just stared at the man in front of her. Jake's admiration for her went up several notches.

"Arrest her," the Russian said as he attempted to push her out of the way and enter the room.

But Madison didn't budge. Instead, she demanded, "Who are you? You're not with the *Polizia di Stato*."

The two cops who were standing next to Jake glanced at one another. They didn't like the Russian either. Interesting.

The Russian leaned down about an inch from Madison's face. "Who I am—"

The older cop immediately moved forward and nudged the Russian out of the way. "I'm *Vice Sovrin*—" He broke off and shook his head. "I am Sergeant Montieri, and the other officer is…Constable San Godenzo." He pointed his thumb at the Russian, "This is Mr. Artyom Petrov. He is…helping us with our investigations in this matter." The older cop finished speaking and looked pleased with himself for getting it all out in his heavily accented English.

"Sergeant Montieri," Madison began, "would you be so kind as to tell me what exactly this is all about? I am at a loss."

Montieri glanced at the Russian and frowned. "*Signorina*, you have been accused of the theft of a very expensive diamond and ruby necklace."

"What?" Madison's eyes got big and her mouth fell open. "I have never stolen anything in my life. Why would someone think I stole a necklace? What necklace is it? Whose is it?"

The sergeant seemed taken aback by Madison's response. Jake didn't know her well, but unless she was capable of Meryl Streep-level acting, she wasn't faking her shock at being accused. The sergeant must have felt the same way because he narrowed his eyes at the Russian and ground his teeth.

"*Signorina*," the sergeant began, "I'm afraid I have to search your hotel room and your person." He turned to look at Jake. "Both of you."

Petrov leaned forward. "Don't pretend you are innocent. We know you stole the necklace. Perhaps we'll even find it in your room," he said with a smug smile. "Now move," he commanded and then pushed both the sergeant and Madison out of the way and grabbed the door handle. It refused to turn. He rattled it a bit but it wasn't budging. "Give me the key."

"It's in my purse." She held up the bag and then started to rummage around in it once more. She knocked the vase with her elbow and Montieri helped her steady it. He offered her a smile as he did so.

Finally, she pulled out the key. "Here—"

Petrov snatched it from her hand and stuck it into the lock. Seconds later, the door bounced against the wall as he forced it open and strode into the room.

Then turning his back on the room, the sergeant signaled the constable, and the man proceeded to pat down Jake. When he did a thorough job, Jake's estimation of the man went up. These guys knew what they were doing, and if he was reading the situation correctly, they weren't so pleased about the Russian's interference either.

Montieri looked at Madison and grimaced. He wasn't sure how to proceed.

"Might I suggest we ask Graziana or one of her assistants to help out with the search?" Jake offered.

Montieri's face broke into a smile. "*Si*, yes. A good idea." He gestured toward the constable who took off across the room and disappeared down the stairs. In the meantime, he put out his hand for Madison's bag and she handed it over. He did a thorough search and then placed it on the floor outside of the room when he was finished. The constable returned a minute later with Graziana in tow.

"*Si?*" she asked and then listened as the sergeant told her in Italian what he needed her to do. "*Si*," she agreed. Then she turned to Madison. "Why don't we just move over here, no?" She led Madison to an area at the other end of the large communal area. "We need to stay in the same room because I am not a police officer, but I will check you quickly. There is no one in the room here." She pointed to the door in front of her. "The guests have already gone out for the day so we will have as much privacy as possible."

Madison smiled slightly before she went over and stood where Graziana had pointed. The hotel proprietress moved Madison so her back was to the gentleman. It wasn't much, but Jake appreciated the effort, and he was sure Madison did, too. Graziana made quick work of patting down Madison's lower body and then she went behind her and searched her arms and then she patted down Madison's chest.

Graziana faced the men. "All good."

Madison turned around and met Jake's gaze. There was fire in her eyes. Jake swore silently. If she didn't hang on to her temper, things could go very badly. He tried to send her that message, but she shifted her gaze from his.

There was a sudden crash that came from the room. Montieri charged through the doorway, but Jake knew instantly what the sound was. Petrov had smashed Madison's laptop. Probably dropped it on the floor. He was a bastard. They'd debated bringing her laptop to town with them but Madison said her shoulder needed a break plus the battery was running low and she wanted to charge it. She'd told him about an encryption program she'd installed so it wasn't like anyone could easily access the information on it either.

Madison walked his way from across the room. When she was level with him, Jake grabbed her arm and stopped her. She whirled on him, eyes snapping angrily, but he simply shook his head. "It won't help anything," he murmured.

The constable was guarding the door to their room. He wasn't going to let Madison past, nor would he be pleased about her charging him. He gave her a stern look.

"Madison," Jake said in a voice so quiet he was sure the constable couldn't hear him, "at the moment, the local police are somewhat on our side. If you go charging in there, all that could change. You can't save your laptop now. It's not worth the risk of upsetting the sergeant."

Madison had opened her mouth to comment when the sound of the sergeant's voice came from the hotel room. He was yelling in Italian. Jake had only a rudimentary understanding of the language, but he was quite sure he heard a few curse words in there.

Then both men came through the doorway, first Petrov and then Sergeant Montieri. "We have a few questions to ask you," the sergeant said.

Petrov was pushing some piece of paper into his pocket as he moved closer to Madison again. "Where is it? Where is the necklace?" There was an urgency to his voice that hadn't been there before.

Madison shook her head. "I have no idea what you're talking about."

"Don't lie," he seethed. "Where is it? We know you stole it."

"Who's we?" Madison asked.

Good question.

The Russian's eyes narrowed. "Don't get smart with me. Where did you put the necklace?"

"I don't know what you're talking about. What necklace?" Frustration tinged her words.

Jake shifted to draw attention away from Madison. It worked. Petrov looked in his direction. "Where's the necklace?"

"I don't know anything about a necklace." Jake kept his voice neutral.

Without his gaze leaving Madison, Petrov directed at the other men, "Arrest the two of them. We'll take them back to Firenze and question them there."

"But you didn't find anything," Madison protested. "How can you arrest us and take us back to Florence if you didn't find anything?"

Jake coughed. "It's true. You have nothing. You can't arrest us because we haven't broken any laws."

"You ran from the other hotel in Firenze through the woods. Guilty people run through the woods. Innocent people exit by the front door," the Russian sneered.

"We ran through the woods because you were chasing us," Madison declared. "You followed me all across Florence without saying one word to me. It freaked me out! I had no idea you were working with the police. You never approached me to tell me. You just chased me down dark alleys.

"Then when I asked Jake for help, you stormed his hotel, looking for me. What was I supposed to do, wait around to ask questions of the man who'd been stalking me all day?" Madison had her hands on her hips and was glaring at Petrov now. "You had me scared to death. Not once did you identify yourself as a police officer or indicate to me that you only wanted to speak to me. No wonder we took off when you showed up. You should be ashamed of yourself."

Jake tried not to laugh. Madison was laying it on a little thick, but the sergeant and the constable were lapping it up.

The Russian was disgusted. "Arrest them."

Sergeant Montieri shook his head. "*Signor* Petrov, they are correct. We have nothing to arrest them for. They have not broken any laws."

"Well then take them in to be questioned," Petrov demanded.

"No." Montieri shook his head. "These people have been questioned enough." His face hardened. "*Signorina*, I am so sorry for disturbing you and your companion. I do apologize. Please try to enjoy the rest of your stay in Italy." He gave her a small nod. Then he turned to Petrov and started yelling at him in Italian.

Jake grabbed her purse off the floor and gripped Madison by the arm and pulled her into the room. He closed and locked the door after them. "Get your blouse on. I want to get out of here as soon as possible. I have no idea what's going on out there, but I don't want to take the chance."

Without a word, Madison went into the bathroom, closing the door behind her.

Jake took a quick look around to make sure he had everything he'd come with, which wasn't much. Then he searched Madison's bag to see if Petrov had left any tracking devices in it. He didn't find anything, but that didn't mean there wasn't one. Although, it wasn't hard to figure out where they would go. Jake needed his clothes, and so did Madison. They would have to go back to her Airbnb and his hotel. The question was, was the whole incident really over?

The voices had died out in the hallway, and Jake heard cars start up in the drive. He glanced out the window. The police were leaving. Did Petrov go, too? He looked around, but he didn't see the Russian anywhere outside.

He hadn't been entirely honest with Madison. He was pretty sure he knew what was going on between Montieri and Petrov. Montieri was telling Petrov off for involving him in something shady. Petrov was no doubt fuming that Montieri wouldn't do his bidding.

The big problem was that just because Montieri wouldn't do what Petrov wanted, that didn't mean the cops back in Florence would be the same. If Jake had to guess, he'd say Petrov had some friends who were high up in the Florence police department. They'd let him search Madison's apartment without any kind of supervision if Madison was to be believed.

The bathroom door opened, and Madison came out fully dressed this time. As much as Jake had admired her guts for just wearing the blazer, he was happy to see her fully clothed. That thought stopped him cold. Since when did he want an attractive woman to put her clothing back on? Since other men were ogling her. He'd like to snap Petrov's neck for making Madison feel uncomfortable.

"Ready?" he asked.

She straightened the hem of her blazer. "Where are we going?"

"Good question. We have a couple of options. We can find somewhere else to hide out for a while or we can go back to Florence."

He looked down at Madison. She seemed so small and vulnerable. Her eyes had dark circles under them, and the fine lines in her face seemed to have deepened overnight. He wanted to comfort her. Wrap her in his arms and tell her everything was going to be alright, but he'd be lying. He had no clue what the hell was going on so telling her it would be okay was bullshit. He didn't want to lie to Madison. Not ever.

"Let's get back to Florence. I just want to get my stuff and get on a plane back home. I'm done with all of this." She turned and grabbed her laptop off the table. She opened the cover and surveyed the damage. The whole screen was smashed. "Do you think it will still work if I change the screen?"

Jake shook his head. "I think you'll be hard pressed to get it to turn on. Petrov must have thrown it against the floor to make that much damage."

"Why would he do that? It doesn't make sense."

Jake ran a hand through his hair. "No, it doesn't. This whole thing is just fuckin' weird." There was more going on here, and Jake hated the gnawing feeling in his gut that was telling him they were still in trouble.

This wasn't over. Not by a long shot.

CHAPTER TEN

"Hello?" Madison answered her cellphone as she walked down the stairs of the hotel. Jake was bringing the car closer since she still didn't have shoes.

"Monty, it's nice to hear your voice. How are you holding up?" Thane Hawkins asked. As Drake's top lawyer, she should have guessed Thane would be the one Drake would assign to deal with all of this.

"I'm hanging in there, Thane." Her voice sounded tired to her own ears.

"I'm sorry you're going through all of this. I am on my way back to Florence. I already have some people working on the issue. I will call you as soon as I know something. I was told you think you're going to be arrested. What's the current situation?"

She reached the bottom of the stairs and stood in the lobby area. She glanced out the window and saw Jake's car approaching the front door. "It looks like I've dodged that bullet. The *Polizia* came and spoke with me and searched our room, but they had to let me go since they didn't find anything. We're just about to leave and head back to Florence. I'm going to try and get a flight out today."

"Uh, unfortunately, you won't be able to do that."

"What? Why?"

"You are a person of interest in a major theft. If you go to the airport, they will arrest you as a flight risk and keep you until they conclude their investigation. The fact that they didn't arrest you at this moment doesn't mean this is over."

Madison's shoulders sagged so that her bag slid off and dropped to the floor. She didn't even try to catch it. It wasn't like her laptop was salvageable. "You've got to be kidding me. I just can't believe this is happening."

"I know, Monty, and I am truly sorry. Is Jake there? I'd like to speak with him if I could, please."

Madison looked up. Jake was climbing out of the car.

She waved him over and handed him the phone when he arrived. "Thane Hawkins. He wants to speak with you."

She trudged over and sat down in one of the comfortable chairs in the lounge area. She just couldn't believe this wasn't over. They didn't find anything. She didn't steal anything. It was all too crazy for words. She rubbed her face with both hands.

"Here." Jake came to a halt in front of her chair and handed back her cellphone. "Hawk says it's better if we stay here. The fact that the Russian, who obviously has connections, couldn't get the locals to arrest you means they're not likely to try again unless they have something more concrete. In Florence, he feels we might not be so lucky."

Madison leaned back in the chair. "I just don't fucking understand any of this." She rubbed her face again.

"Why don't we go into the village and buy you some shoes and clothes. Then we can have a look around and maybe grab a late lunch or early dinner. We can come back and crash early. Things will look better with shoes and sleep."

Madison gave a quick smile to Jake. She appreciated his attempt to cheer her up, but she was past the point where anything but being done with all of this would bring her joy. She heaved herself to her feet. Shoes would be nice, though.

"Why do you call him Thane?" Jake asked. "When he was introduced to us, he said to call him Hawk. That everyone does."

Madison shrugged. "That was in Hawaii, right? From what I understand about those circumstances, Thane wasn't exactly doing his day job. In the everyday world, Thane is a very well-respected and somewhat feared lawyer. Within the company people call him Hawk but in the courtroom and in the boardroom it's Thane. I understand he is a former special forces type where being called Hawk makes a bit more sense. So I guess he's like Jekyll and Hyde. Or better yet, Superman. Mild mannered lawyer by day but fierce superhero by night."

Madison smiled at that thought. If only it were true. She needed a superhero at the moment. Someone who could come in and solve all of her problems for her and then sweep her off her feet. Jake would do nicely as her superhero. She glanced up at him and then snorted. She could fantasize all she liked but he could only do so much. Nope, she was going to have to rescue herself. Now she just had to figure out how to do it.

First, she needed shoes. "Let's go then. I guess we have to ask for a room again." She started walking toward the main door.

"I took care of that. We're good to stay as long as we need to."

Madison didn't say anything, but Jake's relationship with Graziana must be quite something if she cleared the decks for them. She dismissed the small flare of jealousy in her chest as being ridiculous and climbed into the passenger side of the car.

Madison did her best to be companionable with Jake for the afternoon. She bought shoes, black flats and sneakers, some tops, and jeans. He got a few items as well. The day had gotten warm so he switched into one of the new shirts. It was a blue Henley that really brought out his eyes. In town, they had a long lunch in a cafe that served excellent pasta, and Madison indulged in a glass of wine.

A few days in rural Tuscany might not be so bad. She glanced over at her lunch partner as he settled the bill. The scenery was amazing to look at. She was equally sure it would be fantastic to touch. The waitress smiled at Jake and flirted with him as best she could with the language barrier. Jake smiled but didn't seem to notice the woman's attempts to get his attention.

"You ready to go?" he asked as he put his wallet away.

"Yes." She stood up, and they walked from the little outdoor patio onto the sidewalk.

"Is there anything else you want to see?" Jake asked.

You naked? Madison grinned to herself and then coughed to cover it. The wine must have hit her harder than she thought. Probably hadn't been the best idea to have a glass when she was so tired and stressed. It seemed to have gone straight to her head.

"Madison?" Jake touched her arm. "Are you okay?"

"What? Yes. Just tired, I guess. I think I'd like to go back to the hotel. Maybe grab a nap." *With you,* she added silently. Yup, the wine definitely went to her head.

They walked back to the car in silence. Madison tried to focus on happy thoughts but found her mind drifting to either her situation or her protector. She'd never thought of herself as liking the whole macho man type thing, but Jake was different. He was definitely the strong, silent type with her at least. She loved how safe she felt when she was around him. She just hadn't realized how hot she would find that.

Being of a smaller stature, she was always more aware of her surroundings. It wouldn't take much to overpower her, and it didn't matter how many hours she had spent at the gym working out or taking self-defense classes. She just didn't have the mass that others did. With Jake watching out for her, she could relax far more than she normally might. It was refreshing. She felt a freedom she hadn't felt in a long time. It was a luxury beyond anything any label could produce.

When Jake ran a hand through his thick, dark brown locks, Madison had the urge to do the same. He had a square jaw that was runway ready. Models would swoon for his chiseled look and the deep blue of his eyes could strike a woman dead. The way his muscles moved under his new shirt was mesmerizing to watch. The seams on the sleeves were pulled taut as he moved his arms. Yes, all in all, an incredibly sexy man. Too bad they'd met this way. He probably thought she was more trouble than she was worth.

The drive back to the hotel was slow, and with the sun shining down, Madison was quite sleepy by the time Jake pulled into the parking lot.

"I am in desperate need of a nap," she declared as they lifted the bags out of the trunk.

Jake handed her the majority of them and only held a couple in his left hand, which was surprising at first until she realized that he was keeping his gun hand unencumbered just in case. When he'd changed his shirt because of the heat, she'd seen him tuck his gun in his waistband, then settle the new Henley over the telltale bulge. That brought her back down to reality with a thump.

Jake left her standing at the entrance of the room while he did a quick sweep. "All clear," he called as he came back to the living area.

"I think I'm going to take that nap now if you don't mind." Madison put the bags next to the red sofa. She'd go through them later and sort them out.

"No, go ahead. I'm going to make some calls."

She brushed by him and then stopped. "Could I have the T-shirt back? The one I slept in? I didn't think to buy something to sleep in, and I really want to get out of these clothes."

Jake ran his eyes over her, and heat bloomed in her cheeks. She clamped her jaw and tried to will the color back down.

"Sure," he said. Was she imagining things, or was his voice a bit lower, sexier than it had been before?

"Thanks." She let him pass and then followed him down the short hallway to the bedroom. She'd taken off her blazer and was working on removing her new shoes when Jake appeared at her side with the T-shirt.

"Oh!" She let out a small yelp and lost her balance. Jake caught her by the arm and pulled her against his chest to help her regain her equilibrium.

"Thanks." Her body relaxed as if it knew being in his arms meant she was safe.

He made a sound deep in his throat as his eyes fastened on her lips. Whether it was the wine or the general stress of the situation, she didn't know, but she parted her lips ever so slightly. It was an invitation.

"Madison"—his voice was almost a growl—"you've been flirting with me all day. You need to stop."

So much for it being the wine. Had she really been flirting with him all day? Yes. She'd smiled at him and brushed by him more times than were strictly necessary. She'd asked him questions, trying to coax out of him information about himself. He'd been stoic all day. No warmer to her than the waitress. The heat was back in her cheeks, only this time, being so close to him, it was in other places, too.

"You're right. I'm sorry. I guess I'm just…" Just what? Frightened? Scared that she was going to jail in a foreign country for something she didn't do? She blinked back tears.

Jake's arms moved all the way around her and he held her close. "Look I'd promise you it's all going to be okay but…I won't lie to you. I don't know what's going to happen. I can promise you that I will do my best to keep you safe."

She wrapped her arms around his waist. "I know. I know you'll keep me safe." And she did. She knew it in her bones. That wasn't helpful though because it made her want him all the more. She gazed up at him from under her lashes.

Jake let her go and eased her away from his chest. She bit her lip. His eyes darkened. She knew he wanted her but something was holding him back.

His voice rumbled out of his chest. "My job is to protect you. Having sex with you would just cloud that. I don't sleep with clients."

She heard the words, and she knew they were meant to be cold, to make her smarten up, but the fact that he was still holding her close to him said something else. "Technically, we slept together last night."

"You know what I mean."

"Yes, I do. I also know that I like the feel of being in your arms. That it's the only place at the moment I feel safe. I want to spend the rest of the day and all night in those arms feeling all kinds of things as well as safe. Thane is working on getting me out of this mess. I'll be able to leave soon. One night and you're free of your obligation to watch over me. I would like to spend it getting to know you intimately. How do you want to spend it?" She cocked an eyebrow at him.

"Don't bait me." The growl was back.

"Why not?" she asked as she put her hands on his chest.

"You may not like the response."

She tilted her head back. "Oh, I doubt that."

CHAPTER ELEVEN

Jake swooped down and claimed her mouth. He knew it was wrong. Like fucking, career-destroying wrong, but he'd been fighting his desire to kiss her all day, hell, since he'd first seen her. She brought out this fierce desire to protect her but, also, to have her. She tasted like wine and strawberries and so much more. Maybe it was because he was exhausted or maybe it was him being so burnt out but, suddenly, he just didn't give a fuck about his job. He wanted Madison. Here and now and as many times as he could have her.

He broke off the kiss. "Madison," he said in a low voice, "are you sure you want to do this?"

She looked up at him, her hazel eyes filled with desire. "Hell, yes. I want to feel you inside me."

Jesus, she was killing him. He scooped her up and brought her over to the desk where he set her down.

She laughed. "Why the desk? There's a bed right there."

"The desk is higher," he growled and then claimed her lips again. He put his hands on her ass and pulled her to the edge of the desk. When she opened her legs, he snugged her against his cock. When he moved back and forth against her core, she moaned.

Jake rained tiny kisses down her neck and nipped the soft hollow behind her ear.

"Jake," she groaned as she fisted his hair.

The raw need in her voice as she said his name set off a fierce deep-seated desire to possess her. He wanted—no needed her to scream his name when she came. She was going to be his no matter what.

He undid her blouse with one hand while he held her against him with the other. He didn't want any space between them. When he got to her bra, he pushed the strap down and dipped his head to suck her nipple. She moaned when he swirled his tongue around the hard bud.

She stroked her hands from his neck, down his chest, to his waist and then back up under his shirt. He reached back with one hand and pulled his shirt off over his head, then dropped it on the floor before claiming her nipple once again.

He undid her bra and pushed her blouse and bra off and dropped them onto the floor next to his shirt. Then he picked her up and took her over to the bed. After she laid back on it, he slowly lowered himself on top of her.

"Jake," she breathed, "you feel so damn good." She kissed his neck while she ran her hands down his back and cupped his ass. She wrapped her legs around his waist and arched against him.

"Fuck, you're so fucking hot I can feel you through my jeans." He groaned when she rubbed back and forth against his cock. She quickly undid his belt and jeans, then pushed them down over his hips. He stood up and pulled them off. Then he climbed back onto the bed.

Madison lifted her hips and undid her skirt. She shimmied it off, leaving her in nothing but a black lace thong.

"Jesus," he growled.

She was beautiful and so fucking hot. He was so hard he was in pain. He quickly lowered himself on top of her and captured her mouth with a scorching kiss.

Madison's hands cupped his ass as she rubbed against him. "I want to feel you inside me."

"Not yet." He wanted to be inside her, but he wanted other things first. He bent his head to suck her nipple just as she touched him through the fabric of his underwear. He groaned. He couldn't help it. He wanted her touch badly, but he knew if she started, he wouldn't have the power to stop her. And he had so many things he wanted to do to her first.

"You need to wait," he said in between kisses and then grabbed her hands.

"But I want to touch you," she complained as she strained against his grip.

She was so incredibly beautiful. He lowered his mouth to one nipple and then the other. Slowly, he left a trail of kisses down her stomach to her thong. He got harder still, if that was possible, as he ran his fingers across the lace.

When he reached the middle, he let his fingers dip lower.

"Jake." Her voice was breathy, and he doubted that he'd ever heard anything sexier.

The sound of his name on her lips again brought out a wave of fierce desire, and he quickly yanked off her thong. He hovered his mouth over her and blew gently. When she whispered his name again, straining her hips to reach him, he dropped a kiss on her core.

"Oh, my God." Her fingers fisted in his hair as he slid his hands under her hips to bring her to his mouth.

He used his tongue to tease and suckle her, taking her to the brink before stopping. "Madison, say my name," he growled.

She opened her eyes. They were filled with desire.

"Say my name," he said again. He wanted her to know, to remember who made her feel so good. He wanted it imprinted into her brain.

She cocked an eyebrow and smiled slightly. "Jake." Her voice was throaty and so sexy it damn near pushed him over the edge.

He smiled and then brought her to the brink once more, his tongue dancing over her sweet spot. He drove his fingers inside her in a steady rhythm, faster and faster until she crashed over the edge, yelling his name as she arched beneath him. He felt incredibly powerful and insanely protective of her.

None of it made any sense, but he didn't care.

Madison could scarcely breathe. She'd wanted Jake from the moment she'd landed in his lap, but this was better than she'd even imagined. His body was hard and unyielding, and she loved it. The hard planes and defined muscles excited her.

She caressed her fingers over his chest and then locked her hands around the back of his neck. She brought his mouth down to hers and claimed it with a harshness she didn't know she possessed. She wanted him inside. Now.

Their gazes locked as she reached down to push off his black boxer briefs. But he stood and pulled them off himself and then came back to lay on top of her. He swore as her hand stroked him. He was hard as rock.

She rolled him over and climbed on top of him. She rained kisses down his jaw and ran her hands across his chest. She sucked on his nipple and then blew on it. She did the same with the other nipple, and he groaned. She loved that she had the power to drive this man twice her size crazy with her touch.

It was intoxicating.

She shifted her weight until she was straddling his hips. She slowly rubbed her core across his cock. He flexed against her. Her core was hot and wet again. She raised her hips and moved over his cock then lowered herself down onto him. First, she just let the tip enter her. Teasing him, she pulled back.

He swore. His eyes turned midnight blue.

Smiling, she started lowering herself again. This time, she took in more of him. She wanted to tease him longer, but she couldn't handle it. She needed him now.

Jake reached out and grabbed her hips to guide her to his rhythm. She rode him, picking up the pace. The feel of him inside her, filling her up, was exquisite.

Her breath puffed out in small, sharp gasps. She was going to come. She said his name and urged him on, her hips rushing to meet his thrusts. She teetered on the brink and had to bite her lip to keep from screaming.

He drove deep inside her, and she crashed over the edge, euphoria filling her every cell. Jake followed her, and her body kept squeezing him as wave after wave washed over her.

She fell on top of his chest, sweaty and out of breath. That had been fucking amazing. "Round two?"

CHAPTER TWELVE

Madison toweled off in the small shower. She ached in all the right places. They'd had a round two and three, and all had been great until Jake got a call from some guy named Mitch. She sighed. He'd immediately gone into work mode and hadn't spoken to her since. A chill had definitely descended. That was over an hour ago.

She dropped the towel and pulled on her clothes, a pair of faded jeans and a light knit forest green sweater. She'd bought the sweater, thinking it would accentuate the color of her eyes, and it did, but now Jake would be too busy to notice. Why was she so hung up on him? Stupid. She'd known him for forty-eight hours and she was already trying to impress him or at least get him to notice her. Whatever. She'd said one night and he'd given her that or at least he'd given her what she wanted if not technically the whole night. *What they'd both wanted.* He'd been a willing and enthusiastic participant. Now that was over. He was free to do whatever. She needed to accept that. Adulting sucked sometimes.

Madison left the bathroom and found Jake in the living area on the phone. The call was on speaker. She stood beside a chair and listened.

"So, you've got nothing else?" Jake asked.

Another man's voice responded on speaker. "Nah. This guy Petrov or Fedorov is like a ghost. We know he used to work for the GRU, but he disappeared off the face of the planet about five years ago. The fact that he's in Italy, working for some fashion house, has everyone stumped, including our sources in Washington."

"And there's nothing out there on why the Veridanis are trying to pin this on Madison?"

"Nope. And you're right, it's just fucking weird as hell."

Jake frowned. "Okay, well thanks for trying. I think we'll head back to Florence tonight. I was thinking tomorrow, but from the sounds of things, that might be too late."

"It's a tough call, but I agree with you. If you're there, you can maybe mitigate what's going on. Hawk is already at his place. He got your things from the hotel, by the way. Meet him at his place and go from there. Let me know if you need anything," the man said. "I have the boys on the third floor still digging. I'll let you know if we turn anything up."

"Thanks." Jake clicked off the call.

Madison sat down in the chair opposite him. "What's going on?"

Jake met her eyes for what seemed like the first time since they'd finished having sex but he kept his expression blank. "That was my boss, Mitch Callahan. Petrov is actually a guy named Fedorov, and he is former GRU."

She was glad she was sitting down because that news made her knees go weak. "Why would a former Russian military intelligence guy want to follow me around?"

Jake's eyes narrowed. "How did you know what I meant by GRU?"

Madison rolled her eyes. "I read a lot of spy novels, as well as watch the shows on TV." Why was he so suspicious of her suddenly? Things had been fine a couple of hours ago when he was fucking her brains out, but now, she was *persona non grata*.

"I don't have any answers for you yet. I'm assuming Fedorov is security for Veridani and they sent him to find their stolen necklace, but as to why he followed you around all day and didn't approach you right off, it's hard to say." He went back to staring at his phone.

Madison leaned back in the chair and folded her arms across her belly. "I heard you say we're going back to Florence tonight. How come?"

Jake didn't bother to look up. "I spoke with Hawk. He is checking with his source, but he thinks Fedorov is still trying to get you arrested. Hawk feels if that happens, he would like to be there. If they grab you out here, he's not sure what will happen."

Madison's heart stuttered. "What does he mean by that?"

"It means we don't know if they just want to arrest you or if they have…something else in store for you. Fedorov isn't exactly known for playing by the rules." Jake looked up, his expression neutral, but his knuckles were white while holding his phone. He wasn't happy, or at least that's what she thought he was feeling. She didn't know him well enough to read him, which was a bit embarrassing since she'd just spent hours performing the most intimate acts with him. She swallowed and tried to will the heat out of her cheeks.

"Okay. When are we leaving?" she asked in a quiet voice. She just couldn't believe this was happening to her.

"Now." Jake stood up. "Grab your things. I'll go down and sort out the bill with Graziana." He walked to the door but then turned back to look at her. "Don't open this to anyone until I get back." And then he was gone.

Madison blinked back tears. This shit just couldn't really be happening to her. It just couldn't. She got to her feet and grabbed all her new clothes from the bags. Good thing she'd bought lots of underwear; it didn't look like she was going home anytime soon.

Twenty minutes later, they were headed down the mountain. Jake had maintained his cool demeanor, which was killing her because she really needed a hug now.

She sighed. "What the hell do you think is really going on? I mean, do you think it's more than just they think I stole a valuable necklace?"

Jake glanced at her. "I think there's more to it than we know. We only have a few of the puzzle pieces, and it's impossible to get the whole picture from the little we have."

"Do you think it's safer to go back to Florence like Thane says?"

She bit her lip. She wanted to run away, not head back to Florence. It felt like jumping from the frying pan into the fire.

"I think it's risky, but at the same time, coming out here didn't really help us either. Seems to only..." His voice faded out. He shook his head. "If Fedorov gets you arrested out here, there's little I can do. Thane's right on that score. You're better off having him close by in that scenario."

"So we're damned if we do and damned if we don't. Is that what you're saying?"

"What I'm saying is the best thing to do is get out of Italy pronto."

She frowned. "I thought Thane said it was unlikely they'd let me out."

"He did. We're gonna see how it goes. If things start to go south, we'll get out of Italy. Then it's much harder for Fedorov and whoever he works for to hassle you. We can also set up protection for you back in New York, or wherever, for the time being, just to make sure everything is okay."

Great. More money. Her nest egg was going to be shot at this rate. She looked out the window, but it was after midnight and there was no moon. She just saw her reflection staring back at her. "Why do they think I stole a necklace?"

"Don't know. Were you around an expensive necklace lately?"

"No I...well, shit." She straightened in the seat. "Yes, I was. Valentina Veridani created some jewelry pieces before she died. They are on display at Veridani headquarters in Florence. The center piece of the collection is a necklace made of diamonds and rubies. They said it's worth about five million Euros."

Jake whistled. "Well, that would explain a lot if we assume Fedorov works for Veridani."

"Why would they think I stole it?"

"Didn't you say someone named Paloma showed this stuff to you? Maybe you were the last person to see it, so they assumed you stole it." Jake drummed his fingers on the steering wheel. "Still, that doesn't really hold up. I mean, you would have to have access to get it. Why would they think you had access to grab it?"

"Damn," Madison said. "I was there Monday night. No one

seemed to be around, but I just assumed they were in their offices working. I mean, who leaves a consultant in their offices alone at night? Besides, the jewelry was in glass cases like you see at museums. I am sure they were alarmed as well. It's not like I brought a pile of tools with me so I could break into the glass box and mosey out with the necklace. It would take some serious planning and skills to steal that jewelry."

"Why were you there?"

"Paloma called me after dinner. She said there was a mix-up with some of the paperwork and she needed help straightening it out. She implied that my team screwed something up and she was doing me a favor by calling me to come fix it before anyone found out."

"What time was this?" Jake demanded.

"About nine-forty-five, I think. I told her of course I would come, but I took my time and walked over. It's not far, but there were quite a few people on the street so I probably got there around ten fifteen. Paloma was put out that she had to wait. She explained that the paperwork showing the orders no longer matched what was in the computer and asked me to fix it."

Jake glanced over again. "Wait, she said the orders in the computer didn't match the actual paper copies? Why would you have to fix that?"

"Because my team was given paperwork but also access to the online files. Paloma thought someone had done something that deleted some data. The data was actually the same, but when she ran a report, it came out all jumbled up because someone *had* gone in and edited what should be in the report. I can understand why that would be upsetting, but it was an easy fix. I was surprised she didn't realize what had happened. She seemed competent. She should have been able to fix it herself. It only took a couple of minutes. I was out of the building again by ten-thirty."

"Was she with you the whole time?"

"No. She left after about five minutes. She seemed quite anxious to get out of there. Said she had a date."

When Madison looked over at Jake, his jaw was set and his knuckles had turned white on the steering wheel. He said, "I'm guessing she did know how to fix it. She was probably the one that screwed it up."

"What do you mean? Why would she do that?"

"To set you up. She brought you in late at night by yourself for about fifteen minutes by creating a problem you would feel obligated to fix. Just enough time to steal the necklace and blame you."

Madison's stomach rolled. "Oh, my God! Do you really think that's what happened?"

Jake nodded. "The big question is, did she do it on her own or was she doing it for someone else?"

"We have to talk to her." Madison wanted to do more than talk if this woman had set her up.

"No." His response was curt.

Madison glared at Jake. "What do you mean, no?"

"Confronting her is a mistake. There's no proof, and it just serves to warn her that we're on to her."

Madison's pulse ticked up. She fisted her hands. "But I want to talk to the cops. I want to tell them my side of the story. I didn't steal the necklace."

"That's not the smartest way to deal with this. Italy is notorious for having a lot of corruption. Fedorov seems to have some connections. They could get you railroaded in no time flat. We need to move cautiously."

"Drake!" Madison blurted out. "They'll have told him that I stole the necklace!" How could she have forgotten to call Drake? Well, she was being chased by a crazy Russian guy and then she spent most of the rest of the day in bed with Jake. *Shit.* She owed Drake so much. She needed to at least call him and apologize.

She rummaged in her purse for her cell phone. "I have to call Drake. I have to explain. Oh, my God, what if he doesn't believe me?" The purse in her lap blurred and she grabbed the door handle as her world seemed to spin. She closed her eyes.

"Are you okay?" Jake demanded.

Madison put a hand on her head and took a deep breath. She opened her eyes. Everything was in focus once more. "Yeah, fine," she muttered. She went back to searching her purse. As much as she wanted to start a new career, she didn't want to completely torpedo the old one. Plus, with this hanging over her, no one would ever buy her bags. Hell, she probably wouldn't be able to get them made.

Jake's harsh voice cut through her building hysteria. "Calm down. First, Drake is a lot of things, but he's not stupid. He won't believe them because he knows you and knows you wouldn't steal something like that. Second, it's Drake. If he wanted to talk to you, he'd call. I would imagine he'll reach out when he has a minute."

Madison sighed. "I just really want to go home." She looked out the window at the passing scenery. They were driving through a charming little village with people standing on the sidewalk outside what looked like a bar, chatting, looking like they were enjoying life. The place must have just closed. She wanted to get back to that. It had been a while since enjoyment had been the top of her list of things to do, this afternoon excepted.

"Do you have a boyfriend in New York? Someone you should tell what's going on?"

Was he serious? What kind of a person did he think she was? She just spent hours in bed with him. There's no way in hell she would have done that if she had a boyfriend. "No," she said stiffly. "I don't. I don't do well in relationships." And that was the truth.

He glanced at her. "Why not?"

"Because I hate having people depend on me. I want to do my own thing and not have to worry about anyone else. I'm selfish, I guess. I always thought the perfect relationship would be if I could see someone two or three nights a week, and that was it. I don't want to have to build a life around someone. You know what I mean?"

"Yes, I do," he said in a tone that left her feeling hurt. Why was she hurt? She'd just told him what she wanted. He was allowed to want that, too. It was just that maybe she wanted him to say he'd like to see her back in New York and maybe more than two or three nights a week. She shook her head. Now she knew for sure she was losing it. She stared at the darkness.

The sound of a ringing cell phone filled the little car. Jake pulled it out of his pocket while he drove. "Boxer," he said. "Wait, let me put you on speaker, Mitch." He pulled the phone away from his ear and put it on the center console. "Mitch Callahan, my boss." He touched the screen. "There. Tell us what you've found out."

Mitch's voice filled the car. "First, Madison, it's nice to meet you. I'm only sorry it's under these circumstances."

"The feeling is mutual. I've heard a lot about you and your brothers from Drake. Although we haven't met before, I feel like I know you already."

It was clear Mitch was done with the niceties. He got right into it with him. "Nikolay Fedorov, aka Artyom Petrov and twenty more aliases, was born in Moscow fifty-two years ago. He worked his way up first in the military and then in the GRU until he left abruptly five years ago. On paper it looks like he retired, but really he dropped off the face of the earth. Scuttlebutt says he was actually kicked out for overstepping on some big assignment. Apparently, he tortured someone and they died. Not abnormal, but I guess the Russians wanted the victim alive. Fedorov then disappeared but turned up last year as Artyom Petrov, head of security for Valentina Veridani Fashion."

"Any ideas on the missing years? How the hell do you go from the GRU to a fashion house security guard?" Jake demanded.

"Unknown at this time, but we're working on it. What we are hearing is Fedorov seems to have friends in high places in Florence and other cities. Veridani is a popular fashion house. It has some sway with the locals. The brothers who run it are pretty savvy. They donate to a bunch of charities that are rumored to line the pockets of a lot of local officials, so they get what they want when they want it."

"Why do fashion houses need that kind of pull?" Jake asked.

Madison broke in, "The fashion houses need the best space to highlight their work, so they all vie for the top locations for their retail stores. Plus, Veridani does some of the work on their clothing here in Italy as part of Valentina's legacy of loving her home. They have a couple of factories that do some production work, although I've heard it's all for show. On paper it looks good, and they get all kinds of tax breaks for it."

Jake asked, "Wouldn't something like that put Drake off investing?"

Madison shook her head. "No, that's just the cost of doing business, as Drake calls it. All businesses have some sort of scheme set up to help them get breaks and get ahead."

Mitch said, "All this boils down to is watch your asses while you're there. Hawk will have more details on what's going on, but it all looks a little shady from here."

"From here, too," Jake commented.

"Do you need anything?" Mitch asked.

"We may need an extraction for Madison. If this all goes sideways, we'll need her out of here pronto."

"Agreed. I'll start setting it up. I'll be back in touch when everything is in place," Mitch said. "Madison, I am so sorry this is happening to you."

"Me, too, but thanks."

"I'll be in touch." Mitch clicked off the call.

Jake said, "We're going to be in Florence soon."

Madison's stomach knotted. The road had changed from the winding, twisting lane to the marginally wider urban street. Cars were parked along the sides as the city scape grew more condensed around them. Her agitation grew with every passing light. She had no interest in being somewhere where she could be arrested, nor did she want to meet up with Petrov again. He made her skin crawl. The way he looked at her when she was wearing only the blazer had made her want to puke, but she hadn't been willing to give him the satisfaction. What she really wanted to do was smash his nose into his face, but that wasn't a possibility either.

Jake's cell phone went off again. "Boxer." He followed the same procedure and put it on speaker. "Hi, Hawk, you're on speaker."

"Hi, Jake. Hi, Monty. How are you two holding up?"

Madison wanted to laugh. How was she doing? She was a mess. She cleared her throat. "I'm okay, Thane. I've had better days, but we're getting there. At least we didn't get arrested."

"Hmmm, about that. I'm sorry to say, you shouldn't celebrate just yet."

"Oh, God. Now what?" Madison demanded as her heart started hammering against her ribs and sweat broke out on her palms.

"Why don't we discuss this in person? Where are you?"

"Just coming into Florence," Jake said.

"Come to my place. I'll text you the address. Monty, do you need anything? Clothing or toiletries?"

"No, I'm good. Thanks, though. I appreciate you asking." Trying to relax, Madison made a concerted effort to open her curled fists. She took a deep breath and held it in before she released it slowly. Thane Hawkins was a great corporate lawyer. Hopefully, he could help her with this situation. He certainly was good at getting things organized.

Jake's phone beeped. "I got the address. We'll be there in about twenty minutes."

Thane said, "Parking might be an issue, especially at this time of night. I have a spot, but I don't have a spare."

"Don't worry, I'll find something." Jake clicked off the call.

"Thane to the rescue," she mumbled. "I guess he's living up to his superhero stature. I sure hope he's got something good up his sleeve." Madison was numb. The whole thing was surreal. She just couldn't wrap her brain around it.

CHAPTER THIRTEEN

Jake ground his teeth. *Hawk a fucking superhero?* Not fucking likely. Hawk was a good, maybe even great operator, from what Jake had heard, but that didn't make him a fucking superhero. No more than Jake was, at any rate, because Jake knew he had been a fucking top-tier operator when he was in the SEALs, and he hadn't lost a beat.

He swallowed. Jealous much? What the fuck was wrong with him? He glanced at Madison. She was what was wrong with him. There was just something about her that made his male instincts and ego go into overdrive. Yeah, she was beautiful, but he'd been with a lot of beautiful women before and none of them had him this green with jealousy. None of them had him wanting to keep them safe no matter what the cost. None of them had been as good in bed. Jesus, this woman was a handful. He was getting hard just thinking about what they'd done that afternoon. He needed more of that in his life. A whole hell of a lot more. Madison in his bed was pure bliss.

He gave himself a mental shake. He must be more tired than he thought. It was just burnout, had to be, that was making him act this way. Pursuing this line of thinking was stupid. He needed to focus on the job at hand. Being distracted by the client was unprofessional, not to mention that fucking the client was *very* unprofessional. Jake had prided himself on being professional. It was all he had. Now what did he have? A fucking awesome afternoon of mind-blowing sex and a deep abiding desire for more. His career was over if this came out.

Hawk was a lawyer. Mitch ran a company with his brothers, and Logan, Mitch's brother, also worked at being a chef. The only thing Jake had was being a tier-one operator. He didn't have a degree or a trade or anything he could fall back on. His family relied on him to send them a bit of his wages every month and then some. He didn't have any hobby or interest he could turn into a new career. When he was no longer able to do protection work, he was done. There was no second act for him. He tightened his hands on the steering wheel.

When he made a quick right turn, Madison smacked into his shoulder.

"Sorry," he mumbled. He'd been so caught up in thought he almost missed his turn.

"Are we being followed?" Madison asked, her voice quivering a bit.

"What?" Jake glanced at her and then realized she thought he had made the tight turn to lose a tail.

He glanced in the rearview mirror. "We're not—" Shit. A car made the quick hard right just like they did. Now it was dropping speed and hanging back. Were they being followed? It was a Mercedes. He knew because he recognized the headlights but he couldn't determine the color. He guessed black. That was one of the most common colors but it could've been dark blue.

"We're being followed, aren't we?" she demanded as she started to turn to look out the back window.

"Don't look!" he commanded.

She shrank back in her seat.

He glanced at her. *Shit.* He'd scared her. "If you look and they see you looking then they'll know we're on to them." He glanced in the rearview mirror again. The Merc was further back and now they had another car between them. "I'm not positive we're being followed but I'm going to drive around a bit just in case."

He made another couple of turns down the quiet streets and then the Merc was gone. He glanced back but the street behind him was empty. His gut unknotted just a little.

"Are they gone?" Madison asked.

He glanced at her and she looked so scared it almost broke his heart. "I—" They were going through an intersection and he saw the Merc one block over driving through the other intersection. "Fuck," he growled. "We're being followed." He should have known Fedorov wouldn't have let them leave Mugello without following them. Or did he have them followed from there? Jake had kept his eye out for a tail but hadn't seen one until now. How could he have missed it? Because he'd been too focused on his jealousy and Madison rather than focusing on his job. *Fucking asshole.*

"Hold on. I'm going to try to lose them."

Madison bit her lip while she grabbed on to the door.

Jake rolled through the next intersection and the Merc was keeping pace one block down. He glanced in his rearview but didn't spy a tail. He stopped. Then he reversed back to the intersection. He turned left away from the Merc. Then he made another left two blocks over. He kept a sharp eye on the rearview mirror. Nothing. He tried to see if the Merc was running parallel but they were now in the labyrinth that was Florence so nothing was really a grid pattern anymore.

"Did you lose them?" Madison asked. Her voice shook.

He silently cursed himself for being irresponsibly negligent one more time. "I think so. How far are we from Hawk's?" he asked and pointed to his phone directing her attention there. He didn't want to take the time to look down at it. He might miss the Merc.

"It looks like he's not far. Maybe ten blocks but it's a serpentine route."

They rolled to a stop at a red light. The intersection was small, just a one-way street crossing another one-way. The buildings blocked his view. A tingling sensation started at the base of his skull. A bad sign. There were no cars in his rearview and the street ahead appeared quiet. He started to roll forward through the red light when the Merc came out of the side street and barreled across the intersection in front of them. He saw the surprised look of the driver through the side window. There was a man in the passenger seat but he didn't get a good look.

"Shit!" Jake's grip tightened on the wheel.

The Merc slammed on the brakes trying to stop their progress down the one-way street to their left. Jake immediately turned right and went the wrong way down the street. He floored it. Madison let out a small squeak and caught his phone as it flew off the center console.

"Jake!" She yelled as they careened through another red light almost taking out a car in the intersection.

He turned a hard right and they were suddenly in the middle of Florence next to the carousel in the Piazza della Repubblica. Jake slammed on the brakes and turned to the left. There was a parking spot open on the street and he quickly jammed the car into it.

"Grab your stuff. We need to move. Now!"

Madison grabbed her bag and got out of the car. Jake pulled his gun out from under the seat and tucked it into the waistband of his jeans under his shirt. He grabbed his go-bag from the back seat and met Madison on the sidewalk and grabbed her hand. "We've gotta run."

"Okay." Madison's eyes were the size of softballs, and her hand trembled in his. A fierce desire to protect her rose in him and he had to slam it back down. He needed to focus on his job, not react like a Neanderthal, although breaking the necks of the men in the Merc would make him feel damn good right now.

He pulled Madison along behind him as he ran down the sidewalk. They made the first block and were halfway down the second when the sound of an engine turning the corner bounced off the surrounding buildings. He didn't bother looking back. They were at the target. He turned into a very narrow alleyway and jerked Madison in behind him. It wasn't an alley so much as just the space between two very old buildings. But it led to the same type of alley at the back of the buildings. Then from there he could get them closer to Hawk's.

"Jake?" Madison huffed as they turned right onto another ally. "I need to catch my breath."

They'd slowed to a jog and now Jake stopped. He turned to her. It was hard to see her clearly in the dim light that shone from someone's apartment above. She was sucking in oxygen and her eyes were darting all over the place. Damn. "Take deep slow breaths, Madison," he instructed.

She shot him a glance that said, *what the fuck do you think I'm doing?*

"Slowly," he admonished. "Breathe slowly and deeply." A drop fell on his head. He glanced up. It was starting to rain. That was good. Rain lessened visibility. He looked back at Madison. She leaned against the wall, her head tilted upward, rain drops splashing on her skin. He wanted her so badly at that moment it scared him. They were in a back alley in the middle of Florence with men chasing them and all he could think about was how much he wanted to take her, here now against the wall.

Stupid. "We have to go."

"I know," she huffed but she kept her face upturned to the rain.

He took a step toward her, closing her in. Her eyes fluttered open as he lowered his mouth to hers. She opened her lips and he claimed her, leaning his body against hers as his tongue tasted her mouth. Heaven.

He broke off the kiss. Madison blinked. Her eyes were focused again and her breathing regulated. "We have to move now," he rasped. He grabbed her hand again and tugged her down the alley. Within minutes they were back out on the street and only a block from Hawk's.

They made it half a block down when someone stepped out of the shadows. Jake immediately pulled his weapon from his waistband and pushed Madison behind him.

"It's me." Hawk stepped out into the light. He was six feet with dark hair and blue eyes. He was of a similar build as Jake and, like Jake, had kept up his workouts since he left the SEALs so he was still in excellent shape. His white button-down was crisp, and the crease on his light gray dress pants was sharp. Some things just don't go away when you leave the military.

Jake glared at him. "Son of a bitch. I could have killed you."

Hawk smiled slightly. "Sorry. I was just doing a bit of recon. I wanted to make sure it was safe. I saw you coming, so I thought I'd wait."

Jake's heart rate started to settle, but he was still amped up. Being so close to Madison throughout the car ride hadn't helped him remain calm. Her scent had driven him to distraction and kept conjuring up a mental image of her naked on the bed. It had distracted him from knowing they'd been followed. Asshole rookie mistake. And then kissing her in the alley. It had been enough to drive him over the edge.

"Thane," Madison said as she stepped out from behind Jake. "It's good to see you." She had her hand on her chest and her voice had a tremor in it.

"Monty. Good to see you, too. Sorry it has to be in these circumstances."

Jake looked down at Madison, who still seemed like she was recovering from the shock. "I'm sorry if I scared you." He was gutted that she was terrified. It made him want to punch Hawk.

She put her hand on his arm and looked directly into his eyes. "No. Don't apologize. You were doing your job. I appreciate you taking such good care of me. It makes me feel like I am in good hands."

Jake swallowed. He had a fierce desire to pull her into his arms and kiss her like he had earlier. He broke the eye contact and turned to Hawk. "Take her with you. I'll go do a little recon of my own and meet you at your place shortly. We were followed. I want to make sure we really did lose them."

Hawk must have seen something on his face because he didn't ask any questions. "It's the doorway in the corner. My silver BMW is parked out in front. Let's go, Monty. I have wine waiting and some snacks. I wasn't sure if you'd had a chance to eat."

He pulled his go-bag off his shoulder. "Here, take this." He handed it to Hawk and the man slipped it over his shoulder. "Let's go," he said and they disappeared through the entrance to the courtyard of Hawk's building.

Jake had given in to his desire to kiss Madison, and that just wasn't acceptable. He was getting way too attached to his client in all the wrong ways. He needed to forget what happened earlier. It had been colossally stupid. He broke the cardinal rule and slept with the client, and now he desperately wanted to do it again. *Fuck!* He had to get himself under control.

With that thought, he walked to the end of the block in the soft rain. He turned right and went to the next street down. He did the same again until he came to the corner of Hawk's street. He took in the view before him, memorizing the street and the cars. Nothing stood out to him, which was good. Jake knew he was good, and he trusted his instincts completely when it came to work. It was just around Madison that he had to fight them.

The cobblestone street was narrow, with a very limited walkway, but here, people just walked in the street. There were some parked cars, but only the smallest of the small cars could fit. If anyone with a larger car even attempted to park there, they'd lose their mirror or probably a lot more.

Old stone buildings lined both sides of the street. There were storefronts in the bottom of some of the buildings with apartments on top. Other buildings were all apartments by the look of them. The narrowness of the street and dim streetlamps cast most of the street in shadows.

Jake took his time and walked the length of the block. Then he zigzagged for a few minutes to make sure no one was following him. He circled back and stood at the top of the street, watching the area while pretending to look at his phone. The two people who went by didn't pay him any attention and, better yet, no one paid attention to Hawk's building.

Satisfied that the street was clear, Jake walked down the right side of the street and turned into a narrow driveway that tunneled through the stone building around it. He came out in a wide cobblestone courtyard open to the sky where there was parking for residents. He saw Hawk's BMW parked in one corner, facing outward, ready for a swift getaway if necessary.

Jake went over to the doorway in the corner and hit the doorbell to Hawk's apartment.

Hawk opened the door a few seconds later. "All good?" he asked.

Jake nodded. The apartment was more like an American townhouse. The door opened right to a stairwell. Each apartment must have a separate entry. He followed Hawk up the stairs to the main floor where Hawk handed him a towel.

As Jake dried off, he checked out his surroundings. The room was all one open space, which was odd for Europe. The windows were tall, which would allow in a lot of sunlight. Jake loved sunlight. Bad things happened in the dark. There was a modern kitchen in the left corner along the back wall that included American-sized appliances. Another anomaly in Europe. How the hell had Hawk gotten the fridge up that narrow staircase?

Hawk smiled. "It came through the window." He pointed to a floor-to-ceiling window that overlooked the courtyard. "Don't worry, I'm not a mind reader. It's the first question everyone asks. Can I get you something to eat? Drink? Coffee?"

Jake just shook his head as he continued to look around. He was starving, but he needed a minute to settle. The kitchen counter swept around into the room, creating a breakfast bar with a couple of white leather and chrome stools in front of it. Beyond that was a set of French doors that led to some sort of outdoor space. Jake walked over to look and realized they led to a grassy area outside that was about twenty feet wide by thirty feet deep and surrounded by stone walls. "How was this done?"

"It's built on the top of the stone building below. I don't know how they did it, and I didn't ask. It was here when I bought the place. It was why I bought the place actually. I have my own private garden in the middle of Florence.

"There's no way they'd let me do something like that today. The weight from the grass and the soil, not to mention the water when it rains, it's a lot. I am terrified I'm going to be here one day when the building beneath it gives way under the weight. The neighbors say this has been here for hundreds of years in one form or another and the building underneath is made of thick stone. They're all convinced it will be there for at least another hundred. I can live with that." He grinned.

"It's beautiful. It must be stunning in the daylight," Madison said as she came and stood beside Jake. "The flowers… Are those roses? They look amazing." She'd taken her hair down out of the messy bun so it now hung long over her shoulders. It looked like it was still damp. She'd put on a dark green wrap over her top, emphasizing the shade of her eyes.

He looked down and noticed her matching socks. "How are your feet?"

"Much better." She smiled. "Thane has this amazing cream that I put on them. Helps with the pain and the swelling. I managed to cover all the cuts and get them cleaned up nicely."

Jake's heart did a little dance at her smile. If only he'd been the one to put it on her feet. He grunted. *Of course,* Thane *did.* Jake sighed to himself. He really needed to get a grip. He was turning into an asshole. He swallowed hard and took another look around the apartment.

There was a dining area on the other side of the doors with a wooden table and six chairs. To the left of that was a doorway leading to another set of stairs and a small bathroom. To the left of the doorway was a seating area with a large white sofa and two oversize white chairs. They all had different color pillows on them that complemented the colors in the paintings on the walls.

There was a glass coffee table in front of the couch and a couple of matching end tables next to the chairs. But where was the TV? And then he noticed the slit in the ceiling. The TV had to be lowered when he wanted to watch it. Interesting. A small wooden desk and chair in the corner by the stairwell rounded out the room.

"It really is a nice apartment, Thane. I'm jealous." Madison smiled at their host.

"Thanks. I love it, too. I just don't get to spend enough time here," he said as he handed her a mug of tea. "I bought it a few years back thinking it would be my escape. A great place to relax but that only works if you can actually get away." He chuckled. "You sure I can't get you something?" Hawk asked Jake.

"I guess I'll take a cup of tea," Jake said as he settled on one of the white leather stools.

Hawk handed him a mug. It smelled good, like berries. He took a small sip and decided it tasted damn good, too. Hawk also placed a plate with cheese and crackers on it next to Jake and one on the coffee table in front of Madison.

Jake grabbed a cracker and some cheese and popped them into his mouth. "So, what have you found out about Fedorov, or whatever he calls himself?"

Hawk, coffee in hand, went over and sat down next to Madison on the couch. "Monty, first just let me say how sorry I am you're involved in this mess."

Madison favored him with a slight smile. "Thanks." She took a sip of tea. "I'm sorry, too."

Jake swiveled on his chair so he faced the two of them. "Is there really no chance to get her on a flight out of here? Even private?"

Hawk shook his head. "I get it, Jake. It would be nice if we could give Monty some distance from Fedorov, but I don't think that's going to be possible. I spoke with a source here in Florence, a local cop. She said that as far as they're concerned, Monty is their only suspect in the robbery at the Veridani offices. If she tries to fly out of the country, even private, they'll take her into custody."

Jake's gut knotted. "That's not good. Her being the only suspect means they aren't even trying to pretend that they're doing an actual investigation."

"Yes," Hawk agreed. "It also means that Monty will likely be arrested in the next day or so."

Madison made a small squeaking sound and began choking on her tea. Hawk reached over, took the mug out of her hand, and tapped her back gently. "Are you okay?"

She nodded as her coughing began to subside. "I'm sorry," she coughed again. "I just didn't realize the situation was so…dire."

Hawk nodded. "I didn't either. I'm working on finding you someone who can represent you in court if it comes to that, but let's hope we can stop it from getting that far."

"You have any ideas on that?" Jake asked.

"Maybe. I think it's wise to keep a low profile. If they can't find you, they can't arrest you."

Madison frowned. "But we just came back to Florence. You think we should leave?"

"No. Being here makes it more likely you'll be found eventually, but leaving makes you look more guilty, and how it looks matters a lot here. I also want to be there when they arrest you. If they know someone is keeping an eye on you, it will be harder for them to do anything…stupid."

Jake exchanged a look with Hawk before he looked back to Madison. Her cheeks had lost the bit of color they'd had. The dark circles under her eyes looked even more pronounced. She'd curled her legs under her on the couch as if she were cold.

She was terrified, and Jake didn't blame her one bit. The reality was both he and Hawk were afraid that, at some point, things could go horribly wrong, and Madison could wind up dead. Just that thought was enough to make Jake lose his appetite. He dropped the cracker and cheese he'd been ready to eat back onto the plate.

Instead, he took a sip of tea. "I think the best thing we can do is to figure out who is the real thief and why they chose to frame Madison in the first place. There has to be more to all this than they just randomly picked her."

Hawk was silent for a moment and then nodded. "Agreed. There's definitely more going on here. Fedorov is barely containing himself, according to my source. He's charging around, demanding they find Monty and arrest her immediately. The only thing holding the local police back is the absolute lack of evidence. If they had anything at all, they might be able to make it work. My source says they have nothing other than you were in the building the night it went missing. So were a lot of other people. It's not enough to arrest or detain you, Monty, but it won't be long before something turns up that will incriminate you."

"How do you know that?" she demanded. "I didn't steal the necklace. How could there be anything that could incriminate me?"

Jake snorted. "Because this is Italy, which is known for its corrupt government, and because a former member of the GRU special forces has it out for you. If nothing exists, they'll create it, and there's not a fucking thing we can do to stop that from happening. But," Jake said, catching Madison's gaze, "we're going to do our best to make sure whatever they create, we can tear it apart."

Hawk nodded. "Jake is right. We may not be able to prevent them from making something up, but we can rip it apart so the charges won't stick. In the meantime, we need to keep a low profile and figure out what the hell is going on."

CHAPTER FOURTEEN

Madison was totally numb. She was so shocked that she couldn't think straight. Thane had just said she was likely to be arrested based on fabricated evidence. The men continued talking, but she couldn't move, couldn't speak, couldn't comprehend. She wouldn't survive in jail. How could she go to jail for something she didn't do? Didn't know how to do. Never even dreamt of doing. She could not get her mind to take it in.

"What's wrong with running?" she asked. The words came out in a quiet voice, but Jake stopped speaking mid-sentence and shifted his gaze to her. She cleared her throat. "Why should I care how it looks if they're just going to fabricate evidence anyway?"

"Hawk, get Madison something stronger than coffee." Jake's gaze had pierced her protective layer of neutrality. He had to know she was frozen on the inside. Terror flowed through her body, mixing with the blood in her veins.

"Monty," Thane started and then stopped.

He stood and went over to the kitchen where he grabbed a bottle and then poured her a healthy glass. He came back and put it in her hand. She automatically took a sip and then another. The burn from the scotch hitting her belly started to thaw her insides ever so slightly.

"Madison," Jake said, "I have Mitch working on an escape plan. If worse comes to worse, we use it, but…if you run, it's harder to sort this mess out, and you will be looking over your shoulder until you do. Once we're out of Italy, Fedorov will have more flexibility. Believe it or not, he does have to work within certain rules here. They may manufacture evidence, but if we leave, Fedorov has free reign. Until we know why they picked you, we don't know the level of danger you're in."

"What do you mean?" Her voice was a frightened croak.

Jake took another sip of tea then set his cup aside. "The first problem is this—why did they pick you? I mean, if you are in town to get Drake to invest in their company, why would the Veridani brothers want to frame you? It makes no sense. There's no way Drake will invest now."

"Maybe Paloma framed me, not the Veridanis." Madison was struggling to get her brain around all of it.

Thane shook his head. "No. Paloma wouldn't have the connections to pull this off. Even if she teamed up with Fedorov, they still need Veridanis' contacts to make the connection with the local *Polizia* happen. The Veridani brothers are involved."

"But, if we run, at least it will put space between me and Petrov. We can use that time to find out what's really going on," she argued.

Thane spoke quietly, "Assuming we can get you out of Italy, where would you go? You would have to pick a country without extradition because as soon as you turn up anywhere else, the Italians would demand you be arrested and sent back to Italy. More time for us also gives them more time for them to fabricate evidence. The more evidence there is, the harder it is for us to fight it."

"I— It just doesn't make any sense." Madison took another sip from the tumbler. The cold was receding, and in its place was a hard stone in the pit of her stomach. Reality really was a bastard. Running wouldn't help. "You're right, Jake. They went after Drake. They really wanted him to invest with them so framing me seems counterintuitive…unless, of course…" She looked at Thane. "I haven't spoken to Drake yet. He knows I'm innocent, right? Maybe I should call him right now."

She made to put down her drink, but Thane reached out and stopped her. "Yes, he knows you're innocent. He is doing what he can to figure out what's going on. He's got a call scheduled with the Veridani brothers tomorrow morning. He said he would call after that."

"Something changed," Jake stated flatly. "Something is different now than when they first approached Drake. If we figure that out, we'll be a long way into figuring out what's going on."

Madison nodded. Jake was right; something must have changed. "They were very excited when we arrived. They couldn't be helpful enough."

Thane leaned back on the sofa. "Was there anything different about this audit? Anything that stood out to you?"

Madison shook her head. "No. It was a normal audit." She hesitated.

"What?" Jake demanded.

Madison cocked her head. "I… There was nothing wrong with the books. They were very clean and organized, but…I just had a gut feeling there was more going on. I couldn't find anything but, I don't know, something just didn't feel quite right."

Thane asked. "Do you think they're in financial trouble?"

"No. That's just it. Usually if a company is looking for investors because they're in trouble, they give you a good sense of what's going on but not all the details. They don't want you to see the real level of difficulties until you've already agreed to most of the deal. Once the investor is that far in, it's unlikely a bit more bad news will make them pull out. With these guys, there was no bad news so no reason to hide anything."

Jake rose off his chair and went to pour himself another cup of tea. "Anyone?" Thane and Madison both shook their heads. After filling his mug, he asked, "So, if Veridani isn't in trouble, why do they want Drake to invest?"

Thane smiled. "Legitimacy. It always helps to have big name investors and board members. If the big names have confidence in the company, then it inspires others to have confidence in the company. If, say a year down the road, they decide to go public, having Drake as a major investor goes a long way to guaranteeing other big names will buy their stock. It's not just about the bottom line. It's about market share and, to a degree, popularity."

Madison nodded. "Jameson Drake, believe it or not, is an influencer. Not on social media, obviously, but in business. If he says something is good, then others are likely to invest. Veridani, as a fashion brand, also has to rely on being popular to get a larger share of the fashion market. If someone like Drake invests, then chances are excellent that he and/or his girlfriend will be at the fashion shows to support their investment, and they'll wear the products.

"Then, if he gives the products to his friends as gifts and they start wearing the clothes or carrying the bags, it filters down through social media and creates a buzz that the rich are into the brand. Once it has that kind of cachet, the items start flying off the shelves. And it wouldn't just be Drake. They would start with him and go from there. Celebrities, fashion icons, influencers. That's what sells fashion these days."

Jake's eyes narrowed. "So then I go back to what changed? It seems like they're giving up an awful lot by losing Drake's investment. What would make that loss worth it?"

Thane's eyebrows went up. "When you put it like that, you're right. It's absolutely crazy to frame Monty."

"Unless… Madison, did the level of friendliness or helpfulness change at any point?" Jake asked.

Madison started to shake her head, but stopped. "You know, I think it was all good until late last week, just before the rest of the audit team left. Paloma, who had been easy to work with, suddenly became distant. She wasn't as quick to be helpful. Brian, one of my team, commented on it. We all thought maybe something had happened in her personal life that upset her. We were mostly finished by that point. The team was packing up to leave, and I was clearing up a few loose ends this week."

"You're saying it was all good until Friday, then?" Thane inquired.

Madison nodded. "We invited Paloma and a few others out with us for drinks, but she didn't come. The others did, though. Once the team flew out, I spent the weekend reviewing things. I made a few more phone calls on Monday, and that was it. I was set to send my final report until Paloma called me and asked me to come in and fix the files, like I told you earlier, Jake."

"And that's when the necklace was stolen. Monday night. At least according to the *Polizia*." Thane got up from the sofa and went over to his laptop. "According to the officer I spoke with, they received the report of the missing necklace first thing Tuesday morning. They reviewed the security tape and spoke with Veridani's security people. Monty, you were the only person in their offices who was there during the timeframe the necklace was reportedly stolen."

"Well, that's not true, because Paloma was there with me at least for the first five minutes or so. She was very put out about her file and let me know in no uncertain terms how unprofessional she thought we were for deleting important information. I explained to her that the information wasn't gone. The settings had been changed on her reports. It had nothing to do with my people, but I would happily fix it for her. She didn't seem to believe me, but she hustled out of there anyway. She'd been glancing at her watch since the moment I arrived."

Thane nodded. "The *Polizia* cleared her. Said they had interviewed her and believed her to be a credible witness. She is a trusted employee who 'would never do such a thing' was the exact phrase."

Madison snorted. "And I would?"

Jake cocked his head. "The team was leaving on Friday night…"

"Saturday, actually."

"Saturday," Jake amended. "Paloma changed her attitude Friday morning? Friday afternoon? What time did you notice the change? Was she the only one?"

Madison rested her head back on the sofa. Drinking without eating enough was becoming a theme while she was in Italy. She needed to be smarter than that. "Paloma was fine first thing Friday morning. She was chattering away like usual. She offered us pastries and was excited to go out with us that evening. It wasn't until later in the day that her attitude changed."

"And did anyone else's attitude change as well?" Jake asked.

"Not that I noticed, but by that time, we were getting ready to go out for drinks. Very little work was being done."

Jake nodded. "What were you doing when you noticed the change in attitude?"

Madison blinked. "Um, good question." She thought back to Friday. What had she been doing? "When I got to the office in the morning, I made sure the team had copies of all the files they would need. There was still more review to be done back in New York, but more just confirming certain details, that type of thing. We reviewed the bible—"

Jake frowned. "Reviewed the bible. What does that mean?"

Thane laughed. "Monty is famous for her spreadsheets. She is the most organized accountant I've ever met, which is truly saying something. She has a spreadsheet that lists step-by-step what needs to be accomplished at each onsite audit. The auditors say it's saved their asses more times than they can count, so they call it the bible. No one arrives at or leaves a site without going over the bible multiple times first."

Madison nodded. "It's important not to miss anything when we do these audits. One wrong move, and we could cost Drake billions. So, I created a template to use. Anyway, we reviewed everything. We'd covered ninety-nine percent of the spreadsheet, so we were pretty much good to go. We also discussed how we would divide up the remaining work on the project. There were a few outstanding accounts that required closer scrutiny and, as I mentioned, a few charities to call and get some tax data from. That sort of thing. I said I would take care of all of that since I was staying a few extra days."

"It took until midafternoon to do the review and divide up the few remaining tasks. Then we went out for early drinks, which lead to dinner for some." The men didn't say anything but exchanged a long look. "What?" she said, looking back and forth between them. "What are you two thinking?"

Thane cocked his head. "We're wondering if you *did* do something, even if it was minor, that it could have changed things somehow. Did you tell Paloma which way you were leaning with your recommendation to Drake? Which way were you leaning, by the way?"

Madison shook her head. "I never say anything about it to anyone during my audits. I keep it all very neutral so Paloma wouldn't have any idea from me what my recommendation would be. Plus, I don't really make recommendations to Drake, more just tell him about the financials. *He* makes the decision."

Thane smiled. "But he asks your opinion. I've seen him do it. He holds you in high regard."

"Thanks, Thane. That's kind of you to say."

"What would you have told him when he asked about Veridani?"

Madison stood up and moved out from around the table. She walked over to look through the glass doors to the courtyard beyond. Her feet were only slightly sore now. That cream really was a miracle worker. She glanced down at them and then turned around to face the men.

"I would have told him to proceed with caution if he wanted to do it. There are other much more established fashion houses that he could get involved with and still make money. Veridani under Valentina was more of a sure thing. Since her death, I think it's less so. It wouldn't surprise me to see it flourish briefly and then crash out in a few years. The Veridani brothers don't have their sister's design abilities and taste, nor do they have her charisma."

Jake spun his chair slightly, almost facing her. "You don't like their chances long-term."

Madison nodded. "I think it will go under or be bought out by some other fashion house and rolled into their brand. The Veridani branding isn't strong enough, and it's just not different enough to stand out in a crowd. I think Valentina could have done it, but looking at the products the brothers are selling now…" She shook her head again.

"Do you think Paloma knew that?" Jake asked.

"No. My team was very enthusiastic. I think they all thought I would recommend it because, from a financial perspective, it looks strong. I'm quite sure Paloma believed I would recommend it. Drake was having good calls with the brothers as well, so it all looked like it was headed in the right direction for them."

"And yet they still blame you for the theft, thereby tanking the deal." Thane shook his head. "It makes absolutely no sense."

Madison took another sip of the drink she'd carried over and sat down on the stool next to Jake. She liked being near him. Just his presence made her feel steady, safe, and she needed that right now. Her whole world was crumbling. She needed to feel like all hope was not lost. Of course, she would rather be in his arms, but if all she could do was be close to him, she'd take it.

"You know," Jake said, "something has been bugging me for a while."

Thane cocked an eyebrow, and Madison turned to look at Jake.

"Why did Fedorov think the cops in Mugello would arrest you? He obviously had no pull there, so why was he so confident the officers would go along with his request to take you into custody?"

Madison stared at Jake. That hadn't occurred to her, but it was true. Fedorov just assumed the cops would arrest her on his say-so, but if he had no pull there, then why would they? "You think there was something else going on?"

Jake nodded. "Remember how he rather desperately wanted to search the room and how smug he was about it?"

She nodded. "He destroyed my laptop on purpose. I won't forget that anytime soon."

"Maybe that was his goal," Thane suggested. "Maybe Monty had something on her laptop that would cause them issues, and he went there purposely to destroy it."

"Maybe. That is a distinct possibility. Still, he really thought the police would arrest us. He was angry when he came out of the room." Jake leaned back in his chair. "What if he thought they would actually find the necklace."

Madison gasped. "You think he had it on him, and what? Just didn't get the chance to plant it in the room?"

Jake shook his head. "No. My theory is that he thought it was already there or somewhere on us. He searched your place first with a whole group of cops. I think he expected to find you and it there. When you weren't at your *pensione*, he started pushing the cops to search the whole city for you. I get that the Veridanis have pull, but they must have been pretty confident that you would be arrested and found guilty if they were making those kinds of demands so quickly."

Madison frowned. "What would make him think I would have it

on me or even close by? Wouldn't that be sort of stupid? I mean, when you think about it, if I had stolen it, I would have had the rest of that night plus all the next day to hide it. Why would he think I would still have it with me?"

"Maybe he thought you were meeting someone to fence it in Mugello? Or your buyer was there?" Thane suggested.

Jake took a sip of coffee. "Maybe. Or maybe he thought you had it on you because someone gave it to you."

"What?" Madison started at Jake. "What do you mean? I think I would have known if someone gave me a diamond and ruby necklace."

"Would you?" he challenged.

Madison frowned. "I don't understand."

Jake turned and put down his mug on the counter. "Didn't you tell me that Giovanni Veridani gave you a purse or something, and when you refused it, he got really mad and stormed out, leaving the purse at the restaurant?"

"Yes, but I don't get…" She trailed off. "You think the necklace was in the purse?"

"You said it seemed heavy. Stones usually are."

Madison shook her head. "But what if I opened the purse? I would have seen it."

Thane cut in. "Not if it was sewn into the lining. That's what you're thinking, right Jake?"

Jake nodded. "They assumed you would have the necklace because they gave it to you. Giovanni probably thought you would keep the purse because it's expensive and it's from their collection. He must have been furious when you turned it down."

She nodded. "He *was* livid. You think he left the purse on purpose so I would have to take it?" She paused. "It was a gamble, though. What if I left the purse at the restaurant?"

"I'm sure Giovanni was either close by or he had Fedorov watching you to see what you did with the purse. If you left it behind, he would have had someone grab it, and then he could have found you at your place later and tried again to get you to accept it, or he could have sent it over with his apologies. Either way, the purse would be at your place when the cops showed up."

Thane stood up and walked over to the kitchen area. Madison and Jake turned in their chairs to face him. He leaned against the counter. "It makes a lot of sense. That's why they were so confident that they could get you arrested. They'd given you the stolen property. All they had to do was catch you with it."

"I still don't get why Giovanni didn't even mention the necklace at lunch. I had no idea it had been stolen."

Jake turned toward her. "My guess is he didn't want to give you an opportunity to figure out the setup. Why give away the element of surprise?"

Thane nodded. "It really makes sense, Monty. It's why they hadn't concocted any false evidence before this. They thought they didn't need it because you would have the necklace in your possession. And speaking of which, where is the purse with the necklace now?"

Madison blinked. "About that…"

CHAPTER FIFTEEN

"You what?" Hawk said.

Jake started to laugh. He couldn't help it. He must have been more tired than he imagined because he laughed so hard he couldn't breathe. It was priceless, really.

"It's not that funny!" Madison said as she folded her arms across her chest.

Jake snorted. "It's really fuckin' funny. Come on, the only reason we didn't get arrested with the necklace was because you couldn't find the room key and knocked the purse into that vase? That's funny." He glanced at Hawk who was grinning. "See, he thinks it's funny, too."

"Sorry, Monty, but Jake is right on this one. It's really funny. And fortunate. Look at it this way, being slightly clumsy kept you from being arrested."

"I'm not clumsy," she stated firmly with her arms still crossed. "My feet hurt, and I had to move off the tiles that were causing me pain."

Jake smiled and tried to keep the laughter in, but it was no use. He had a good laugh while Hawk chuckled and Madison fumed. It felt good to just let it out. Finally, he stopped. "Sorry, Madison, but if you only knew how many times stupid shit like that happened and it saved us from getting our asses blown off, you'd laugh, too."

Hawk nodded. "Sometimes, it didn't matter how much planning we did. It was incidents like that that saved our bacon. You do have to see the humor in it."

Madison's eyes narrowed. Obviously, she still wasn't seeing the humor.

Jake sobered up and put his hands on the breakfast bar in front of him. "Well, I think it's safe to leave it where it is at the moment. That vase has been there for the last who knows how many years, so I don't think the necklace will be found anytime soon. There's no point in getting anyone to pull it out and confirm things. That would likely cause us more problems, so let's just go with the necklace being in the purse and the purse in the vase."

Madison frowned. "What about Graziana? Should you tell her? She could put it in the safe?"

"Yes, but then she would have knowledge of it. This way she has plausible deniability. I wouldn't want to drag her into this mess."

Madison nodded but still did not look pleased. "Where does that leave us?"

Hawk said, "I think we're at least in a better position because we know they can't find it to plant it on you again. It does, however, mean they are most likely manufacturing other evidence against you."

Jake agreed. "I think the smart bet is that they are going to leave something incriminating in your apartment."

"How do you know they haven't already planted something at my place? Fedorov could have done it when he was there the first time," she said.

"If he'd done that, then they would have arrested you already. The Russian would have had the proof for the two officers in Mugello. The fact they didn't find the necklace wouldn't have mattered as much."

With a groan, Madison rubbed her face with her hands. It was obviously getting to her. Jake reached out to rub her back but dropped his hand. It was so damn tempting to touch her, but it wasn't going to help the situation any, and he needed to focus on what he was doing. "Don't worry. I have a plan."

She rested her arms on the countertop. "A plan?"

Jake looked at Hawk. "Your source… he'll tell you if or when the arrest warrant goes out?"

Hawk nodded. "Yes, *she* will tell me if anything changes."

A woman. Why was he not surprised? Because he would do the same thing if he were Hawk. Developing a source inside the *Polizia* was key. It had the potential to be a more pleasurable experience if it was a woman.

"Good." He glanced at his watch. It was close to one-thirty a.m. "I suggest we get some sleep. Tomorrow, I'm going to stake out your apartment and see if they break in."

Madison nibbled on a cracker. "How do you know they won't go tonight and plant something?"

"I don't, but it's logical to assume they need some time to manufacture the evidence. They tried to arrest you around eleven this morning. It hasn't even been twenty-four hours yet. I'm guessing they'll do it tomorrow night."

Hawk nodded. "I agree. Chances are good it will be tomorrow night. The evidence has to be good. If it's too flimsy, it won't stand up, and there'll be a lot of eyes on this. Drake is calling in favors."

"Are you going to catch them in the act?" Her voice was filled with hope.

He hated to crush her, but that wasn't the best plan. "No. I'm going to let them plant it."

Madison shook her head. "I don't understand."

"If I catch them, it will be their word against mine, and with the pull these people have, my word won't account for much. The better plan is to wait until the person leaves the stuff and then remove it again. When the cops show up, there will be nothing for them to find."

"But don't you think Fedorov will have someone watching my place just in case I come back?"

Jake agreed. "Probably."

"So how will you get in?"

"Don't worry. I'll find a way." And he would. He just had no idea yet how. He wouldn't really know until he got there.

Hawk smiled. "It's what we were trained to do, and Jake does it very well."

Jake looked up at Hawk, eyebrows raised. It was high praise coming from another former Navy SEAL but he wasn't sure how the lawyer would know that unless, of course, Hawk had done some digging. Hawk gave him a barely perceivable nod. Interesting. Maybe he should be upset about it, but Jake just couldn't see the point. Hawk had probably dug into his background for Drake back when he first hired Callahan Security. Either way, it was good to know that Hawk trusted him.

"Will you be in a lot of danger, do you think?" Madison asked, her voice quiet.

"Not overly." What was he supposed to say? The truth was he had no fucking clue until he got there and checked it out. He could be arrested, but if these guys were serious and they caught him, they might see fit to work him over in trying to find out Madison's location. It was a crapshoot and the type of situation that he absolutely hated being in, but he didn't have a choice.

"Do you want me to come as back up?" Hawk asked.

Jake frowned. "It would be helpful, but I think it's better if you're here with Madison. She needs protection just in case they figure out where she is and try to arrest her."

Hawk nodded. "Let me know if you require…anything. I do have some useful connections here."

"I'm good. I was on a job here already, so I am set for equipment."

"Okay then, why don't we go to bed? Tomorrow, er…today is going to be a difficult day, to be sure." He turned to Jake. "I have your stuff in the first room on the right at the top of the stairs."

"Thanks." Jake stood up and looked at Madison. "I'm going to grab a quick shower and go to bed. You would be wise to do the same thing."

She didn't say anything. He gave a mental shrug. They'd unpacked a lot, it had to be difficult for her to digest. Knowing some asshole was out there trying to set her up for a crime she didn't commit was a lot to deal with. It didn't help matters that they'd spent all that time in bed. He was exhausted. She must be as well.

He got up off the stool, and a thought occurred to him. He said to Hawk, "I can take first watch if you want."

Hawk shook his head. "I'm willing to bet I've had a lot more sleep than you two have. I'll stay up. I'll wake you in a few hours."

Jake nodded and then headed up to his room. He took the stairs two at a time. His bedroom was similar to the first floor. Same wood flooring, similar furniture design. A white comforter was on the bed and a colorful rug on the floor. The window was also floor-to-ceiling and overlooked the courtyard. There was a tiny balcony, not even large enough to stand on. It was just for show.

The bathroom was off to the right. It had a small shower stall with a toilet and a sink. It wasn't huge but would do nicely. Hawk had left his bag on the bed, and Jake got out some clean clothes and his shaving gear. He brought the necessities into the bathroom with him and turned on the spray. A minute later, he was letting the hot water sluice down over his tired muscles.

He hadn't realized just how stressed he really was. This wasn't a normal job. Madison wasn't a normal client, no matter how much he would like to pretend otherwise. As much as an unnatural jealousy had flared because of Hawk, he was damn glad the man was here. Jake desperately needed some downtime.

What he really needed was a vacation. A break from the back-to-back jobs he'd been doing for more than a year now. Madison in a bikini on a beach somewhere. That would be ideal. *Shit.* He was getting hard just thinking about it.

Enough. He was a professional, and no matter how much he liked Madison, if his behavior with her ended up costing him this job, he was up shit creek.

When he'd first gotten out of the SEALs, he'd been happy to go home to Pittsburgh and bum around for a while. He'd visited with his parents, saw old friends, but then became bored out of his mind.

His father had tried to encourage him to get a job at one of the local manufacturing plants. His brother worked at the one his dad had retired from, and he had cousins at two more. But he just couldn't bring himself to do it. The reason he'd joined the Navy in the first place was that he just couldn't see spending his life working at the plant. Not that there was anything wrong with it. It just wasn't for him. He needed…more. He'd found it in the SEALS, but he'd been a bit lost after he got out. The call from Mitch had come just in time, and he hadn't looked back since. Until now.

He washed his hair and scrubbed his skin. What had Mitch meant about changes coming and they had to discuss his future? If Callahan Security was thinking of letting him go, Jake wouldn't do well in the regular nine-to-five world. He wasn't built that way. Was Mitch unhappy with his work? He hadn't said anything.

On the other hand, they were hiring a lot of new people and making some changes to different areas of the company. Maybe Mitch had something else in mind for him. After that crack about the numbers Mitch had made, Jake was doubtful. It was true. He hated working with numbers. He had no problems writing the reports and keeping things organized, but numbers always defeated him. It was a weakness, and he knew it, but he was too old to do anything about it. It hadn't mattered until now. He could do the math he had needed in the SEALs, and that was what was important.

Numbers. It was one of the things that made Madison so damned impressive. She was a numbers whiz. She was his opposite in so many ways, and didn't opposites attract? Fuck. He had to stop thinking like that.

Jake got out his shaving cream and razor and started to shave. What he hadn't mentioned to Madison was that tomorrow night's little adventure was just a stopgap. He'd find whatever they were going to plant, but it wasn't like that was going to stop them permanently. No. It seemed very important to someone to frame Madison for the necklace theft. Until they knew why, they would only be triaging the problem, not solving it.

Jake finished up in the shower and then dried off. He tied the towel around his waist and opened the bathroom door.

Madison was standing in the middle of his room.

"Oh, sorry," she said looking quite startled. "I…" She licked her lips. "I just wanted to say thank you for sticking with me. This has all gotten…so out of control…and I…just well… I appreciate what you're doing."

Jake stared at her. She couldn't be fucking serious. She was standing in the middle of his bedroom while he was wearing nothing but a towel, and she wanted to thank him for his service? Un-fucking-believable.

Madison blinked. She opened her mouth and closed it again. She looked so vulnerable standing there. Her hazel eyes were tired. He really wanted to hold her close and promise that everything would be okay, but he had no fucking clue how all this was going to turn out.

"Um, was there something else you needed?" Jake asked as he leaned against the doorjamb.

Her eyes flicked to his chest and then lower. Finally, they came back up to his face.

"Madison," he growled, "you need to leave now." He was having a hard time not crossing the room, throwing her down on the bed, and going for round four. He dropped his hands in front of his body to hide the developing situation under the towel.

She really needed to go.

"I— I just wanted to say that I'm a—I'm nervous about tomorrow night." She bit her lip. "I really don't want you doing anything that could get you in trouble, or worse."

She was worried about *him*. "Madison, it's my job to protect you. That's what I'm doing. I've been trained to do this type of thing and have quite a few years under my belt. This is nothing compared to some of the things I've done. You can stop worrying."

"It's just, this is all so overwhelming. I just…it's…"

"Madison, this is your last warning. You need to leave now, or I will spend the rest of the night making you scream my name just like you did earlier, and I don't care who hears us."

Her cheeks turned pink, and she spun around. Jake sagged against the doorframe and closed his eyes. The sound of the closing door reached his ears. It had taken all of his willpower not to kiss her and comfort her. That's really what she wanted. Comfort.

But if he had started, he wouldn't have been able to stop. He straightened, his hand clutching the knotted towel. He opened his eyes. Madison was standing in front of him.

"I need you, Jake."

That was it. That was all it took to break him. He swooped down and captured her lips once more. She was so scared and sad and she needed to be held. God help him, he couldn't say no. Not to her. Madison had wormed her way under his skin and now he was defenseless against her pleas.

He brought her against him again. His cock was rock hard under the towel. He wanted to touch and taste every inch of her. He wanted to help her forget and give her comfort even if it was only for a moment. It was all he could offer her.

Madison stepped back and pulled her sweater up and over her head and dropped it on the floor.

Jake raked his gaze over her skin. While he watched, she reached around and took off her bra as well and dropped it too. Then she shimmied out of her faded jeans and underwear. She stepped back into the circle of his arms.

The feel of her breasts against his chest was a step closer to heaven. He kissed her, the kiss turning fierce. She matched every stroke of his tongue with one of hers. His last vestiges of control gave way and he picked her up. He turned and carefully carried her into the bathroom and put her down on the counter. Then he captured her mouth once more as he closed the bathroom door with his foot.

She sunk her fingers into his hair as he kissed her neck.

"Jake," she whispered as he captured her nipple in his mouth. She ran her hands down his back and then cupped his ass as he brought her to the edge of the counter so he could rub against the apex of her legs.

"Are you sure this is what you need, honey? I don't want to—"

She put her finger to his lips. "This is heaven. I need you. I need to feel good even if it's just for now. Please don't stop."

He was being stupid. He should stop and focus only on his job but he couldn't let her down. She needed him at the moment and in this way. He kissed her and then kissed the hollow of her neck.

Madison moaned then reached down and undid his towel. He stepped back and took a look at her.

"You're beautiful," he ground out before capturing her mouth in a scorching kiss. She curled her fingers around his neck and deepened the kiss before she reached down and stroked him until he broke the kiss and cursed. "If you keep doing that I won't last."

She continued and even picked up the pace. She wrapped her legs around his waist. He entered her slowly, but she reached around him and cupped his ass, pulling him in deeper. "Take me, Jake. I need to feel you deep inside me."

He let out a soft curse and then pulled out and entered her again. He tried to maintain a slow, smooth rhythm, but she wouldn't stop urging him on with her words and her hips. Within seconds, he was pumping into her in a mad frenzy. Her head dropped back and her mouth opened in a silent moan, as if she reveled in the moment.

"Jake," she moaned, "harder," she whispered and lifted her hips higher. He couldn't stop himself. He pulled her hips hard against him and buried himself to the hilt. She said his name as she came. He pushed himself even deeper inside her and two seconds later followed her into bliss.

Finally he straightened. "Madison," he said as he reached up and brushed her hair out of her face, "that can't happen again, honey. This was reckless and stupid."

She nodded. "I know. I'm sorry but I needed to feel something other than fear even if it was only for a few minutes."

He nodded. "I get it." And he did.

She looked up at him with her soft hazel eyes. He knew she was willing him to tell her it was all going to be okay. That this nightmare would soon be over but he wouldn't—no, he couldn't—promise her it would all work out. He made a vow a long time ago not to lie in this type of circumstances because it had been his experience that once he made the promise of safety, no matter what, that's when all hell broke loose.

CHAPTER SIXTEEN

Madison bit the inside of her cheek and willed the heat out of her face. She wasn't sure what made her go into Jake's room. *Bullshit.* She knew exactly why she'd opened his door. Lust. Pure and simple. Jake Boxer standing there in nothing but a towel was a sight to behold. His body looked incredible, from his washboard abs to his broad shoulders, and it felt even better, like when she'd been pressed against it all that afternoon. And that kiss in the alley. It was so damn hot. She'd needed him. Needed to release the pressure he'd built in her. God, it was mortifying how much she wanted him. She was getting all tingly even now just thinking about him.

She was totally objectifying her bodyguard. It was so wrong on every friggin' level, but she just didn't give a shit. He was hot, and she was completely overwhelmed. Being in his arms just felt so right. Like she could relax for the first time in…well, forever. He was sexy as it was, but the fact that he made her feel secure added fuel to the fire already burning within her.

She wanted to feel his body on hers again. She wanted to get lost in him. That's why she'd gone in there. And he knew it.

Yesterday afternoon had been a mistake. At least, that's what he must think. He'd taken great pains to distance himself from her. It stung, but she understood. She was his client. Correction. Drake was his client, but she was the one getting the benefit of his services. *In more ways than one.* She had to smile. Still, after Petrov left, she'd thought sex with Jake would be a fun way to pass the time. A distraction. Now she knew better. He was an addiction. She'd just whetted her appetite in Mugello, and now she'd wanted more. She'd had him again and she still wasn't satisfied. She wanted to think it was just the crazy situation that had her acting this way but she had a sneaking suspicion, she'd be addicted to Jake no matter what the circumstances were.

She let out a long breath. Nope. He was right. It all had been a mistake. She needed to remember that. Once this ordeal was over, it was back home to New York and maybe, just maybe, she'd start her new career as a handbag designer. If she didn't end up in an Italian prison.

Madison crawled under the thick white duvet and tried to go to sleep. She was exhausted but she just couldn't turn her brain off. Why her? Why would the Veridanis choose her? She had no answers. Why steal the necklace? Maybe it was an insurance job. They wanted the money, but that didn't make any sense. They had money unless their entire balance sheet was a lie.

She rolled onto her side. No. No matter how good their in-house accounting was, they couldn't hide it if they were that broke. And also, although the necklace was north of five million euros, that wasn't much for a company like Veridani. It wouldn't save them from bankruptcy or anything.

She closed her eyes, and an image of Paloma showing her a brochure flashed in her brain. The charity. Paloma had been proud of the work they were doing with Hope For Kids Foundation. Madison had called and emailed the charity to ask for verification on certain numbers, but they hadn't responded. She threw the covers back and got out of bed. No time like the present to check. She wasn't going to sleep anyway. It was one of the very few things that were outstanding on the audit, and she hated leaving loose ends.

She threw a sweater on over her navy tank top and pulled on a pair of shorts over her underwear. She quietly opened the door to her room and then padded down the stairs. The light over the stove was on, casting long shadows in the room. Thane was lying on the sofa. Shoot. She didn't want to wake him, but she should probably ask if she could borrow his computer.

Maybe this wasn't such a great idea.

"What do you need, Monty," Thane said as he opened one eye.

"Oh, sorry. I didn't mean to wake you. It just occurred to me that I didn't hear back from a charity about Veridani."

"I wasn't sleeping just relaxing. You want to check to see if they responded at this hour?" Thane sat up. He was wearing jeans and a black sweater. He looked like he was ready to go out for a nice dinner.

She weighed her options and then decided the truth was her best course of action. "I just have a feeling about it. The charity, I mean. Jake was asking me earlier about Paloma and when her attitude changed. It was right after I asked her to reach out to someone at Hope For Kids. They weren't getting back to me, and you know I hate loose ends."

"You think there could be something off with the charity?"

Madison shrugged. "I don't know. I just wanted to see if they emailed me back. I can't seem to sleep anyway."

Thane's expression softened. "Go check. My laptop is right on the desk. Why don't I make you some tea to help you sleep?"

"Thanks." She went over and sat down in front of the laptop. She clicked the mouse and brought the screen to life. She logged into Drake's network and checked her personal email. She had pretended to be interested in donating. Since her calls had garnered no response, she'd sent a message from her private email account, hoping she'd find the name of the person she needed to speak with to get the information. About twenty from the top, she found the email she'd been waiting for. She clicked on it.

The email thanked her for her interest in their charity and, yes, they attached a list of projects they had completed and where they were located. Did she want to set up a time for a call to discuss further?

"Not just yet," she mumbled and then put her mouse over the attachment. "Thane, do you have good security on this? I'm about to open an attachment that may or may not come from a reputable source." She glanced at him.

His back was to her, making tea at the stove. "Well, Drake's system is really quite good so if it came through there, then you should be fine. I will run a local scan on my machine when you're finished."

"Okay, thanks." She clicked on the attachment, and it opened on the screen. She then downloaded a file that she had stored from her now destroyed laptop and opened it. Damn good thing she saved everything to the cloud. She compared the two lists.

Madison leaned back in her chair. It was as she suspected. The lists were different. Now she needed to make a phone call. When she'd seen the original list, she'd been surprised but thought maybe she wasn't as up on current events as she thought. Now, the kernel of an idea that had started earlier grew into a solid thought. She was on the right track. The same spidey-sense that tingled when she was on the trail of hidden information during an audit was buzzing away.

She glanced at her watch. It was late at Deandra's location, but this couldn't wait. Dee would just have to forgive her. Madison would buy her dinner the next time they were in the same city together. Dee losing a couple hours sleep was nothing compared to knowing the why behind what was happening to Madison. She would just have to convince her friend of that.

She started to get up to get her cell phone but cursed softly when she remembered that Jake had taken the sim card out of hers. She glanced around the room and spied the burner phones Thane had left out earlier. She asked to borrow one and Thane nodded. He handed her the tea and then went to the restroom.

She dialed her friend Deandra's number. It was one of two she knew by heart. Her dad being the other. Dee was one of the few people from her hometown that she'd stayed in touch with other than Drake, which was a different scenario all together. Dee had gone to college in D.C. to study world politics. She had gone into the foreign service and was now stationed in Gabon. Madison wanted to get out there to see her but, so far, their schedules hadn't meshed.

"Hello?"

"Hey, Dee," she said.

"Maddy!" Dee's voice was like a balm to her nerves. They'd been best friends since they were in kindergarten, pre-volleyball days when everyone else started calling her Monty. They'd be friends forever as far as Madison was concerned.

"How are you? How's life in Gabon?"

"Good. I was just out with some friends."

Madison made her voice deep. "Ummhmm. I am sure you were. Did you look at the clock, young lady? I know what you were out doing."

"Oh, my God! You can still imitate my father to a tee." She started to laugh. "I have missed you, girl. You have to come visit."

"I'd like that very much." She'd go right now if she thought she could get out of the country. Hiding out in Gabon sounded like a great plan.

"So, it's really late and you're calling me. What's up?"

"I'm working on a client's taxes, and they said they donated to this charity called *Speranza per i Bambini*. Hope For Kids. They said this organization builds schools and playgrounds in Africa. They listed Gabon as one of the countries they've built stuff in, along with a host of others. Have you ever heard of them?"

"Um, no, but if they're small, I might not have. Where else do they say they are doing work?" Madison listed off a bunch of countries in Africa. Dee yawned. "I'll see what I can find out for you."

"I know it's a big ask, but can you do it quickly? I really need that information."

"I'll do it first thing when I get to work. It shouldn't be too hard to find out if they're doing work in the country. I have friends in a couple of those other countries you listed. I'll send an email right now, asking if they've heard of this charity. I should have something for you tomor — I guess it's later today," Dee said with a chuckle. "Can I ask why this is so important?"

Madison hesitated. "It's a long story, and I promise I will explain it all once this is over."

"That sounds ominous, but okay. Can I reach you at this number?"

"Um, yeah. This will work." She'd just have to keep this burner with her.

"Alright. I'll call as soon as I have something. Love you, Maddy."

"Love you, too, Dee." Madison clicked off the call.

She took a sip of her tea as she walked across the room and sat down on the sofa. She should go back up to bed, but she knew she wouldn't be able to sleep. Thane came out of the bathroom and sat down on one of the comfy chairs and put his feet up on the ottoman in front of it. "Did you get your answers?" he asked.

"Working on it. Sorry"—she started to rise—"I should go back upstairs and leave you in peace."

He waved her back down. "I'm fine. Relax. I can sleep anywhere." He grinned.

She nodded and sat back down. She took another sip of tea. Dee had been her lifeline when they'd been kids. Madison's mother had multiple sclerosis with other complications. She'd been sick as long as Madison could remember. She spent her childhood helping her dad take care of her mom. Dee had invited her for sleepovers and spent many long hours on the phone with Madison, talking about anything but her mom's illness. Dee's parents had always taken Madison with them when they went to the city to see a play or go to a museum.

Madison's father never took her to New York City, or anywhere else for that matter, because her mom couldn't manage it and her father wouldn't even think about hiring a nurse to stay with her while they went away.

Madison had longed to escape after high school, but she'd missed out on college because they didn't have the money to send her. Her mother's medical bills had eaten away all of their savings. So Madison had stayed in town and worked, not only to help her dad financially, but also to take care of her mother.

She was sad when her mom finally passed away, but she was also relieved. It was awful, and she felt extreme guilt over it, but she couldn't help her feelings. Her mother had been a drain Madison's entire life. It wasn't just the illness; it was the complete helplessness in the way she lived. She protested that she just couldn't do anything. Madison had tried to force her to get out more, but her father would just do whatever her mother wanted. It led to huge fights between her and her dad.

After her mother passed away, Madison thought she and her father would grow closer, but that didn't happen. He still didn't want to go out and do anything. He didn't want to move away and start again. He just stayed in the same house without changing anything.

Madison had been so grateful to Drake for the scholarship. She'd loved university, but loved living in New York City even more. By the time Drake offered her the first contract job, Madison had already traveled to five or six different countries. Contract work was the best of both worlds for her. She got to travel and see some place new, and do it on someone else's dime. She also got to do a job that she loved.

She drained her mug. If she were being honest, though, over the last six months, something had changed. It wasn't that she didn't want to travel anymore, but more that she was feeling it was time to set down roots of some kind. She was thirty-four. It was time to find a more permanent home. She loved New York, but it was expensive and, in truth was also a bit isolating. She traveled too much to have real friends.

Madison leaned her head back on the sofa. What she really wanted was a job that she loved with more vacation time so she could travel but also some free time so she could work on her bag designs. Oh, and a hot man there to share it with her. An image of her and Jake cooking in her tiny kitchen came to mind. She smiled.

When the cell phone she'd used buzzed, Madison almost dropped the mug. She put it on the coffee table and picked up the phone.

"Dee. I didn't think you'd get back to me so soon."

"Yeah. Since I was up, I decided to poke around a bit about your charity."

"And…" Madison's stomach fluttered like butterflies had set flight.

"Hope for Kids Foundation doesn't exist, or at least it doesn't do work here in Gabon. I spoke with a friend in the local government here, and they can't find the charity registered anywhere. So if they're doing work here, it's under the radar. But…Maddy, you said they're building schools and playgrounds, etcetera. There's no way they could do that under the radar here."

"You must have a good friend to be able to get them up at this hour and ask questions," she said.

Dee giggled. "Yes, he's a very good…friend."

Madison smiled. "Can you ask your friend if there are any other charities that do this type of work in Gabon that are based in Italy?"

"Um, sure." Muffled sounds of voices came out of the phone.

So it was like that. Good for Dee. She was the nicest person. She deserved some happiness. Madison tucked her hair behind her ears. Someday she would like to have a partner, too, if she survived this mess. Jake would be nice to wake up to, but even better to go to bed with. She sighed and shut that thought down. It wasn't helpful.

"Okay," Dee said, "there are no charities registered in Gabon that do that kind of work that are Italian based. There are only three charities listed in those categories. One is from the UK, one is American, and the other is a Chinese charity."

"Thanks, Dee. That helps. Sorry for keeping you up all night."

"No problem. I want details on this, though, when you get the chance."

"For sure. I will fill you in. Promise."

"I'll email you when I hear from my friends in the other countries as well. Take care. Talk soon."

"Thanks again, Dee," Madison said and then hung up.

She'd been right—the charity was a hoax. What did that mean? And how was it linked to framing her for theft?

CHAPTER SEVENTEEN

Jake rolled over and groaned as he looked at the bedside clock. He was exhausted. He'd tossed and turned until it was time to take his watch. Hawk had waved him away, so he'd gone back to bed, falling asleep as the sun came up. His dreams had been filled with how good Madison had felt in his arms, and worrying about her safety. As he pulled on a pair of jeans and a black sweater, he came to the conclusion that he needed to stay well away from Madison Montgomery if he ever planned to sleep again.

He made his way downstairs, only to find Hawk and Madison eating breakfast.

"Morning," Hawk said in a cheery voice.

Jake grunted as he sat down at the table.

Hawk immediately got up and poured him a cup of coffee. "Would you like some breakfast?" Jake started to stand again, but Hawk motioned for him to stay seated. "I've got it."

"Thanks." Jake took a big swig from his mug. He glanced over at Madison. She hadn't slept either if the dark circles under her eyes were anything to go by. She gave him a wan smile.

Two minutes later, Hawk set a plate with eggs, bacon, and a grilled tomato in front of him. "Anything new, Hawk?" Jake asked before he took a bite of his eggs. They were delicious.

Hawk shook his head. "No. No arrest warrant has been issued."

"That's good." Jake took a piece of toast from a plate in the middle of the table. He didn't think they'd be waiting long however, maybe one more day before they tried to arrest Madison, but that gave them twenty-four hours to prepare for it.

Madison put down her fork. "I spoke with Drake this morning."

Jake stopped his fork halfway to his mouth. "What did he say?"

She tilted her head. "He says the Veridanis are sticking to their story. He is no longer being asked to invest."

Jake frowned. "But I thought they wanted people like Drake."

"They do," she confirmed, "and losing him is a big hit, but there are more investors out there. According to Drake, he's already heard rumors of some Russian oligarch wanting to invest.

Jake swallowed his bite of food. "Russian. That's interesting." Alarm bells were going off in his head. Anytime he'd ever heard the phrase "Russian oligarch," it was always followed by a shit ton of trouble.

Hawk nodded. "I thought so, too. Drake sent me the name, and I'm working on pulling up some background on the guy. It may be nothing, but it might also give us a clue to what is really going on here."

Madison put the last forkful of food in her mouth and then set it down again. She finished chewing and then took a sip of her coffee. "As to that, I think I know."

Jake took a bite of his bacon and eyed her as he chewed. She was wearing a soft pink sweater that clung to her curves and a pair of jeans. Her hair was pulled up into a messy bun again. He liked it better when it hung down over her shoulders, but it was cute this way, too. She looked pale, and he wanted to reach out and pull her in for a hug but, instead, he looked down at his plate. So she'd been up all night working the problem while he'd tossed and turned, doing nothing but driving himself crazy. *Shit.*

Hawk pushed his plate away. "Your phone calls went well then. Tell us what you learned."

Madison took a deep breath. "I believe the Veridanis are laundering money."

Jake stopped chewing. That had come out of left field. "What makes you think that?"

"Well, it was you who actually got me thinking. You asked me when Paloma turned sour. It was after I asked her for more details about the charities they were making donations to. I had contacted all on the list, and they'd all gotten back to me except one, the one the Veridanis donated the most money to. I'm talking millions every quarter, supposedly, through various fundraisers."

Jake took a bite of his toast. "So, they didn't hold the fundraisers?"

"No, they did, but I'm guessing they donated waaay more than they reportedly raised. Let me explain. The Veridanis raised two million for a charity, *Hope for Kids,* at their fundraiser. Then through corporate donations and matching, they say they raised another ten million. Now the charity is getting twelve million that the public knows about. In reality, they could be getting another twenty million off the books."

Jake cocked his head. "Okay, so they donate this money to a charity. Then what?"

"Then the charity says they spent that money on building supplies and architects, playground equipment and furniture. Whatever they want basically. They can even say they spent it on real estate. They have to buy all the sites where they claim they are building schools and playgrounds."

Hawk got up and brought the coffee pot over, refilling everyone's cup.

Jake pushed his plate away but still munched on a piece of toast. "So you're saying they have twenty million and they tell the world they're buying property and supplies with the money, but really they don't do anything?"

"Yeah, it's all done on paper but doesn't exist in real life. They own all the companies involved in all of the countries. They may have to pay a bit of tax in some countries, but as a charity, it would be minimal. So what appears to be a charity for children is actually a front to wash money for someone. The Veridanis do not have that kind of money, but they have a high profile so they can hold all of these fundraising events that make laundering that level of cash appear legit. I would imagine they also get a chunk to keep the fashion house books looking healthy."

Hawk leaned his elbows on the table. "How do you know all of this?"

"And can you prove it?" Jake asked.

"Paloma showed me a brochure from Hope For Kids Foundation about a week ago. She was gushing about all the good work they do. I think she was super proud of the brochure because she had helped create it. She said something along the lines of their in-house printing department had done it because it would save the charity money, and since they had an art department to do all their catalogues, they might as well use it for a good cause.

"The whole exchange stood out to me because they said they do work in Gabon. On the brochure, there was a picture of the mayor of Libreville, the capital city. I recognized her because my best friend happens to be stationed in Gabon. She works in the foreign service, and she interacts a lot with local governments.

"I reached out to the charity that day, but I hadn't heard back by Friday so I asked Paloma to talk to her contact there and get them to call me. That's when she got weird."

"So you think Paloma sounded the alarm about you looking to speak to someone at the charity, and then the Veridanis panicked? Why didn't they just have someone call you pretending to be from the charity." Jake asked. "I'm sure they could have supplied you with enough false information to cover their asses."

Madison grimaced. "That's my fault. I told Paloma that I had a friend in Gabon and that I recognized some of the officials in the picture on the brochure."

Jake's gut churned. She'd made herself a target without even realizing it. Hawk caught Jake's eye and gave a slight nod. They were both thinking the same thing. They'd been lucky to this point that all the Veridanis had done was try to frame her for a theft. If it didn't work, he had no doubts they'd kill Madison.

The tension in Jake's shoulders tightened significantly. "Do you have any proof of this?"

She nodded. "Some. I called my friend in Gabon, and she says the charity has never done that kind of work there. There are only three charities that have, and none of them are Italian. Also, she emailed me this morning and said no one has built a school or a playground in recent months, so there's no way the charity is doing what they say they are doing. She put out feelers to the other countries that the Hope For Kids Foundation supposedly does work in. She's waiting to hear back.

"Perhaps most telling is that I checked the Foundation's website, and Gabon is no longer listed as one of the countries they do work in." She glanced across the room to the laptop, as if willing it to ping with an incoming mail message. She sighed loudly.

Hawk leaned back in his chair. "They've erased it that quickly. Interesting."

Madison nodded. "I did have a brochure. I took one of the ones Paloma showed me. She had a whole drawer full, but now I can't find it. That would have at least been enough to spark an investigation."

Jake swore. "Fedorov took it. I saw him shove it in his pocket right after he searched our room in Mugello. I didn't know what it was at the time." He grimaced. "Now we know why he smashed your laptop. It was a distraction so you wouldn't notice the brochure was gone."

"So"—Madison looked at Jake—"what do we do now?"

That was a fucking good question. One he didn't really have an answer for. "Well, I still have to find whatever they're going to plant in your apartment. That's step one."

Hawk stood up and grabbed his phone off the counter. "I will start by trying to get more information on the Hope For Kids Foundation. Do you know if those brochures were ones the Veridanis had used before?"

Madison shook her head. "Paloma said they were new. They're holding a charity ball tomorrow night. They had them printed for that."

Jake cocked his head. "Do you think they would have gotten rid of the flyers?"

Hawk looked at him. "What are you thinking?"

"If we could get a copy of the flyer, we could at least prove the charity is being dishonest. Are there a lot of rich and important people going to this event?"

Hawk whistled quietly. "I see where you're going with this."

Madison frowned. "I don't."

Hawk explained, "If the people who already donated to this charity discover that they've been had, then there will have to be an official investigation. We don't really need to have enough proof for the authorities. Only enough to piss off the high society crowd. None of them will tolerate being played for a fool."

Jake got up from the table. "It's something to think about." He was already turning over ideas in his mind. There just might be a way out of this for Madison if they didn't kill her first.

He spent the majority of the rest of the day getting ready for the night's incursion. He went over to Madison's neighborhood and scouted it for a while. He wore a disguise, but no one appeared to be watching the place, which led him to believe that one of her neighbors had been paid off to let Fedorov know if she showed up.

After making sure he didn't have a tail, he arrived back at Hawk's just after dinner. Hawk handed him a plate, and he scarfed down the chicken and potatoes like a man who hadn't seen food in days. Then he stayed at the table and asked Madison to join him. He had a few questions for her. What he really wanted to know was which one was spying on her, but he didn't want to come out and ask. It would just freak her out and, in the end, he wasn't sure if it mattered.

He started, "I am familiar with the area, but now I need to know about the building itself. The layout. How many apartments? Did you meet any of the renters? That type of thing."

"Okay, well there are only six apartments in the building. Two per floor. It's not a big building. The landlady, Mrs. Rover, lives in the bottom right if you're facing the building. The D'Antoni's live on the bottom left.

"I have the place on the middle floor on the left above them. The apartment across from me was empty while I was there. It's owned by the same people that own mine. An Italian American couple, Carmine and Paola Ricci. The renter who was supposed to have it this week is sick and didn't come to Italy.

"The top two apartments are rented out to two families. The D'Elias on the left and the Bernardis on the right. They both have two kids."

"That sounds promising. Is there a back way into your building?" Jake asked.

"Not that I'm aware of."

Jake sat back in his chair. "Do you have the contact info for the Ricci's?"

"Yes, why?"

"I want you to reach out to them and ask them if I can rent that apartment across from you for the rest of the week. That will give me access without hassle. I'll wear a disguise so Fedorov and his people don't recognize me.

"I can help there," Hawk said. "Actually, why don't you let me and Monty take care of all that while you get ready to go. It's going to take you a bit to get there and to scope it out before you make the approach. Just because no one was there earlier doesn't mean Fedorov won't have guys waiting for you now."

He made a good point. Jake was going to have to be careful during his recon of the place in case there were eyes on it.

Hawk continued. "You want to be in early so you can get set up. We'll make sure the rental is sorted for when you're ready for your approach. I have a jacket and a scarf you can wear so it's hard to see your face. It will be dark out, and I'm betting there're lots of shadows on the street." Hawk went over to a closet and came back with a brown cashmere scarf and a new phone. "Here. You'll probably need both of these."

Jake took the scarf. "Okay." He glanced at his watch. "Assume I will be ready to enter at ten. Do you have this number?" he asked Hawk as he held up the phone.

"Yes. We'll call if we run into any complications."

Madison spoke up. "Mrs. Rover will want to talk your ear off when she gives you the key. You should tell her you're not feeling well. She's a hypochondriac. That should keep her at bay."

Jake nodded. "Good." He stood and put the phone in his pocket and tossed the scarf over the back of the chair.

A couple hours later, Jake put his backpack on the chair and picked up the scarf. He'd changed into a midnight blue sweater and a darker pair of jeans. He'd put on his shoulder holster and adjusted it for comfort. Madison had been pacing in front of him for the last hour. It was stressing him out.

Finally, she turned to him. "I want to come with you."

"No," he said as he wrapped the scarf around his neck so he could pull it up over his face.

She glared at him. "Jake, I can't ask you to risk your life for me."

"It's my job." He pulled on the jacket Hawk had given him.

"Jake!"

He stopped what he was doing and looked at her.

"I just can't let you do it on your own."

"I'll be fine." He needed to get moving. He also needed to stay away from her. She looked so scared he was struggling not to lean in and kiss her fears away.

"But if I come with you, I can help you search. It's not a huge apartment, but there are some weird hidey-hole locations that you might miss. When the new owners renovated the building, they cut it up weird and left some odd spaces, at least according to Mrs. Rover. That's why things are a bit odd in the layout. It's not something anyone ever mentions when you Airbnb."

She was trying hard, and he appreciated it, but there was no way in hell he was going to let her come. "If *I* can't find it, then *they* couldn't find it."

She shook her head. "You don't know that. They've already searched it once. They've had days to search it as often as they liked."

Jake sighed. "I get that you're scared, but it's more dangerous for you out there. Besides, how would you get into the building?"

"You said they aren't watching the building."

"They weren't watching the building *at the moment*," Jake corrected her. "Do you know what that means? It means one of your neighbors is spying on you." He didn't think it was possible but Madison's cheeks got paler. "It's just better if you stay here."

"I'm going with you," she said. Her voice was quiet, but her eyes glinted with determination.

"That's not a bad idea," Hawk said as he entered the room. Jake whirled around and stared at him. Hawk raised his hands to calm Jake down. "Let me rephrase. Drake called in a favor from a friend, Enzo Valardi. We were supposed to meet tomorrow, but he says something has come up and it's better to meet now. Drake wants me to get Valardi's assessment of the situation since he's lived in Italy for years and he's...connected."

"Valardi. Isn't he the guy who helped Drake with the Hawaii situation? They were good friends years ago or something?" Jake asked.

Hawk nodded. "That's him. I can take her with me, but Valardi is Italian mob, or was. Apparently, he's retired. I didn't know mobsters could retire." He shrugged his shoulders. "The point is not only are we meeting in a not great area, as her lawyer, the last place I want Madison is anywhere near anything unsavory. Fedorov and his people will paint her with whatever brush they can, and I would rather not give them any ammunition."

Jake ground his teeth. "I'll be breaking into an apartment. That's not exactly savory."

"Actually, you won't because if I'm with you I can let you in. It's still my place."

Hawk smiled. "She's got you there."

"I hate this idea. I do not want her anywhere near these guys," Jake argued.

Hawk shrugged. "The alternative is leaving her here alone."

Jake wanted to yell and smash things. The last thing he needed was Madison anywhere near danger. Just the thought of it had his stomach in knots. On the other hand, he couldn't leave her here alone and unprotected. It was his job to protect her, but she'd become more than that. Leaving her alone just wasn't an option. Ever.

"Fine," he snarled. "Get a coat and whatever you can find to disguise yourself. You'll have to arrive after me because your landlady will recognize you." He blinked. That meant she *would* be alone for a bit. His pulse ticked up.

"I'll stay with her until she can go in. I should still be able to make my meeting." Hawk went to the closet and started pulling out more coats and hats.

Twenty minutes later, they were ready to head out.

"I'll take Madison with me, and we'll meet you over there." Hawk offered his hand. "Good luck. Call me if there's trouble."

Jake nodded as he shook the man's hand. "You, too. Be careful."

Hawk grinned. "It's my middle name."

Jake looked at Madison. "You will do exactly as I say when I say it. Do I make myself clear? And you will do the same for Hawk. This could easily turn out badly, Madison. It's important you follow directions."

She nodded. Her hazel eyes were big, and the fear he saw in them gutted him but he refused to think about that now. He turned and started down the stairs. He let out a long breath. They were going to need all the luck they could get.

Jake glanced at his watch. It had taken him forty-three minutes to get to Madison's place. Hawk and Madison were around the corner, waiting on him. He checked out his reflection in the plate-glass window. With his collar turned up, the scarf wound around his neck, and a new fedora on his head, it was hard to get a good look at his face. Of course, it wouldn't really fool anyone who was seriously looking for him, but he was willing to bet Fedorov wasn't the one doing the looking. As a matter of fact, he was pretty damn sure.

Now, it was time. Hawk had sent a text that everything was a go so Jake was going for it. He started down the street but then slowed his steps a bit. There was a large group of men walking together behind him. He let them catch up and then pass him. He kept pace then so he was only a step or two behind the group. When they reached Madison's building, he broke off and went up the steps.

The landlady, Mrs. Rover, was waiting for him in the foyer of the building. She was an older woman of medium height with salt-and-pepper hair. She was a bit heavy around the middle but looked like she kept herself in decent shape. She was probably in her early sixties.

She hustled right over and opened the door for him. "You are Mr. Homes? Peter Homes?"

"Yes, and you must be Mrs. Rover. So pleased to make your acquaintance." He smiled at her as he offered his hand. They shook, and then he coughed, putting his hand over his mouth. "Pardon me," he said. "I seem to have a bit of a cold."

Mrs. Rover stared at her hand and then back at Jake. "I see," she stammered as she backed up a bit. She frowned.

"I do apologize for the late hour of my arrival," Jake forced his voice into a rasp that was devoid of any accent. In his experience, if he spoke softly and made his word choices formal and his pronunciation clipped, people remembered him as having an accent of some sort but could never place from where. It was also the polar opposite way of his natural speech.

"Yes, well, it's not ideal but one does as one must. Let me show you to your apartment."

He allowed her to lead the way up the stairs. At the top, she turned right and walked across a large landing. There were two doors, one on each side with a blank wall in between. No window meant chances were good that this building was built flush against the next building with no space in between. That's what it had looked like from the aerial maps, but it was good to have confirmation.

Mrs. Rover pulled out a key and opened the door for him. She stepped into the apartment and turned to him. "I'll just show you where everything—"

When Jake broke out into another coughing fit, a look of sheer panic crossed Mrs. Rover's features. She took a large step back.

Jake finished coughing. "I think I will be fine. If I have any questions, I can always call you, yes?"

"Yes! Yes!" She turned, pointing down a long hallway. "My number is on the piece of paper on the kitchen counter."

"Good. Thank you for being so kind and staying up to greet me." He put out his hand, and she practically threw the keys into it as she scurried past him and went out the door.

He closed the door after her and grinned. That went well. There's no way she'd be able to describe him now. She was so terrified of catching something she'd stayed far away. She'd barely looked at him. Now they just had to get Madison into the building.

They agreed to wait twenty minutes before Madison would enter.

"Down to work," he mumbled. He took off the hat, scarf, and jacket and dropped them on a small bench that was next to the wall in the hallway. The hallway itself ran the length of the apartment from back to front with all of the other rooms leading off it. It was painted a nondescript shade of white with no other furniture than the bench.

It was a bland sort of apartment but about what he expected. The rooms were all painted white and the decorations all done in neutrals. He was sure people were thrilled to stay here because of its central location if not for its lack of personality.

Jake found the place small, but he was a large guy. Assuming the one across the hall was the mirror image, he could see why Madison had picked the place. It had everything she needed and was in a great location. She was here to work, so she didn't need any frills, or even much space.

Nothing to do but wait. He pulled out a stool that had been tucked under the counter and set it quietly next to the window. He needed to keep the noise to a minimum since the landlady lived beneath him. After getting settled on the stool, he pulled out a monocular from his backpack and looked through the slit he'd created in the blinds. He studied the street. It was clear. It just had to stay that way until Madison was inside. Ten minutes. It was going to be the longest ten minutes of his life.

CHAPTER EIGHTEEN

Madison crossed the street and went up the stairs to the building. She opened the door and entered as quietly as she could. If Mrs. Rover looked out her peephole, she would see a youngish man dressed in a navy peacoat with a brown scarf and a news cap. Her new tenant had a visitor.

As soon as Madison got to the landing, Jake opened his door. She moved swiftly across the threshold and into the apartment.

Jake closed the door and turned to face her. He spoke in a quiet voice. "Did Mrs. Rover see you?"

"I don't think so. Her floor squeaks by her door so I think I would have heard her."

"Okay, take off your coat and stuff and leave it on the bed. Move very quietly. We don't want to attract any attention." Jake went down the hallway to the kitchen.

Madison walked into the bedroom and took off the hat, letting her hair fall loose. She took off the scarf and jacket as well, leaving everything on the bed as directed. She went back out into the hallway and walked down to the kitchen. A weak light over the stove gave enough light to see without the apartment appearing to be occupied for anyone trying to look in from outside.

Jake rested on a stool, looking through a crack in the blinds. He looked damn good in his navy sweater and dark jeans. His clothes hugged his body, and Madison felt a small spark of heat in her core. There was something so incredibly sexy about a man protecting her. Add to the fact that it was Jake, and she was so turned on it was shocking.

She walked over to stand beside him. "See anything?" she asked just above a whisper.

He shook his head. He turned and looked the other way down the street. "It's clear."

"What time do you think they'll come?"

"Probably not before midnight. They won't want too many witnesses, and the street is still pretty busy."

Madison nodded. "So we have an hour to kill."

Jake looked at her sharply. "Madison." His voice held a warning.

She chose to ignore his cautionary tone. "Jake." She smiled slowly. If she was going to go to jail, she might as well enjoy her last night as a free woman. If this plan didn't work, it did not look good for her.

"Stop," he growled. "This is not the time or the place."

"If this doesn't go well, it's the only time and place before I get locked up."

"You're not going to get arrested."

She cocked an eyebrow. "Can you guarantee that? Promise me, Jake. Promise me I won't get locked up."

He opened his mouth and hesitated. He closed it again without uttering a word.

"See? You know as well as I do that this is a Band-Aid at best. They plant evidence. We remove it. How many times can we do that before they find another way to get me?"

"Madison, we're working on it. You figured out they are laundering money. We'll get the rest of it sorted soon. You just have to be patient."

"I'm tired Jake. I don't have any patience left. I just need this to be over." To her mortification, tears threatened to spill down her cheeks.

He sighed and pulled her against his chest. "I know this is hard." He dropped a kiss onto her hair. "But we're going to get it sorted. You aren't going to jail even if I have to smuggle you out of the country myself." He smiled down at her.

She laughed and then gulped back a sob. "Please don't let it come to that."

He went to hug her again but she kissed him instead. He froze at first and then he kissed her back. It was a tender kiss. One that melted her heart. She wrapped her arms around his neck and moved her body against his. She needed this. His warmth, his understanding. She was rubbed raw with every nerve jangling and he was the balm that soothed her.

He ran his hands down her back and cupped her ass. He deepened the kiss keeping it slow and tender. It was like he understood exactly what she needed. He pulled her tight against him. She buried herself in his embrace, the fear receding even if it was only for a little while. He was her port in a storm.

He broke off the kiss. "We have to stop. Now is not a good time for this."

She leaned back slightly so she could see him a bit better in the ambient light. "Jake, I need this. I need your arms around me. I need to feel safe and cared for even if it's just for a few minutes." She begged him with her eyes. She swallowed hard as a lump built in her throat.

He got off the stool and moved away from her. He couldn't do this again. He wouldn't. "I'm sorry Madison. I can't help you like that. I have to keep you safe." Then he sat back down on the stool.

She bit her lip, then hung her head as she tiptoed out of the room.

But he was quite sure she didn't realize what had just happened. He'd jeopardized everything by just kissing her. He'd taken his eye off the ball. He could have missed the men's arrival. And it was not just their safety, but his job, his career, his entire way of life. He thought about what had happened last night. If it got out that he screwed a client it would be bad enough but during a job, when danger was imminent? Hell they'd been followed and he'd missed it because he'd been distracted by her. Just because they were at Hawk's didn't mean it was safe. Sleeping with Madison was a career killer move. The worst part was he'd do it all over again if she pushed him too hard. She just couldn't ask. Not ever again.

"See anything?" Madison reappeared beside him.

"No. Not yet." He didn't look at her or say anything else. He was still reeling from having risked everything for her. He needed to get his brain in the game. He'd been lucky so far but his luck wasn't likely to hold. It was a rookie mistake, sleeping with the client, and he hadn't been a rookie in a long time. His stupid, dangerous errors were how people got killed.

He kept his eyes on the street outside the window. He couldn't bring himself to look at her. She was his weakness. He couldn't seem to resist her. If he didn't smarten up, he'd get her killed.

Madison paced quietly in the kitchen for the next half hour. Then finally she came next to him again. Her scent swirled around him. He blinked and scoped out the street. He tensed. They'd arrived.

"Are they here?"

He nodded just once. She moved over beside him and tried to peer out through the small crack in the blinds.

"The blue car on the right." His voice was soft.

There were two men in a car half a block down from the building on the opposite side of the street. They finished parking the car but didn't get out. They were definitely watching the street.

"How do you know it's them?"

"They circled the block a couple of times. And, no, they weren't just looking for parking. They were checking out the street." Jake reached for his monocular and peered out the window again.

The car lit up inside briefly. The driver had lit a match. "Did you see anything?" It was too fast for her.

"Two men. I think both are Italian; neither are Fedorov."

She hooked her fingers in the front pockets of her jeans. "How long do you think they'll wait?"

"Not long."

Sure enough, a couple of minutes later, the two doors opened and the men got out. The driver was heavyset and dressed in a navy suit with black hair slicked back from his forehead. He wasn't overly tall, maybe five-feet-eight inches or so. They moved across the street.

Jake pulled out a cell phone and held it up to the window. The only light on the street came from the store signs and one lamp post so it wasn't great, but he snapped a couple of pictures anyway.

"I'll send them off to Mitch and Hawk. Hopefully, someone will recognize them. You should know the driver is wearing a shoulder holster and probably has another gun tucked somewhere else. Ankle possibly. I can tell by the cut of his suit. You need to be aware."

That was all he said, but he knew she understood what he was telling her. In case things went bad, the driver had two guns and, most likely, so did the passenger. She swallowed hard and his gut knotted. She shouldn't have to know this shit. She shouldn't have to go through this.

The second man was taller. Curly brown hair grazed his shoulders in a typical Italian style. He was also wearing a suit, but his was a gray color, possibly a pinstripe. He also wore a straw boater-style hat so it was harder to see his face. He was carrying something. Whatever it was, he had wrapped it in a cloth bag of some sort. That had to be the evidence they were going to plant. The package wasn't too big, no more than eight, maybe ten, inches in length and the man could hold it in one hand.

"What do you think he's carrying?" Madison asked.

Jake shrugged. "Tools maybe. Not sure."

The men walked slowly across the street and stopped in front of the building. After they came up the steps, he lost sight of them. He got up off the stool.

"Stay in here." He handed her a phone. "Call for help if shooting starts." He wanted to say more but there really wasn't much to say. He gave her a quick smile.

Then he walked out of the kitchen and down the hall.

CHAPTER NINETEEN

Jake stood beside the door. He crouched low and pulled out his gun. If they knew he was there, they could easily start shooting through the door, and standing just made him an easy target. He glanced back to make sure Madison was not behind him. *Madison.* He immediately shut down that line of thinking. He'd have to deal with the consequences of his actions later.

He cocked his head and listened. Down the stairs, the building door opened and then murmuring voices floated upward. There was some more quiet chatter and then silence until…very soft footfalls on the stairs. Someone was walking up, but it wasn't the men. The steps were too light. The sound paused on the landing but then continued past Jake's door and continued upward. Interesting. One of the women that lived on the floor above had let the men in. Good to know. She was the one spying for Fedorov or these guys.

The sound of the men climbing the stairs reached Jake's ears. They were quiet, but not like the woman had been, or at least he assumed it was a woman. The men reached the landing. A distinct scrape of a key in the lock and then a door opening. A few seconds later, the door closed.

As Jake waited near the door, the tension gripping his shoulders intensified. He focused on calming his breath and praying that Madison remained quiet and hidden.

Ten minutes later, the men came out, locked the door, and left the building. Jake hurried back to the kitchen, moved around Madison, and positioned himself at the blinds again. He watched them walk across the street. They got into their car and sat for a few minutes.

"What are they doing?" Madison asked as she clutched her throat.

"Sitting." Jake grabbed the monocular again and studied the men. They were chatting about something, but it didn't appear that they were arguing. What was the hold up? Were they waiting to see if Madison showed up?

The tall guy pulled a cell phone out of his blazer pocket and spoke into it. He nodded and gestured and then nodded again. The driver started the car and pulled out of the parking spot. They drove down the street and disappeared. "They were waiting for a call. They're gone."

"What now?" Madison's already large eyes were huge. She fidgeted with her hair and then the cell phone on the counter. Fear came off her in waves.

It crushed him to see her like this. "Now we wait a few minutes, and then I go over to your apartment." She nodded and then opened her mouth, but he wouldn't let her speak. "No, you can't come with me," he said flatly. He didn't care what argument she came up with. He wasn't letting her go over there. She'd almost proved too tempting, and he couldn't let it happen again. She stared at him for a minute but then pulled out the other stool and sat down.

Jake gave it another twenty minutes in case they came back, but the street remained clear in both directions.

"Here"—he handed Madison the monocular—"make yourself useful. Watch the street. I'll leave you one of the cell phones. The number for the one I have is already programed in. Text me if you see anything strange or if the men come back. Stay in the kitchen out of range of the door."

He didn't wait for a response. He walked out of the apartment, over to the opposite door, and let himself in with the key Madison had given him.

The apartment was the mirror image of the one he'd been in. Jake pulled a pen light out of his backpack, aimed it at the floor, and turned it on. He entered the bedroom and stopped dead. Madison's scent surrounded him, and it threw him off guard. He just hadn't been expecting it. Stupid. He knew she had lived there. He took a few seconds to gather himself and get back into the right mindset.

Methodically, he searched the room. Hawk had paid someone to come by and retrieve all of Madison's things, but thinking about it now, it might not have been such a good idea. Now Fedorov knew she wasn't coming back. Was that a good thing or a bad thing?

Jake finished in the bedroom and moved over to check the hall closet. It was empty. He searched the bathroom next, but came up dry. He even checked behind the toilet. Nothing. Where the hell did these guys hide whatever it was? He crossed the hall and went into the living space. There wasn't much there to search other than the furniture, and there was no way they would put it there. That would be too amateur hour. So, Jake headed for the kitchen.

It was the same as the other one except it was decorated in the yellows and oranges of Tuscany. It also had more appliances on the counters and the breakfast bar had a floor length blue cloth with tiny yellow flowers that covered where the stools were stored.

Jake started searching the cupboards, but still found nothing. He opened the fridge door. It was a tiny fridge so there wasn't much room, but Madison had bought some vegetables and there were some leftovers in a plastic container. It was the wrong shape to hold whatever had been in the bag, but he reached out for it anyway.

Then froze. The cell phone was vibrating in his pocket. He cursed and almost ignored it but thought the better of it. He checked the message. *Fedorov is crossing the street coming to the building. Get out now!*

Shit. He still hadn't found the package yet. He straightened and quietly closed the fridge door. There was nowhere to hide in the apartment, and he didn't have time to leave the kitchen anyway. He pulled out his gun and turned to face the doorway. The sound of a key in the lock made his gut knot up. The apartment door opened. There was some rustling, and then the door closed, but there were no footsteps. There was mumbling and what he assumed to be cursing in what sounded like Russian.

Jake replaced his gun in the holster, then turned and lifted the curtain that was in front of the stools. As quietly as humanly possible, he picked up the first stool and placed it in front of the window then placed the other stool next to it. Without a sound, he grabbed his penlight from the counter where he'd put it down and crawled into the space vacated by the stools. He squatted with his back to the outer wall and his knees against the cabinet. Then he pulled the curtain back into place. He got his gun out and rested it on his leg.

Footsteps came closer, and the grumbling became louder. The kitchen light went on. Jake gritted his teeth and aimed his gun at an upward angle to catch whoever it was in the chest should it become necessary. The fridge door opened and then another sound that Jake assumed was the tiny freezer. More rustling and then "*Da*," followed by a long string of words in Russian. Jake mentally cursed himself for never bothering to learn the language for other missions. It would have come in handy right now. There was silence for a few moments that ended with, "Fuck."

Floorboards creaked as Fedorov shifted around the room. Cupboards were opened and closed loudly and the clank of dishes being moved around. "It's me," he said, followed by some words in Italian. Then Fedorov switched to English. "I'm at the apartment. Where do you want me to put the necklace?"

Wait. They had the necklace? No fucking way! It was likely that no one had looked in that vase for eons, so why now?

"With the other stuff?" He grunted. "It's too obvious. I will hide it somewhere else." There was silence. "No, I won't make it too difficult for the police to find. Why don't you just tell your man where it is? Then they can find it right away." There was a pause. "Okay, I'll make it look good." He must have hung up because then he let out a string of curses, first in English and then in Russian. "Fucking moron," Fedorov grumbled, and then Jake heard more rustling. Fedorov was putting whatever it was back into the freezer.

The doors of the freezer and then the fridge banged shut. The sound of tapping reached Jake quickly followed by Fedorov speaking in rapid Russian. Jake cursed silently. He fervently wished he knew who the hell the Russian was speaking to.

"English. Bah. You need to go to Russia more. Your Russian sucks. Your mother should have taught you better. The girl is not coming back. Veridani wants me to plant evidence in her apartment so she can be arrested. I think it's a waste of time."

If Jake remained crouched in his hiding spot much longer, he wouldn't be able to move when the time came.

"We need to get rid of the problem in a more permanent way."

Icy fingers clutched Jake's heart. Fedorov wanted to kill Madison. Jake put his finger on the trigger of his gun. He could kill the man now. One quick shot to the heart, and it would be all over for Fedorov. But it wouldn't be over for Madison. They would just send someone else to kill her. Whoever *they* were.

"Yes, I can find her. I will make a call." Fedorov paused. "Yes, I will take care of it."

Fedorov must have ended one call and started another because he was speaking in Italian again. Suddenly, the apartment door opened. Fedorov immediately stopped speaking. Footsteps came down the hallway toward the kitchen. They were heavy, and there were two sets. Jake let out a small prayer of relief. For a moment, he had thought Madison might have decided to come rescue him. It was something she would do. The thought brought a weird flutter to his chest.

Jake's gut churned, and he put his finger back on the trigger. It would be so easy to kill all three of them right now. He had the element of surprise, and he was a crack shot. But it wouldn't help Madison long-term. In fact, it might make everything worse. He gathered himself so he could spring into action if necessary. He tried to keep his breathing even.

The footsteps came closer and then stopped. Fedorov swore again. "What are you two doing here? I almost shot you."

Then one of the men broke out in Italian. All Jake understood was Veridani. Fedorov answered back and it sounded like things were getting heated.

Then suddenly, "Fuck," Fedorov swore. "I know what I'm doing."

One of the other men said, "Veridani said you need to put the necklace where it's easy to find, yes? He's worried you will get a bit too creative, eh? He said we should hide it."

"Jesus Christ," Fedorov muttered.

"But the boss says to help you, so we are here to help. Give me the necklace. I hide it in the bathroom."

Fedorov must have given over the necklace because footsteps retreated down the hallway. Then a few minutes later, more chatter and footsteps. The apartment door opened and closed again. Jake stayed where he was for another few minutes and then slowly moved the curtain back. He slid out from underneath the counter, stood up, joints and tendons creaking after being crouched for so long. He slung the backpack onto his back. His feet were still numb but the cramps in his legs had subsided.

Jake moved over to the kitchen doorway and took a quick look into the hallway. He listened closely. There was no movement, and his senses told him he was alone in the apartment. He opened the fridge and retrieved the package from the freezer. He shoved it into his backpack. He'd look later to see what it was. Now he had to get the necklace. He walked down the hallway.

In the bathroom, he looked around for the necklace. He found it stuffed behind the pedestal of the sink. He pulled it out and looked at it in the penlight beam. It was diamonds and rubies in a wide band, that went into a deep V. It had the shape of a neckerchief if someone tied one around their neck.

A few months back, he'd asked Mitch's other half, Alexandria, who just happened to be a thief, to educate him on the world of jewels and artwork. She'd taught him a lot. Enough to know that this necklace would be worth a fortune if it were real and that it was a bit cliché. Valentina Veridani needed to think a bit more outside the box when it came to her jewelry designs as far as he was concerned.

But the necklace was paste. A good job, but still paste. They had a fake necklace made and decided to leave it at Madison's apartment as proof that she'd stolen the original.

Jake straightened and put the necklace in the backpack. At the door of the apartment, he checked the landing through the peephole. He needed to get out of there and call Hawk. Fedorov had said he had a way to track Madison down and then he was going to kill her.

Over Jake's dead body. His fingers itched. He'd make sure Fedorov didn't see another sunrise if he hurt one hair on Madison's head.

CHAPTER TWENTY

Jake entered the apartment and shut the door quietly behind him.

"Oh, my God!" Madison said, "I was so scared." She threw her arms around his neck and hugged him.

He hugged her back quickly then let her go. "I'm okay. Thanks for the warning."

"What happened? I saw the other guys go in, too. I wanted to text you but even in silent mode, sometimes the cell phone vibrates and you can hear it. I didn't want to take the risk."

"We have to get back to Hawk's place asap. There's a lot going on. More than we thought. I'll fill both of you in at the same time."

She nodded. She ached to throw herself into his arms again but now wasn't the time. They'd taken a major risk and it had been stupid. She was sure he was trying to make up for their lapse in judgement but as far as she was concerned, there was no lapse.

He pulled out the cell and called Thane. As soon as the man answered he said, "Can you pick us up where you dropped her off?"

"Yes. I'll be there in ten."

"Good." Jake clicked off the call. "Put your disguise back on. We need to leave."

She nodded then reached out and touched his arm. Their gazes locked. "Jake I was really worried about you. I am glad you're alright. All of this…you risking your life for me, you…comforting me, well I won't forget it ever. You have done more for me in the short time I've known you than any other person I've ever met. Saying thank you just doesn't seem like it's enough but it will have to do." She squeezed his arm again.

Jake swallowed hard and turned away from her gaze. He was uncomfortable. Well, that was fine. He'd have to get over it though. She was going to thank him again and again until it actually felt like he understood how much she cherished his help and understanding.

She put her disguise back on. A short while later, with his disguise in place and his backpack over his shoulder, Jake slowly opened the door to the landing. They left the apartment, and he locked the door once again. He took the lead down the stairs and stopped just inside the front door. He checked the street. It was clear.

Out they went. Jake moved so quickly Madison almost had to run to keep up. They walked the three blocks over and met Thane. Jake opened the back door, and Madison climbed in. He got in the passenger side, and Thane pulled away from the curb.

Thane glanced over at him "How'd it go?"

"It turned to shit, but I got the stuff." Jake dug the package out of his backpack. He unwound the bag and looked inside. "Jesus. Lock picks. There's no way she could have stolen the necklace with lock picks."

"That doesn't sound too bad then," Madison piped up from the backseat. If she could prove there's no way she could have grabbed the necklace with just lock picks maybe they'd stop suspecting her.

"Yes. It would have been fairly easy to dismiss those," Thane agreed.

Jake reached into the bag again and pulled out the fake necklace. He kept it low in his lap so no traffic cam could pick it up. "This is what they really wanted to hide. It's what Fedorov had."

"What?" Madison leaned forward over the seat. "Shit. That can't be the real necklace. They didn't find the real one, did they?"

"No. This one is fake."

"Fedorov came himself? That's surprising." Thane made yet another turn, checking to see if they were being followed.

"The two goons I sent you a picture of came with the lock picks. Fedorov showed up separately with the fake necklace. I was in the apartment at the time."

Thane grunted and then glanced over, eyebrows raised.

"I managed to hide. There's something weird going on. I don't speak Russian or Italian, but it seems like Fedorov might be working with two different sets of people. The Veridanis and some Russian guy or group. He had calls with both while he was in the apartment."

"Hmm," Thane mused. "Do you think they're all part of the same group, or are they two separate entities?"

Jake grimaced. "That's the thing. I'm not sure one knows about the other."

"Why do you say that?" Thane made the turn onto his street.

"Because the Italians want to frame Madison, and the Russians want to kill her."

Madison's heart stuttered and she gasped. *Someone wanted her dead?* "But…but why?"

Jake glanced back over the seat at her. She wanted to reach out and hold on to him but she knew he wouldn't like that. Not in front of Thane. But someone wanted to kill her. She closed her eyes. This just couldn't be happening.

"There's more." Jake gave her an apologetic look. "Fedorov thinks he has a way of finding Madison. My guess is we don't have much time before he shows up at your door."

Thane parked the car. "I'll make sure we're not walking into an ambush. You look out for Monty." He was out of the car in seconds and at his front door. He disappeared inside.

"They want to kill me." Madison's voice was barely above a whisper.

"Yes." Jake reached his arm over the seat and she grabbed his hand. "I'm so sorry Madison. I didn't want to tell you that way but it's better if you know the truth."

She blinked back tears and sniffed. "What am I supposed to do?"

"There's nothing you can do other than follow our directions when we give you an order. Hawk and I will do our best to keep you safe." She nodded. "Madison," his tone changed, "what happened earlier, at Hawk's, and then tonight with that kiss, cannot happen again. It was a stupid thing to do. I lost track of my primary objective, which is to keep you safe. Almost missing those guys heading into your apartment was dangerous. It could have gotten us both killed."

"I know," she whispered. "I'm sorry."

"Don't be sorry. It's my fault. I should have stopped you. I should have stopped us both but I didn't and that's on me. It's my job to protect you and I didn't do it. I won't make that mistake again."

She nodded but couldn't speak. She couldn't get the words out. He was telling her they weren't going to be together anymore and for some reason that was even more crushing than the fact that someone wanted to kill her. Breath dammed up in her throat. She squeezed his hand. He tightened his fingers briefly over hers, then let her hand go and faced forward again.

His phone buzzed. "It's clear. Let's go." The two of them left the car and went into Thane's apartment.

Thane was already packing a laptop and other equipment. He turned to Jake. "Do you need more weapons?"

Jake shook his head. "I have my go-bag. I'll grab a few changes of clothes, and I'm good to go. Madison, put some clothes in your shoulder bag and leave your laptop behind. We're leaving in five minutes."

Madison went around the corner and up the stairs. She just kept telling herself to put one foot in front of the other, but she was barely managing it. She went into her room and did as instructed. Coming back out to the hallway, she found Thane striding out of his bedroom, a backpack over his shoulder, and Jake with his bag in his hand.

"Ready?" Thane asked, and then his cell phone chimed. He glanced down at the screen. "Fuck. We're too late. He turned the screen so they could see it. It was Fedorov and at least three other men. They were standing in the courtyard directly in front of Thane's door.

"What do we do?" Madison whispered. Her eyes bounced back and forth between the two men.

Jake frowned. "Is there a way over the back wall?"

Thane nodded. He glanced at Madison and then back at Jake. "We'll have to climb down two stories on a drainpipe."

Madison blinked. That was not something she wanted to try. "Are there any other options?" she asked as they heard the chime alert that the front door was opening.

Thane nodded and went back to his bedroom. Jake and Madison followed suit. They entered the bathroom to find Thane standing on the closed lid of the toilet, pushing up a piece of the ceiling. It was the access to the attic. He shoved the board out of the way. Then he hauled himself up and disappeared inside.

Jake grabbed Madison around the waist and lifted her onto the toilet. Then he hopped up with her and lifted her until she could crawl into the attic as well. He hoisted himself up into the attic after her. He swung his legs out of the way and Thane settled the board back in place.

The attic was cold. Thane had turned on a flashlight so they could see. There was very little insulation between the studs. The roof above them was peaked so they could stand if they were in the center, but it sloped so much on the sides they would have to crawl. There didn't appear to be anything to stand on, however. Madison shivered in the darkness. There had to be a way out. She wasn't going to die in a cold attic. No. Just no fucking way.

Jake looked at Hawk and cocked an eyebrow. *Are we staying here?*

Hawk shook his head and then pointed the flashlight beam at the eaves. There were boards placed over the trusses in a path that lead across the entire attic. Jake nodded. Hawk took the lead. He turned sideways and moved very carefully over to the boards. Then he shone the flashlight back so Madison could do the same.

She looked at Jake, and even in the pale light, terror glowed in her eyes. He grabbed her hands. They were shaking. "You can do this," he whispered. "You don't have a choice." He wanted to hold her so badly it made him ache, but he was determined to keep his distance. His job was to protect her, not love her. Loving her would only make things worse.

Madison nodded once. She turned and got on her hands and knees, then crept along two studs until she got to the boards. Hawk started down the boards and Madison crawled after him.

Jake waited and listened. He couldn't hear anything, but he didn't want to be crawling, facing the wrong way, if Fedorov or his guys decided to come up here. Hawk and Madison made it to the other end of the attic and then disappeared. Jake blinked. Where the hell did they go?

The attic went dark. Jake quietly pulled out his pen light and held it in his mouth. Then he crawled over to the boards and followed the route Hawk and Madison took. He was three quarters of the way to where they disappeared when he heard it. The voices from below were getting louder. He picked up speed. If they lifted the board before he got out of sight, he was in trouble.

When he came to what looked like the end wall of the attic, he realized there was a space. The "floor" they'd been crawling on ended, and there was a gap. It had to be five feet by seven feet or so. When he had looked at it from across the attic, it appeared as if the "floor" went all the way to the wall.

He looked down. Madison and Hawk were sitting in the space. He quietly slid down between them. The space was made out of stone, and the cold and damp immediately sunk into his bones. The sound of the access board being moved reached him. He clicked off his pen light and pulled his gun from his waistband. Flicking off the safety, he rested it on his knee with his finger next to the trigger. A beam of light danced above their heads.

A voice said something in Russian. There was a response and then nothing for a few seconds. Then the first man spoke again. The man's voice receded, and it went back to being quiet. They heard the occasional thump, but then a few minutes later, nothing.

"How long do we stay here?" Madison whispered in the dark.

Hawk shifted his legs slightly. "We have to give it at least an hour, if not more."

Jake leaned over slightly toward Madison. "We have to be sure they've left and aren't sitting downstairs waiting for us to come out."

Madison squeezed his leg to indicate she heard him. In the silence, he heard her breathing. It was a little fast. Then he heard another sound. It was her teeth clicking together. Her teeth were chattering. He pulled out his penlight from his pocket and turned it on. He shone it next to her. She was shivering, and her lips were blue. She must have taken her jacket off when they'd arrived back at Hawk's and didn't get a chance to put it back on again.

Fuck. As quietly as he could, he pulled off the coat he was wearing and wrapped it around her. Hawk caught his eye. He glanced at Madison and then back at Jake. *Yeah, she wasn't doing too well.* Shock to go along with the cold.

Hawk whispered in Jake's ear, "We gotta wait for at least another thirty minutes. She's not looking good. Keep her warm. I'll check things out as soon as it's time."

"How about you keep her warm and I'll go check," he countered. It wasn't about Madison, although having her in such close proximity was driving him a bit mad. It was the fact that whoever went to check was taking the greatest risk. The first man over the wall. He would prefer it be him than have anything happen to Hawk. Jake didn't know him well, but he knew enough to know Hawk was a good man and, ultimately, this was Jake's job, not his. Hawk was a lawyer, here to help Madison, yes, but not in this way. "Hawk, I got this."

"She's closer to you, and we can't move around that much. She's yours to protect. Sorry, buddy, but this one is mine."

Jake frowned and then looked back at Madison. She was dwarfed by the huge jacket. Her eyes darted everywhere, and he'd bet she was seeing nothing. Her hands trembled. He cursed a storm in his head. He lifted his arm and put it behind her, moving her so that she leaned on his chest. He realized it wasn't just her hands that were shaking, but her whole body.

As quietly as possible, he scooped her up and cradled her in his lap. He hugged her to him. Her head rested on his chest. He bent his head and kissed her hair. It was just a natural thing to do. He didn't even think about that or how she fit perfectly in his arms. He bit back a sigh and tried to think of other things.

They didn't have a chance to discuss how Hawk's meeting with Enzo went. Would Enzo know who those two men were? Were the Veridanis involved in money laundering with the Italian mob or the Russians? Or both possibly? Nah, they didn't seem smart enough for that. The Italians wouldn't stand for sharing resources like that with the Russians. The Veridanis would most likely be killed if that were the case. He could only hope. He'd like to see them in Hell for what they'd done.

Thirty minutes later, Hawk leaned over to Jake again. "I'll check it out. I'll text if it's clear. If you hear shooting, do not come out." He patted a storage bin next to him, a soft *thump thump* sounding. "There's extra guns and ammo stored here. It isn't ideal, but it beats the shit out of having nothing."

"Good luck," Jake said, and he meant it. Hawk was risking his life for Madison and for Jake. He hated that Hawk had to do it alone, but there was no way he would leave Madison on her own.

A week ago, he didn't even know her, and now he didn't want to leave her side. Not just because it was his job but because there was something so fierce about her nature. The way she didn't flinch when that animal Fedorov had leered at her. She wasn't intimidated in the least. He loved that. The way she demanded to go with him, and her behavior at the apartment... It was over the top, and yet she had no regrets. She could have sat there and cried and moaned, but instead she faced everything head-on.

He also was impressed by her intelligence and openness. She'd been telling him about herself since they'd met, and not once did she clam up and apologize for it. She was basically saying, "This is who I am. Like it or not, I don't care." And he absolutely thought that was the sexiest thing ever.

If he'd met Madison at a bar or through friends, it would be game on. He would have done his damnedest to make sure she was in his bed at the end of the night, and chances were good, he wouldn't have let her out again for a long time. He would spend hours making her happy. The memory of her screaming his name was making him hard.

But she was a client. One that was in serious trouble, and an intimate relationship between them never should have happened. Not ever. He let his personal needs interfere with his professional assignment. As much as he wanted to go with Hawk and kick some ass, he had to stay and do his duty.

Hawk got himself organized, placing a gun in his waistband and one in his sock. He tucked extra ammunition in his pockets. Madison struggled to sit upright and then leaned over to kiss Hawk on the cheek and whispered, "Good luck."

Hawk winked. "Don't worry, Monty. It'll be fine." He stood up and hoisted himself out of the hole.

Madison watched Thane disappear over the top of the wall. Her heart thudded against her ribs. She hated this. All of it. Every single bit except for Jake. *Jake.* She didn't want to think about him, but curled up in his lap it was hard not to. At least she was finally warm and feeling a bit less woozy. The shock of being in this situation was getting to her.

Being attracted to the man hired to protect her was not something she'd anticipated. She hadn't initially wanted to start anything with him because this was just a shit situation. Plus, he probably had all kinds of women throwing themselves at him. He was sexy as hell, and she was sure he knew it.

Oh, God, was she just another client who had the hots for him? Did this happen all the time? *Yuk.* Okay, being one of a crowd always annoyed her. That was enough to stop her brain from remembering how hot the sex was. Almost.

But she had started something. At the hotel in Mugello, Madison had thought, *What the hell?* Go for it. Truthfully, she was glad she did, but looking at it now, she could see what Jake was saying. She had seduced him to make it seem like they were dating or together. To take the edge off her reality.

Heat flooded her cheeks. She was so grateful for the darkness so he couldn't see how red her face must be. She showed him her weakness and he'd nearly done exactly as she asked. It didn't matter how reckless it was, he would have done what she wanted because she needed it. Needed him. Even though he'd put a stop to her advances, she knew deep in her bones she was falling for him.

Stupid. It wouldn't work anyway. He probably thought she was crazy, and even if he didn't, she'd done nothing to make him want to date her. Plus, she was constantly flying around the world for different jobs and staying for varying lengths of time. It was hard to date someone when you weren't in the same place for more than a few weeks.

It was what she wanted, though. A life of travel and adventure. Well, it was what she *used* to want. Now, she was just tired and missed her apartment back in New York. Everything hurt, and she couldn't begin to process the fact that someone was trying to kill her. It just boggled her mind.

She snuggled deeper into Jake's chest. He closed his arms around her. It felt good. Great even. The idea of having someone like Jake to come home to sounded nice. At least, in theory. She'd never been much good at sharing her space, nor did she do well if she didn't have enough alone time. Boyfriends had always been relegated to the nice-to-have once in a while category, as long as they didn't become too clingy and didn't want too much from her.

She knew her needs were unrealistic. She wanted a guy to be loyal to her, but only see her on her terms. A couple of nights a week when she was in town worked for her. Having someone in her space all the time would drive her crazy, or so she'd always told herself. Maybe it would be different than she thought.

Nah, she liked to be on her own. She liked a life where she didn't have to depend on anyone, worry about anyone, or be responsible for anyone. That was the key. She didn't want any more responsibilities. She had enough with work. The idea that someone might depend on her really freaked her out. She just didn't have it in her to be responsible for anyone ever again. She'd loved her mother, but once was enough.

There was a sound. She cocked her head, and her palms dampened. She remained perfectly still.

"It's Hawk moving around."

She gritted her teeth because she was afraid they would start chattering again. Not because she was cold, but because she was terrified. She closed her eyes and tried to do some deep breathing exercises. They were supposed to make her relax, but it ended up making her lightheaded, so she stopped. "How can you be so sure?"

"If it was someone else, we would have heard a gunshot."

"What if they used a silencer?"

Jake chuckled softly. "Suppressors make it quiet, but they don't completely muffle the sound. I have faith Hawk would have gotten a warning shot off to let me know there was trouble, if nothing else, and he doesn't have a suppressor on his gun."

"Oh." It felt like hours since Thane had left. "How long has it been?"

"About twenty minutes. It's going to take a while. Hawk is going to check for people, but also bugs and cameras."

Well, shit. She'd thought it had been at least forty-five. She really needed to get a grip on herself. She shifted slightly in Jake's lap. Maybe it was better if she moved over to sit on the stone again. Being warm in his arms was making it difficult to stay focused.

The loud crash was so unexpected she started to scream, but Jake put a hand over her mouth. She froze. He dropped his hand and then shifted her off his lap. He reached back and pulled out his gun. Then he grabbed another from the ones Thane had left behind. Then setting the gun down, he turned off the penlight leaving them in inky darkness.

She had no idea what Jake was doing, but she felt rather than heard him move. Icy fingers grabbed her heart, and fear clawed their way out of her chest. A scream built in her throat, but she just couldn't let it out. If she did, it might get her killed. Worse, it might get Jake killed, and she couldn't deal with that. She bit her cheek and tasted blood. That quelled the scream, but it didn't stop her hands from shaking.

The pitch black was endless. She held up one of her hands in front of her face, but she couldn't see it. She only knew Jake was there because she hadn't heard him leave. He was so still it was like she was alone in the hole. She couldn't take it. She reached out and felt around until she touched Jake's leg. She grabbed his thigh. He didn't make a sound but didn't shake her off either.

Suddenly there was a beam of light dancing around above them. Jake was eye level with the floor. He had the guns pointed in the direction the light came from.

"It's me," Thane called.

All the air whooshed out of Madison's lungs, and she slumped against the wall.

"Jake, come on over here. We need to talk."

Jake put one gun down on the ground and pulled the penlight from his pocket. He turned it on and handed it to Madison. "I'll be right back."

She took the penlight and nodded. She didn't trust herself to speak. There was still a scream lurking somewhere in her chest, and she didn't want to take the chance and let it out. What could have caused the crash? Did that mean there was a dead guy down there? Suddenly, the thought of sitting there while the men decided things just pissed her off. She knew it was just another reaction to the stress, but anger felt a whole lot better than fear.

Madison grabbed the penlight and climbed out of the stone hole. She crawled on her hands and knees along the boards until she reached the two men.

Jake shot her a glance and shook his head.

"What? What's going on? You would've had to crawl back over there and tell me anyway," she said. She sat on the boards and crossed her arms over her chest.

Thane grimaced. "Sorry if I scared you. The neighbor's cat was on my balcony. He knocked over a potted plant I had on the deck, and it smashed."

"So there's no dead guy downstairs?" she asked.

Hawk smiled. "No. No dead guy."

"Well, that's a relief." She wiped a hand across her face. "So, what do we do now?

Jake stared at her. "That's a damn good question."

CHAPTER TWENTY-ONE

Jake put his hands on her waist and brought her down from the attic. Then he stepped down and walked out of the bathroom. Madison followed suit. Hawk waited for them in the hallway. "We can't turn on any lights or turn off lights that are already on. One of Fedorov's men is watching the apartment from the inside wall of the courtyard. I almost missed him. If he hadn't lit a cigarette, we might have had some major issues."

"So should we go out the back?" Madison asked. "Where can we hide? Maybe another hotel, not one of Drake's?"

"We're not going anywhere," Jake stated flatly.

"Pardon?" Madison's eyebrows went up.

"What Jake means is that this is the safest place for us at the moment," Hawk explained. "The guy outside is looking for us to enter this place. He doesn't know we're already here. As long as we don't mess with the lights and we stay away from the windows, we should be good." He glanced at his watch. "It's almost five-thirty. Mrs. Conti, a retired schoolteacher, lives in the corner unit. She gets up around five-forty-five every day. I'll call her in a bit and ask her about the man standing outside. She'll call the cops on him. Then he'll have to at least watch from the street, outside of the courtyard. It will buy us a little breathing room."

He leaned on the wall and wiped his face with his hands. "I don't know about you two, but I am bushed. I think we're safe enough for now, so why don't you both grab some sleep while we can?"

Jake looked over at Madison. She was pale, but at least she was no longer trembling, nor were her eyes darting around like they had been when they were in the attic. She seemed to be relaxing a bit.

"Madison," he said, "I think it's a good idea if you do get some sleep. You're looking a bit pale, and I know you're tired."

She arched an eyebrow at him. "Is that your way of telling me I look like shit?"

He blinked. "Um, no. Earlier, I think you were suffering from a big shock. It takes its toll. That's all I'm saying. I'm going to grab some sleep as well, if that's okay with you, Hawk?"

Hawk nodded. "I'll call Mrs. Conti and then crash myself. I am expecting that the police will go back and search Madison's apartment today. I will get a call about that in a few hours. Once they don't find anything, I expect there will be some confusion and then they'll have to abandon the idea of arresting Madison. At least for today. I would guess that we've only bought a day or so before they manufacture something else." He touched Madison's shoulder. "One day at a time."

She nodded but didn't say anything.

"Hawk, at some point we need to hear what Enzo said."

"Right. It was enlightening. But grab some sleep, and then we'll debrief."

Jake stood there with his arms folded across his chest. Madison stood next to him. He suddenly realized she wasn't going to move unless he did. She was looking for him to say it was okay to sleep. While he wasn't happy about all of them sleeping, she certainly needed to get some rest. He shot Hawk a look. *Wait.* Hawk nodded slightly.

Jake took her by the arm and led her to her room. "Get some rest. I promise you it's fine to sleep." Those words made Jake uncomfortable since he hated making promises, but he knew she wouldn't let herself relax if he didn't say it was okay. The anger he'd seen in her eyes in the attic was long gone. Now she looked tired and sad.

"You're sure?" she said as she walked into the room.

"Yes. Sleep for as long as you need. If anything happens, we'll wake you."

She nodded. "Thanks." Her voice was soft. Fatigue dripped off every word. She started to close the door.

"Just remember, no lights. Here, take this." He handed her the penlight. "Stay away from the windows.

She took the light, nodded her thanks, and closed the door. Jake stood there for a moment, wondering if he should go in and make sure she had everything she needed and understood to keep the penlight pointed at the carpet.

Hawk touched him on the shoulder. "She'll be alright. It's almost daybreak. You need to get some sleep as well."

"What about you? You're just as tired as I am."

Hawk smiled. "Not quite, but yeah, I'll crash on the sofa downstairs. I have all the alarms on the entry points hooked to my phone. The cameras point outwards, so if they're hacked, they only see the outside. We're good. I'll call my neighbor and sic her on Fedorov's man, and then I'm going to sleep."

Jake nodded reluctantly. He didn't want to recheck everything Hawk did because that would be insulting and unnecessary, but he couldn't deny the uneasy feeling tightening his gut. Not that anything was wrong, but that he was leaving something undone.

"You can check for yourself if you like. I won't be insulted," Hawk offered.

He grimaced. "That obvious?"

Hawk laughed. "Yup. But only because I would be the same way."

"I guess I'll trust you then." Jake turned to go into his room but turned back. "Hawk?" When the other man stopped on the top step, Jake said, "Thanks. It's good to know someone has my back."

Hawk smiled. "Always, brother." Then he went down the stairs.

Five hours later, Jake grabbed a quick shower and then went downstairs. Hawk was making coffee in the kitchen area. "Morning, Sunshine." Hawk held up a cup.

"Hell yes, and keep it coming." Jake sat down on one of the barstools. His eyes felt like sandpaper and his body ached. He'd managed to get a few hours' sleep. It wasn't really enough, but it would have to do for now. "Did you get any sleep? How'd it go with the neighbor?"

"Yes, I got a few hours. Mrs. Conti not only called the cops, but she chased him out of the courtyard with a broom. By the time the cops got here, she had him out on the street. I chanced it and took a quick peek. Fedorov's guy is still there, but he's halfway down the block. All he can do is watch the driveway. It buys us a bit of space."

Jake grunted as he took his first sip of dark Italian roast. It tasted like he needed a hundred more. "Any news? What did Enzo say yesterday?"

Hawk grabbed his coffee and came over to stand at the counter. "He said—"

Jake's cell rattled. "It's Mitch." He answered the call and immediately put it on speaker. "Hey, Mitch. I'm here with Hawk."

"Hey, Jake. Hey, Hawk. How are you? How did the raid go?"

"It was a bit of a shit show, but it's under control. What about you? Any more information on Fedorov? I would love to know who he's really working for besides the Veridanis."

"What makes you think he's working for someone else?" Mitch asked.

Jake took another sip of coffee. "I'll fill you in, but why don't you go first? What did you find out?"

"Not a whole lot. Fedorov is a very cagey guy. It doesn't help that the *Polizia* are keeping a tight lid on this whole thing, which is quite unlike them. Someone either has major pull, or someone is getting cold feet."

"You think someone has helped the Veridanis but is now worried about backlash?" Jake asked.

"Yeah. I mean it should be all over the news about the necklace, and yet it's not. I think the Veridanis asked a favor of someone high up to keep a lid on things and promised a swift outcome in return. Now that it's being dragged out, I would be willing to bet the person is getting worried. A scandal like this could take someone down. Or not. It's Italy. Who the fuck knows?"

Hawk picked up the coffee pot and filled his cup. Jake finished his coffee and pushed the empty mug toward Hawk. "I hear that. Anything is possible."

Hawk refilled Jake's mug. "That sounds plausible. My source at the *Polizia* said the cops were not pleased when they did the search of Madison's place but came up dry. There was some screaming in the offices of the higher-ups. People are getting antsy."

"That's not good," Jake commented.

"No," Mitch agreed. "But at least you managed to retrieve the planted evidence. Maybe if we can prolong this, whoever is granting the Veridanis and their Russian muscle access will get cold feet and shut the whole thing down."

"It would be good but, honestly, how long can we play this game? At some point, they're going to plant evidence that we're not going to find. Or, even worse, they won't even bother planting it and just say they found it in her place or in some place she frequented and have someone swear it's hers. We're bailing water out of a sinking ship with a small bucket, and we can't keep up."

Mitch let out a long sigh. "I know. I know. Drake is calling in some favors with friends over there. Hawk, you spoke with Enzo. What did he say? Did he provide any clue as to what's going on?"

"Actually, we have some information about that," Hawk said.

Just then, Madison entered the room. She came over and sat down on the stool next to Jake. "Morning," she said to Jake. Then at the phone, "Hi, Mitch." She smiled at Hawk. "I would love some of your amazing coffee."

"Coming right up." He pulled out a mug and poured her a cup. He set it on the counter in front of her and then pushed a small pitcher of cream and a bowl of sugar toward her.

"Hold on. I want Drake in on this call as well as my brothers." When Mitch put the call on hold, Jake watched as Madison doctored her coffee. He rubbed his knee. Somewhere in the last couple of days he must have dinged it. It hurt like hell at the moment.

He'd told Mitch he was exhausted, but maybe it was more than that. Maybe he'd just lost his edge. Losing his edge meant losing the ability to function at the level he needed to do the job. Maybe he had already been there and that was the reason Mitch wanted to speak to Jake.

"Jake, Monty, and Hawk." Mitch came back on the line. "Logan and Gage are here, and I patched Drake in on the call."

"Are you making any progress on this, Jake?" Drake asked.

"Yes and no. There's more going on here than we thought. Fedorov seems to have two masters. One that wants Madison arrested and one that wants her dead. We think we know why, but—"

"Jake, maybe you can provide us some context so we can understand what's happening," Logan said.

Jake grimaced. Logan was being all conciliatory and lawyerly, a sure sign he thought Jake had fucked up.

"I went to Madison's apartment to intercept the evidence they were going to plant—"

"Start from the beginning," Gage interrupted.

"Okay, you know that Madison is being framed for the theft of a very expensive diamond and ruby necklace that was designed by Valentina Veridani." He glanced over at Madison. She still looked exhausted but better than she had last night. Pride swelled in his chest for the way she was hanging in there. He continued, "We think we know why, but it's complicated. It would be better if Madison explained it."

Madison took a deep breath and then said, "Jake asked me a lot of questions about my interactions with the Veridanis, and it triggered a memory for me. I made a call to a friend, and she was able to confirm my suspicion about why the Veridani brothers are trying to get me out of the way. Drake, the Veridanis are laundering money. They're using a fake charity to do it. I stumbled across it when I was doing my due diligence for the audit, only I didn't realize it at the time." Madison went on to explain the whole story. "Anyway, I'm waiting to hear if the other countries are also just a front for the laundering. My friend has reached out to her contacts. She'll email me when she hears anything."

"Do you have any proof of this?" Drake asked.

"That's the thing. There's no real proof. At least not on their books." Madison tapped the rim of her cup. "I have to say the way they cooked their books and covered it up is very impressive. Top level. Extraordinarily clean."

Jake studied Madison as she spoke. A bit of color had bloomed on her cheeks. She was still exhausted, but she appeared more comfortable. Work was her refuge from the world. *Takes one to know one.*

Jake gulped more coffee. "So, what do you think that means?"

Madison tucked her hair behind her ear. "Well, Jake heard Fedorov on the phone with two different groups of people when he was in the apartment."

Jake picked up from there to explain that part of the story.

"What are you thinking then, Monty?" Logan asked.

Drake cut in. "A safe bet would be the Italian mob."

"Yes, but my guess is the Veridanis are laundering for the Russian mob as well as the Italians. I'm assuming they couldn't get away with dealing with the Russians if they weren't doing it for the Italians, too."

"My turn," Hawk cut in. "I spoke with Enzo Valardi. He said that no one knows anything about what the Veridanis are up to, or at least no one is admitting to it. He was adamant that if they were actually laundering money for the Italian mob, people would know, especially in the numbers we think they're moving. I sent him the pictures of the two guys that Jake took, and he texted this morning that they're two low-level enforcers for the local mob and have no clout whatsoever. He thinks if the Veridanis are using them, then they definitely do not have connections higher up in the organization."

Drake sighed. "So he doesn't think the money laundering is a mob thing?"

Hawk grinned at Madison and Jake. "I didn't say that. He was very interested about Fedorov's involvement in the whole thing. After what Jake said last night about Fedorov seeming to have two masters, I called Enzo and asked the question. Could the Veridanis be laundering the money for the Russian mob and not the Italians? He said if they were, they had a death wish. No one gets away with doing something like that without paying a tax to the local mob boys, and a setup like that would mean the locals would want in." He paused. "The presence of two goons in the picture means that didn't happen. They would have brought higher level thugs with them as muscle."

"So, to summarize," Gage said, "we believe the Veridanis are laundering money for the Russian mob, and because Monty stumbled on the scheme, the Veridanis decided to have her arrested for theft so that her story of money laundering would be discredited, and because that would draw less attention than an American woman being murdered in Florence. The Russians, on the other hand, just want her dead because it's more expeditious." Gage paused. "Sorry, Monty."

She cleared her throat. "I'm getting…used to the idea."

Jake's head started to pound. Madison should not have to get used to the idea that someone was out to kill her. He cleared his throat. "My guess is Paloma told the Veridani brothers, and they hatched the scheme to have Madison arrested. It wasn't like they could suddenly say to Drake, 'Hey, we're not interested in having you invest anymore.' That would ring alarm bells for other investors, which I'm assuming they need to cover what they're doing."

Madison nodded. "If they want to launder more money, they need to bring in investors and start new projects to make it look like the money is going out and coming back again."

Jake continued, "So they hatched a plan to have her arrested in order to discredit her and get them out of the deal with Drake. They could also control the narrative around it and keep the police at bay. I think Fedorov's Russian bosses got impatient and decided to have Madison killed as a way to solve the problem. I think the Veridanis are shitting themselves right about now. Er, sorry, Madison."

She smiled and waved off his apology.

"I agree with you, Jake," Gage said. "That makes perfect sense. With Monty out of the way, the problem disappears and they start again with another investor. Chances are good no one else will bother to track down the charities they 'donate' to and see if they're legit, especially if those investors are Russian oligarchs with money to burn."

Jake nodded. "Yeah. The other part of this is, I don't think Fedorov told the Veridanis about killing Madison. He certainly didn't tell them when I was in the kitchen, and he had every opportunity. Two of the Veridani's henchmen showed up to 'help' Fedorov hide the copy of the necklace in Madison's apartment. I don't think the Italians trust the Russians."

"So, how do we use this to our advantage?" Drake mused. "I spoke to the Veridanis earlier, and they were apologetic to a point but steadfast in their belief Monty took the necklace. Monty, is there any indication at all they were in trouble? Anything in the past?"

"No, nothing, but I think that's because the Russians are taking care of the books now. My guess is the business isn't actually successful and hasn't been for a while. Valentina's fashion house was just taking off when she died. I think if she'd lived, it would have been fine, but her brothers don't have the design talent that she had, nor do they have the feel for fashion." She shook her head sadly. "Valentina seemed to just understand what women wanted to wear. She had an innate fashion sense. Her brothers, not so much. They've hired talent, but it's not the same. They probably thought Valentina's death would bring them even more notice, and they could capitalize on it."

"That's a cold way of looking at things," Jake said.

Madison shrugged. "Not really. It's business. Their sister was dead, and they needed to carry on. Her death gave the brand lots of publicity. She was a media darling, and then she was gone. The brothers probably borrowed a lot, thinking they would expand, and the publicity would take them to the next level, but without Valentina, it just died out. Once they were in trouble, then it was all over. It would be simple to get into the money laundering game."

Jake shrugged. "It doesn't really matter how they got there, I guess, just that you're involved in their mess. Now, how do we get you out of it?"

"That's a great question, Jake," Drake said. "Monty, can you think of any way to prove what's going on?"

"I did see a brochure, like I said, with the mayor of Libreville on it at a supposed event to celebrate the opening of one of their sites. I had a copy, but Fedorov stole it."

Logan asked, "Do you think you could possibly get another copy?"

Madison sighed. "I don't know. Paloma had them in her desk. A copy of one would be a good start. It would be enough to get someone in government interested, as long as we approached the right person."

Hawk took a swig of coffee and leaned against the stove. "The best thing would be to find the original files so we could show how they doctored the pictures in the first place."

Jake cocked his head. Hawk's idea was a good one. It would go a long way to clearing Madison's name with the *Polizia*. Plus, they could actually produce the necklace at some later date. The question was how would they get the files and where would those files be?

"Gage, is Dani around?" Jake asked.

"Why do you ask?"

"Well, I was just thinking of what Hawk said. What if we could get the original files? If Dani could take a quick look around, maybe she could find them."

"You want Dani to hack into Veridani?" Gage sighed.

Drake spoke up. "I would be willing to pay her."

"That's not the point." Gage was silent. Then finally, "I'll ask her, but I'm sure she'll want to help Monty. I'll let you know if she finds anything."

"Okay. I guess we'll stay here until we hear anything from you." Jake glanced at Madison. This was going to be a tough one. Sitting and waiting was the worst part of something like this. If they were doing something, it felt like forward momentum even if it wasn't.

He was going to have to come up with something for her to do. Boredom led to thinking, and thinking led to fear, and fear led to… An image of their limbs tangled together flashed in his head. Yeah, that just couldn't happen again. He needed to come up with something for her to do for both of their sanity levels.

CHAPTER TWENTY-TWO

Madison sipped a second cup of coffee and tried to decide what to do. Jake and Thane were discussing the inner workings of the Italian mob, and she had nothing to add to the conversation. She drummed her fingers on the countertop. Sitting around all day, doing nothing more than waiting, would suck. It would stress her out, and she was realizing she wasn't so good at dealing with stress. Not the normal stress like a bad co-worker or a project that went sideways, but real stress like life-threatening stuff. She freaked out and seduced men. Okay, one man, but it wasn't a good approach, obviously, to handle her stress.

She moved over to the sofa. Better to get distance from said man. Now that she could look back with some clarity, she realized that, even at the hotel in Mugello, she was reacting to the stress level as much as she was to Jake.

He was incredibly sexy, and the fact that he was her protector was just intoxicating. But would they have slept together if they'd met in a bar? Hell, yes! Who was she kidding? There's no way she'd have let him get away.

She closed her eyes and took a deep breath. The truth was she had turned to him because she was panicking, and as much as she enjoyed their time together this was not the best way to start a relationship. Besides, they were both busy people with crazy jobs that had them traveling all over the world. Their relationship wouldn't stand a chance.

Of course, that was assuming he wanted to have a relationship. He'd been keeping her at a distance since the…incident in Thane's apartment, where she'd seduced him a second time. Heat rose in her face. She was mortified just thinking about what she'd done. She'd put him in a truly difficult position, and it had been a stupid thing to do. She didn't regret the idea of more sex with him, but she regretted how she went about it. She really hadn't given him much choice. She owed him an apology for that one. Thank goodness he'd had a clearer head in the kitchen at her apartment building. If they'd gone any farther…

All this just went to prove that Madison Montgomery was not good at relationships or handling life-and-death stress. Fair enough. So what was she going to do now to deal with the stress if screwing Jake's brains out was off the table?

There was always work. "Thane, do you think it would be okay for me to use your laptop?"

"Sure."

She thanked him and then walked over to the desk, careful to avoid the windows even though the blinds were down, and sat down. She booted up the laptop and logged into her cloud account. She still needed to finish the report for Drake even though the deal wasn't going to happen. Madison hated loose ends. Also, looking at the documentation that Veridani had provided was top of her to-do list. Maybe there was something there she'd missed.

Three hours later, Madison rubbed her eyes and sat back in her chair. She hadn't missed anything. The books were pristine. *Too pristine.* She'd felt something was off at the time, but she hadn't really let herself fully trust her instincts. She would from now on because she'd been right. The fashion house of Valentina Veridani was too good to be true.

When she looked around, she realized Jake and Hawk weren't in the room. A shot of adrenaline raced through her, leaving her tingly and slightly nauseated. Where did they go? They would have told her if they were leaving, and Jake wouldn't leave her alone. It was his job to protect her, as he'd pointed out many times. She willed her heart rate back down.

Then Jake's voice carried down the stairs. "I still think you're wrong. Hamilton was robbed. Verstappen did not deserve the win."

"Maybe. I will concede that it was a funky race and there were other methods of handling the issues that came up. It was a good season, though. One of the more interesting ones. I've been watching Formula One for years."

Jake hit the bottom of the stairs and walked into the room. "I'll give you that. It was a good season."

Madison noticed that the two men were keeping their voices low. It had to be a subconscious thing. It wasn't like Fedorov's guys out on the street could hear them, but she understood the feeling that it was important to be quiet.

"You want some lunch, Monty?" Hawk asked.

She nodded. "Sure. I'll help you if you want." She pushed up off the chair and caught herself as her legs started to buckle. She took a second and then walked over to the kitchen area. Jake stared at her with narrowed eyes but didn't say anything, for which she was eternally grateful.

"So what do you want to make?" she asked Thane just as Jake's phone went off.

"Mitch," Jake said as he answered the call. "We're all here. I have you on speaker."

"Actually, it's Gage and Dani. Mitch just went to get more coffee."

Jake pushed the phone so it was in the middle of the counter between him and Madison. Thane leaned against the sink. "Did you find anything in Veridani's computers?"

Madison leaned forward and said a small prayer. She needed this nightmare to be over.

"Well, not exactly," Dani said. "Monty, I just want to say first how sorry I am you're in this situation. It just sucks."

"Thanks, Dani. I appreciate it. Maybe when I finally get back to New York, we can go for that drink."

"You two know each other?" Jake asked, his eyebrows raised.

Madison glanced up at him. "Dani has come by Drake's office on occasion, and we've had a chance to chat."

Dani piped up. "Monty rocks at numbers, and she thinks like a coder. We connected over a computer glitch at Drake's. Anyway, yes, let's grab that drink when you're back. About Veridani, I couldn't pull up anything because their security is top-notch. Like extremely good. Russian, for sure. I'm pretty sure I recognize the coder. If I had more time, I could set up a phishing scheme and get in that way. Everyone loves cat videos. But with no real time to work with, I can't get past the firewall…from the outside."

Madison's stomach knotted. She was glad she was leaning on the countertop with her elbows, otherwise she might have sunk to the floor. This was not what she wanted to hear. Not at all.

Jake ran a hand through his hair and cursed softly. "So it's a no go then on getting the files."

"Not necessarily, Jake," Gage said. "There is another option. If you can get inside their office and install a file on one of the computers, Dani can take over and see what she can find."

"You want me to break into Veridani's offices?" Jake asked while he drummed his fingers on the counter.

"As an officer of the court," Thane commented, "I cannot hear any of this or I have to report it. So I'm officially not listening. And both Monty and Jake are now my clients. I'll draw up a contract later and backdate it. I need to cover my ass in case any of this comes out in court. There, now that I said all that, Dani, please continue."

"I can send you a zipped file. I would need you to break into the offices and go to someone's computer that you figure has the best level of access and then install the file on their system. That will get me around the firewall, and I can search from there. The whole upload should only take a few minutes. I can search whether you are physically there or not, so you could leave right away, Jake."

Madison could not believe her ears. First, she asked Jake to risk his life to protect her, and now she had to ask him to risk going to jail.

"No," she said quietly at first and then more clearly. "No. No way. I can't ask you to do this, Jake. It's too risky. You could go to prison here in Italy, and with the corruption, who knows what would happen to you? Just no. There must be another way."

Dani spoke softly, "I know exactly how you're feeling right now, Monty. I've been there. It's scary as hell, and you just want it to be over. You also don't want anyone else to risk anything for you. I feel you, and I can tell you, you are not alone. We're all right here with you." She took a deep, audible breath then continued, "But Monty, there is no other way to do this quickly. It will take a day or two or three to get someone to download whatever file I embed the code into. Gage says you really don't have that kind of time. If we need to do this quickly, then this is the only option."

Madison rested her head in her hands and covered her face. Asking Jake to do anything else just seemed crazy. She was surprised he was still here. Thane, too, for that matter. It was too big of a risk. "Okay, Dani, send the file. I'll go in and upload it to Paloma's computer. There's a ball tonight, so the whole company will close early and the building will be empty."

Jake's lips turned into a thin line, and when Madison glanced over at Thane, his brow was furrowed. Neither one of them wanted her to do it, but she wasn't letting one of them take the risk. This was her problem. She needed to be part of the solution.

"Okay, Monty, give me a couple of hours, and I'll email where you can download the zipped file from. Do you have a USB stick?"

Madison looked at Thane, who nodded in confirmation. "Yes, we have one."

"Okay, well, that's it then. I'll call you when it's ready and give you instructions. Good luck, Monty." Dani clicked off the call.

Madison rested her head on the counter for a minute then summoned her resolve and straightened.

"You know you're not doing this, right? It's too damn risky for you." Jake got off the stool and folded his arms across his chest.

Madison glared at him. "Look, I have asked you both to do too much already. This—this is just crazy. If you get caught, you'll go to prison. I can't have that on my conscience. I just…can't."

"Monty," Thane said quietly, "Jake is right. You can't be the one to do this. You will be unprotected out there, and with Fedorov and his men out to kill you, it would be too dangerous."

"It would be equally as dangerous for either of you. It's not like Fedorov won't shoot you."

"You're right. It is dangerous, but the U.S. Navy spent millions on training us how to survive this type of situation, and far worse. You are a civilian with no training. Whose odds are better?" Jake's face was blank but a pulse throbbed in his temple and his knuckles were white.

Madison recognized the signs enough to know he was trying to hold his temper in check. "Fine, Jake, you can go, but I'm going with you. I have been in their offices. I know where I'm going. You will need my help."

Jake grunted something non-committal. "Hawk, can you get me a set of plans for the building Veridani is in? We need to figure out the best way in."

Thane nodded and headed over to his computer.

Madison caught Jake by the arm as he walked by. "I'm going with you." He looked down at her but didn't reply. She said, "It's non-negotiable." Only then did she let go of his arm.

Jake walked over and stared at the screen in front of him. Thane worked the keyboard. Two minutes later, Thane stepped back. "I've got nothing. The plans aren't online. We don't have time to go to the planning office and try and get the plans manually. That would take days. I'm afraid Monty is right. She's going to have to go with you."

Jake shook his head. "She can draw me a map, and I can find it myself."

Madison shook her head. "No. I go, or no one goes. I won't ask you to do something I am not willing to do myself." She took a deep breath. "This whole thing has thrown me off-kilter, and I have made some…questionable choices because of it. It's time I took control of the situation so I can make better choices and be involved in the process of clearing my name. So far, riding shot gun hasn't really been great for me."

"Choosing to break into the building of the people that want you dead is not a good choice," Jake argued.

"Isn't it? I'm asking you to assume all the risk while I sit here and drive myself crazy with worry. I can't take that anymore. I need to feel like I am doing something proactively rather than being reactive to everything. My reactions have been…less than stellar. It's time for me to step up. Besides, you don't want to leave me alone, and Thane has to go talk to Enzo again."

Thane frowned. "How did you know that? He just texted me about twenty minutes ago to meet him tonight."

Jake's eyes narrowed. "Did you put him up to it so I would have no choice but to take you?"

Madison shook her head. "Drake emailed me a few minutes ago to tell me good luck and that Enzo had more information for us, so Thane was going to have to go meet him."

"It's true. Enzo says he may be able to help us, but it might not be the type of help we need." Thane read the screen in front of him.

"What the hell does that mean?" Jake demanded.

"Not a clue." Thane shrugged. "But at this point, we should take any help we can get."

Madison nodded. "Agreed. You will go meet Enzo while Jake and I break into the Veridani offices."

Jake grunted and shook his head at her. "You make it sound so simple. This is going to be anything but."

CHAPTER TWENTY-THREE

Jake sighed to himself. "Okay, Madison, in order to leave, we're going to have to go out the back way."

She frowned. "There is no back way."

"Um, there is," Hawk said, "but it's a...bit complicated."

She narrowed her eyes. "What does complicated mean?"

Jake gritted his teeth. It would be so much better if Madison stayed her ass in the apartment. But if Fedorov suddenly decided to check the place again, she'd be a sitting duck. He let out a string of curses under his breath. "We have to go over the wall at the back of the yard."

Madison blinked. "But there's nothing on the other side of it." She glanced through the crack in the blind. "There's sky above the wall, and I know there's a street back there. There's no stairway or anything."

Jake was doing his best to be patient, but it was all just getting to him. "The street is there, and the yard is built on top of a building that is recessed a bit from the buildings on either side of it. There is a small ledge. You just have to trust me. I need to get you on top of the wall and then I want you to lie flat on your belly. I will jump up and go over the ledge and then guide you down. Okay?"

"Okay? Are you fucking serious? A ledge?" She looked back and forth between the two men.

Jake shrugged. "We don't have a choice. We can't go out the front. You can stay here if you want. I can go to the Veridani offices by myself."

Her face hardened with determination. "No. I'm coming." She took a deep breath. "So there's a ledge. Then what?"

"You're going to have to climb down a drainpipe that's in the corner." Jake checked his backpack to make sure he had the lock picks he'd taken from Madison's freezer.

She blinked. "A drainpipe?"

Hawk covered his smile with his hand. "You can do it, Monty. It's not as difficult as it sounds. Just don't look down."

Jake glared at Hawk. *Thanks for nothing, asshole!*

Hawk had turned around and was walking into the kitchen. Jake noted that his shoulders were shaking with laughter. Someday he'd get revenge for this moment. "Okay, are you ready to go?" Jake looked her up and down. She was wearing a short black skirt and the over-the-knee boots again. Not ideal for shimmying down a drainpipe.

"Maybe change into sweats and sneakers. You can change again at the bottom. Hawk's friend is leaving the wig and stuff in the car. You can switch clothes when we are in the car."

She nodded and went back upstairs. Five minutes later she was back. She was wearing the blouse still, but now she was in navy sweats and sneakers. She had her skirt and boots in her hands. Jake took them from her and stowed them in the backpack. He swung it over his shoulder. "Ready?"

"As I'll ever be," she said. "Wait, aren't there streetlights back there? Are we going to be lit up so people can see us?"

"No," Hawk said. "It's a quiet street that's quite dark. There's a light at either end but none in the middle where we are, thankfully. It would be difficult to see you from the street until you're at the bottom of the drainpipe."

Hawk went to stand beside her. "Good luck. You're going to be fine, Monty." He gave her a quick hug. He turned to Jake, and they clasped hands and bumped shoulders.

"I'll get you for this one," Jake whispered.

Hawk grinned. "Good luck."

Jake stood at the door leading to the yard. He peered through the blinds. No one could see into the back yard area, so he wasn't too worried about being seen at this point. He opened the door slowly and nodded to Madison. They walked outside, and Hawk closed the door behind them. The cool night air was filled with the scent of roses. The moon was only a quarter full so it was quite dark. Better not to be seen.

They walked to the back corner of the yard. Jake turned and looked down at Madison. "You can do this. It's not hard. Just do as I say, and you'll be okay. Let me know at any point if you need a break or if you are starting to panic."

She squared her shoulders and lifted her chin. *Atta girl.*

"I'm going to lock my hands together. You'll step into them, and I'll lift you up so you can climb to the top of the wall. I want you to stay there, lying flat. I'll come up and go over. Once I am on the ledge, I'll guide you down, okay?"

She frowned and whispered. "Fuck, here goes nothing."

Madison faced the wall. Jake squatted next to her and linked his fingers together. She put her right foot in his hands, and he lifted her up. She grabbed the top of the wall and pulled herself up and swung her legs so she was lying on her belly lengthwise along the wall. Her head was facing Jake. She rested her cheek on the rough wall as she waited for him to join her.

Jake moved a bit farther and then jumped up and hauled his body on top. Then he slowly lowered himself down to the ledge on the other side. The ledge was maybe six inches wide and ran the length of the wall. Jake held onto the top of the wall and shimmied sideways until he was directly underneath Madison. Once there, he looked up at her and nodded. She started to move and then stopped. "I can't reach," she whispered.

Jake frowned. What was she talking about? "What?"

"I can't reach the top of the wall. From the ledge, I mean. I'm shorter than you. My arms won't reach that high."

Fuck! He hadn't even considered that. It wasn't something he'd never had to plan for before. Because every time he'd done this type of shit, it was with a bunch of guys like him. He nodded. "Okay, you're going to slide down, and I will come around you so you'll be between me and the wall. I'll hold you on."

She stared at him for a minute and then gave a slight nod. She just started to move when the screech of car tires sounded from down below. Her gaze locked with Jake's. Fear was etched into the lines of her face. Jake wanted to tell her it would all be fine, but now wasn't the time for platitudes. He looked down at the street.

A small blue car flew past them. The driver slammed on the brakes, and the car skidded. Then the car started reversing at great speed and stopped directly below them. Jake tensed. The driver proceeded to wedge the vehicle into the tiniest of parking spots. He bounced off the cars ahead and behind him several times before finally coming to a stop. The driver and passenger doors opened, and two men got out. They were laughing and yelling at each other in Italian. They walked off down the street and disappeared around the corner.

Jake breathed a cautious sigh of relief. "Okay, swing your legs down."

She nodded and gingerly lowered her legs until she was upright. Then she started to slide down. Her clothing caught on the rough bricks and the abrasive surface scraped her hands. Jake had an arm around her, guiding her down until her feet hit the ledge. Her hands didn't come close to reaching the top of the wall even though she had them fully outstretched above her head.

"Okay, halfway there. Stay perfectly still. I will swing my leg to the other side of yours. You are going to be between me and the wall. We'll move together very slowly over to that drainpipe to your left. It's only a few feet. Then we're going to climb down to the street. Got it?"

She nodded ever so slightly. Jake inched toward her. When his left side was pressed against her, he moved his hand out to the other side of her outstretched arms. Then he swung his leg around to the other side of her and placed his foot on the ledge. She pressed herself as close to the wall as she could. Jake pressed himself against her back.

"Okay, now," he whispered in her ear, "I'm going to move my left foot a bit then you do the same. Got it?"

"Yes," she whispered back.

Jake moved his foot. Madison struggled to move hers but, finally, she inched it along. Jake held on for both of them as they made their way to the drainpipe. The scent of Madison's hair surrounded him. Her body rubbed against his. He was having a hard time concentrating. It was crazy and stupid, but this woman was a distraction like no other.

The sound of rapid-fire Italian reached Jake's ears. More people were walking down the street. Jake paused and waited until they had passed before he moved his foot for the last time. They finally made it to the drainpipe.

"Honey, you're going to crawl down the pipe first. It's going to be an easy climb, I promise. You'll be fine."

"What do I hold on to?"

"There are lots of foot and hand holds. See those metal zip-tie looking things that fasten the drainpipe to the wall?

"Yeah."

"That's what you're going to use. Be careful because they can be sharp."

She took a deep breath and reached for the first handhold with her left hand. She grabbed the bracket that held the drainpipe to the wall. Then she put her left foot on another bracket below. She moved out from in front of Jake as she grabbed the metal strip on the other side of the drainpipe with her right hand. She swore.

"What?" he demanded.

"Nothing. I cut my hand. It's okay, though." She was finally over the drainpipe. She looked down and located the next bracket. The space in between brackets was large but doable. Madison felt with the toe of her right foot until she came in contact with the bracket and then she rested her weight on it as she inched her left foot down and repositioned her hands.

Jake watched her climb down. It felt like forever, but it probably wasn't more than a minute until Madison put her feet on the sidewalk. He said a silent prayer of thanks. She stepped back from the wall and looked up at him. It took Jake no more than thirty seconds to go down the drainpipe. He jumped down the last few feet and landed beside her. He grabbed her arm and steered her down the street.

Two minutes later, they found the car exactly where it was supposed to be, and it had the disguises in it. Hawk had some interesting friends, but Jake was grateful that they'd come through. After he and Madison got in the car, she started to get changed.

"How's your hand?" Jake asked as he pulled out onto the street.

"Fine." She pulled her skirt and boots out of the backpack.

"Okay, we're going to review the plan one more time." Jake glanced at Madison and then turned right.

"I've reviewed it enough. I got it. We're good."

"See? Right there, I know we're not good because what's rule number one?"

Madison let out a long breath. "I have to do everything you say when you say it."

Jake tapped the steering wheel. "So let's review the plan."

Madison grunted and then glanced down at her palm.

"Is your hand still bleeding?"

"No. The cut isn't too deep. It just stings. I didn't think to bring gloves with me to Italy. It never occurred to me I would be climbing down a drainpipe. Never in my wildest dreams did I think that someone would frame me for theft or try and kill me either, so I guess I can be forgiven about the gloves."

"Madison." Jake kept his voice soft, nonconfrontational.

"I'm okay," she said with a toss of her hair. The long blond hair swung over her shoulder. "This wig is itchy." She scratched her head under the offending hair piece.

Jake remained silent. He wanted to stop the car and tell her to get out and hide in a gelato shop until he was finished, but he didn't have a choice.

"Okay, maybe I'm not doing so well." Madison let out a small huff. "I'm tired and I'm scared and I'm...raw. Turns out I'm not very good at dealing with stress."

"Bullshit. You're doing fine." Jake made another right turn.

"Ha. I don't think so. I've been behaving like an idiot. Thane's was—"

"It won't happen again. It doesn't matter. Just forget it."

"No." She shook her head, making the long blond hair swing back and forth. "I won't forget it. I shouldn't have put you in that position. That wasn't fair. And it was insanely dangerous. I'm sorry."

Jake ground his teeth. "Do not apologize. What we did at Hawk's is all on me. I should have said no. I didn't. It was a mistake. I knew you were struggling to deal with everything, and I let you… It was my fault."

"Jake, I practically begged you to have sex with me. It wasn't like I was going to take no for an answer." She shook her head. "Like I said, my fault. I've been throwing myself at you since the beginning as a reaction to the stress. I didn't realize it at the time but, looking back, it's obvious. I was using you."

Jake's gut knotted. As much as he knew it had all been wrong, it hurt to hear her say. He liked Madison. A lot. Her spunk. Her smile. Her openness. Even now, as she was telling him that sleeping with him had been a huge mistake, she was doing it from a place of honesty. He couldn't fault her for that.

She'd flirted with him, but he was the one who'd said yes the first time when he shouldn't have. Still, it hurt to hear her say she regretted it. He was pissed off about his own behavior, but he couldn't honestly say he regretted bedding her. Or spending time with her. Given the chance to go back and turn the job down, he'd still do the exact same thing all over again.

Madison had gotten under his skin, God help him, and he cherished every moment with her.

"Let it go, Madison." He didn't want to think about her regret. "We're going to do this, and then we'll get your name cleared. You can go back to New York, and I can…" What the hell could he do? Go for his talk with Mitch. There was a light at the end of the tunnel alright, but he had the distinct feeling it would turn out to be a train.

"We're here." He pulled into a parking spot outside the building. It was at the end of the block so he couldn't be blocked in. He'd gotten lucky. *Let's hope it holds.* He turned to face her. She had her head bent over her lap. "I hate contact lenses," she grumbled as she struggled to stick the first one in her eye. She finally managed after much cursing to get both lenses in. She straightened and blinked several times.

"How are they?" He hated the blond wig and blue-tinted lenses, but they really did change her look entirely.

"I'll survive," she grumbled.

Jake was wearing one of Hawk's suits, which was a little tight in the shoulders but not by much. He also had on his hat from the other day. It should keep his face somewhat hidden from any cameras they'd encounter.

"Do you need to go over the plan. We can review it."

She shook her head. "No. I'm good."

The circles were back under her eyes and the fine lines around her mouth were getting deeper by the day. His heart went out to her. If he hadn't been trained for this type of thing, who knew how he would have dealt with it? He didn't blame her one bit. Just himself.

If only they'd met another way. There would have been a future for them. Now she was embarrassed by her actions and, worse, regretted them. If he'd held out any hope that maybe they could salvage a real relationship out of this, her saying she'd been making "poor choices" and her reactions were "less than stellar," had pretty much made that thought DOA.

"Okay." Jake took a deep breath and let it out slowly. Now was the time to focus. The past was dead. Now it was time to fix things for Madison. The future would take care of itself. "Let's go."

He got out of the car and met Madison on the sidewalk. He had a gun in his shoulder holster, a gun at the small of his back under his sweater, and one at his ankle.

Madison was wearing her white blouse with a much shorter black skirt this time. Hawk must have brought it from Madison's place. She also wore her boots. Jake had complained that they might not be the best footwear, but she pointed out they were far sexier than anything else she had, and if the point was to distract, then they would be the best option. He'd reluctantly agreed. Earlier, he'd found it hard to keep his eyes off her legs and her ass and everything else.

"You know you don't have to do this."

She turned to look at him. "Yes, I do, Jake. I really do." She shot him a smile and then walked quickly to the entrance of the building. She pulled open the door and went inside. Jake watched her through the glass. He stood back so the security guard at the desk wouldn't notice him.

Madison immediately went up to the desk and started chatting with the guard. She gestured a lot, pointing to her leg and to her hand. The security guard appeared sympathetic. He nodded and smiled. Then he reached down and grabbed a key off his desk. He offered it to Madison, but she pointed to her hand again. He smiled, and the two of them disappeared from sight.

Jake pushed open the door and hurried past the security desk straight to the elevator. He hit the button, and the doors opened. He stepped in and used the key card Madison had held on to from her time working in the offices and had given him to unlock the elevator and hit the button for the third floor. The door started to close. Madison came running up and hopped on the elevator.

Jake frowned. "Where's the guard?" The guard was supposed to come back with her and Jake was going to send him on a wild goose chase to find a briefcase he'd supposedly left in the building earlier.

"I spilled some disinfectant all over his uniform when he was helping me wash my cut. He went to clean himself up in the men's restroom."

Jake shook his head. How come he could never get away with that shit? The cut on her hand had come in handy. It was a last-minute change in script, but Jake knew it would play well. Who didn't want to help a damsel in distress, especially one that looked like Madison?

"I'm small. No one is intimidated when you're small. Everyone thinks I'm harmless. And I am. Usually." She smiled.

Jake had found Madison a lot of things, but harmless was not one of them. He handed her a pair of gloves and pulled on his own pair.

The elevator reached the third floor, and they got off. There was a reception desk on the other side of the lobby from the elevators, but it was empty. Madison strode over to the glass doors behind the desk. "The company has floors three through six, but the executives are all on this floor." She took the card from Jake. "I'm glad I forgot to give this back. Cross your fingers they didn't kill it." She waved it in front of the security reader, and the light turned green.

Jake's gut unknotted just a little. If it had stayed red, they were going to have to break the glass, and he wasn't sure how well that would go. The other option had been to use the computer on the reception desk and see if it worked.

Madison held the door, and he walked through. Jake's feet sank into the plush pale gray carpet. The off-white walls had splashes of color in the form of artwork. There was a sitting area with a couch and several chairs. All white and modern looking. There were two hallways, one on either side of what must be the waiting area.

Madison started down the one to the right. "Paloma's office is down here."

Jake walked after her, content to let her lead the way. He kept his hand close to his gun in the holster, but his instinct said the office space was empty. Madison had explained earlier that the offices were in the shape of a U. The important people had offices on the outside of the U with windows and a view. The support staff all had cubicles on the inside curve.

Madison stopped in front of an office three quarters of the way down the hall. The door was closed, but when she turned the knob, it opened. "She never locks it." She beamed a smile at him over her shoulder.

The office was done in grays with some pink. The desk was sleek and black but had pink roses in a glass vase in the corner. There was a desktop computer and keyboard and some paperwork. Paloma kept her space clean. There were drawers down both sides. There was a black and chrome desk chair and a credenza behind that underneath the window, which had the blinds already lowered.

"Now for the hard part." Jake went over and sat down at Paloma's computer. He pulled out the USB stick and set it on the desk. He moved the mouse, and the screen lit up. "Any ideas on her password?" He checked all around the monitor, but there were no sticky notes or anything.

"Try—"

He lifted the keyboard. "Never mind. Found it." He held up a folded piece of paper. He opened it up and then typed in the word *Veridani*.

"Seriously?" Madison rolled her eyes. "That's secure. Not." She'd come to stand beside the desk.

Jake agreed. "Most people aren't good at passwords. They stick with the default, which is usually *Password*." He clicked around and brought up her drives then inserted the USB drive and started the upload. Dani had said it shouldn't take more than a minute or two for it to finish.

"Why don't you look around and see if you can find a copy of the brochure?" Jake started by checking the drawers on the left. There were various papers and things but no brochure or anything else that seemed helpful. "Nothing interesting here. What about you?"

Madison had been searching the drawers on the right hand side. She'd stopped searching with the second drawer open and was holding her phone over a piece of paper. It appeared to be a letter of some kind written in Italian.

"What is that? What did you find?"

"Paloma is sleeping with Giovanni. She thinks he's going to ask her to marry him."

"Are you using a translation app?" he asked.

She nodded. "Yes, and it's very good. This is a note from Giovanni to Paloma, telling her he loves her but due to unforeseen circumstances, he needs more time."

"Bullshit."

"Uh huh. He's never going to marry her. He's sleeping with one of the other secretaries."

"How do you know?" Jake asked. "That can't be in the letter."

"No, it's not."

"You know what? I don't want to know. Whatever. Might come in handy later. Maybe we can prove he's sleeping around to her and make her angry enough that she flips on him." Jake glanced at the screen. Another thirty seconds according to the computer.

Madison searched the last drawer and then straightened. "Nothing."

"Why don't you check the credenza?"

Madison went over and pulled open the cabinet doors. "Nothing of interest here." She checked both sides and then tugged on the door in the middle. It was locked. Jake turned around in the chair and gave it a tug, but it wasn't going to open. He reached into his suit jacket pocket and pulled out the lock-pick set that the henchmen had left in Madison's apartment.

"I thought this might come in handy." He chose the tools he wanted and went to work on the lock. A few seconds later, the lock popped. He tugged on the drawer, and it opened. There was a small stack of brochures.

"Jackpot!" Madison grabbed a couple, folded them up and stuffed them in the waist band of her skirt. Jake took a few more and stuffed them in his jacket pocket. He turned back around and checked the screen. The upload was complete. He ejected out the USB drive, pulled it from the port, and then cleared the memory. Then he pulled out his phone and sent a text to Dani.

She replied with a thumb's up emoji.

"Let's go." He stood up and walked to the door and then stopped. Whistling. It was far away, but it was getting louder. He stepped back in the office and closed the door as silently as possible. Paloma had left the light on so Jake left it that way as well, but he backed up Madison so that she was against the wall behind the door. Anyone looking in through the glass on the other side of the door wouldn't see them.

He waited. Madison grabbed his hand. He gave her hand a quick squeeze and then dropped it. He needed to keep both hands free to reach his guns. He listened. There was a faint sound of someone talking. It was getting louder.

He reached up and pulled the gun from his shoulder holster. He glanced at Madison. Her eyes were huge, and her lower lip had turned white around where she bit it. Terror was etched in every line of her face. Jake swore silently and then shifted slightly so he was blocking any access to Madison. If whoever was approaching stopped and opened the door, he didn't want them to see her and start shooting.

The voice got louder, someone speaking in Italian. The voice was right on top of them. Jake caught a glimpse of the man. It was a security guard. He must be a partner to the one downstairs in the lobby. He was probably making his rounds.

Jake glanced at Madison and nodded to let her know it was going to be okay. Once the guard was gone, they could leave. He would make the turn and start down the other side of the U. He should be far enough away that they could take the stairs.

Jake counted off a minute in his head and then turned to Madison. "Okay, we're going to go back along the hallway but we'll take the stairs instead of the elevator. You said they go to the street level and end in an alley out back?"

She nodded. "Yes. Everyone smokes out there. They jam the locking mechanism so they don't get locked out, but the stairwell door will be locked. They all have keys to that but not to the outside door."

"We'll be going out so it doesn't matter.

He opened the door and ushered Madison out. Then he closed the door and started down the hallway back toward the stairs. He moved quickly to make sure they got there before the security guard. As they reached the waiting area, Jake looked up and saw Fedorov opening the glass door.

"Shit!" He pushed Madison into the nearest cubicle as Fedorov opened fire. Jake returned fire, but he was a beat too late. Burning pain bloomed in his left shoulder. Fedorov had dived behind the wall in the waiting area. Jake wasn't sure if he'd hit the man or not. He grabbed Madison's hand, hauling her out of the cubicle. He had his gun raised and pointing where Fedorov had disappeared. "You need to run back and secure yourself in one of the offices. I'll do my best to hold him off."

Fedorov's head popped out and Jake took the shot but missed. "Run!" he commanded, and Madison took off down the hallway, back the way they'd come. Fedorov stuck his hand around the corner and started firing wildly. Jake had been backing up so he dove into the nearest office.

There was a pause in the gunfire, and Jake snuck a peek out the office door. Nothing. He listened, but he didn't hear anything. Jake glanced toward Paloma's office. Where was Madison? Where the hell was the guard? He quietly stepped out into the hallway and moved swiftly down toward the back of the U. He glanced into Paloma's office, but Madison wasn't there.

He kept going. There was another gunshot.

Madison!

His heart slammed against his rib cage. Fear raced through his veins. She couldn't be dead. Just no. He took a steadying breath and relied on training and instinct to propel him forward.

He cleared every office and every cubicle. He assumed Fedorov had gone to the other side of the U. They would meet in the back. As long as Jake got to Madison first, they still had a chance to escape down the stairs. Assuming she was alive. He needed to find her. Now.

Jake's shoulder was throbbing, and he was losing the ability to use his left hand. He'd been through this enough to know he wasn't going to bleed out, but he needed help and he needed it soon. Where the hell was Madison?

CHAPTER TWENTY-FOUR

Madison was crouched low in one of the workspaces at the back of the u-shaped space. She didn't want to get too far ahead of Jake. She was hoping that the security guard would come and help her. She was on her hands and the balls of her feet. She stuck her head out around the partition and scanned both directions. *Nothing. Damn.* She ducked back inside the cubicle. Where was Jake? Where was the guard? Where the fuck was Fedorov?

Her heart rate was in the stratosphere. All she could hear was the sound of her blood pounding through her veins. She didn't want to die. She didn't want Jake to die. This was all so stupid. She choked back the building scream. She couldn't—wouldn't—give herself away. She bit her cheek to quell the panic.

Madison stuck her head out again. The guard was coming slowly down the hallway. *Oh, thank God.* She waved at him and got up. She had started out of the cubicle toward him when she heard the loud bang. The guard's eyes got big, and his mouth formed an *O*. Then he sunk to the ground face first.

Fedorov was standing behind him. "Come here," he demanded.

Madison was incapable of moving. He could threaten her all he wanted. He could shoot her. She just could not get her body to react to her brain's directions.

Fedorov walked over and stuck his gun in her face. "Where is the necklace?"

Madison opened her mouth but couldn't force out a single word.

"Where is the necklace?" Fedorov demanded again, putting his finger on the trigger.

Madison shook her head, and a breath she didn't even realize she was holding came out with a whoosh. "I don't have it," she managed to whisper.

"Where is it?" Fedorov barked, but Madison just shook her head. "He has it?" Fedorov asked, gesturing down the hallway with his gun. "Does your friend have it?"

Madison didn't say a word. Was it better if he thought Jake had the necklace? Fedorov wouldn't kill him then. At least not until he knew for sure where the necklace was.

Fedorov smiled. "Your friend has the necklace. Let's go find him." He pulled her forward with a punishing grip on her bicep, then spun her around, wrapping his left arm around her neck and holding his gun to her head with his right. His body repulsively snug against hers, he marched them cautiously down the hallway.

Suddenly, Jake popped up from the top of the cubicle on the right. Fedorov let off a couple of shots, but Jake disappeared behind the cubicle. *Please let him be okay*, she prayed. Her ears rang because of the sharp noise from the gun, muting Fedorov's harsh breathing. He pushed her forward, his gun pointing toward her head once again.

But she clearly heard his shout to Jake. "We make a deal, you and I. I will let the girl go. You tell me where the real necklace is."

There was no response. Madison thought she might pass out. Could Jake really be dead? No! No way! It just couldn't be true. She couldn't live with herself. She made a strangled sound.

"Shut up," Fedorov growled, jamming the muzzle of the gun into her temple. He redirected his attention to Jake. "You need to tell me where the necklace is." He slowly moved Madison forward once again, coming to the turn in the hallway. He pushed Madison out in front of him as they rounded the turn.

Jake stood there, leaning against the doorway of Paloma's office. Madison's knees went weak with relief. His shoulder was stained red, and his left arm was hanging at an odd angle. He was shot but he was alive. *Oh God! Was he leaning because he couldn't stand upright?*

"You are going to kill her no matter what," Jake said. "What incentive do I have to tell you where the necklace is?"

Jake was speaking the truth. She knew it in her heart. Fedorov would kill her no matter what he or she said. There was a weird calmness about accepting that.

Suddenly, she didn't fear dying as much anymore. It was inevitable, but her blood still pumped wildly through her veins. If she was going down, she would do everything in her power to make sure Fedorov went with her and Jake survived. She fisted her hands until her knuckles ached. Jake was not dying because of her. *No fucking way.*

Fedorov shifted his weight so that his head had moved out slightly from behind her. She widened her stance a bit. She tried to catch Jake's eye. An idea was forming in her brain. A way out. The sound of sirens hit her ears. If the cops came, was that good or bad? It was hard to tell.

"You make a good point." He squeezed off a shot, but Jake was already gone into Paloma's office. The shot hit the glass, and it shattered.

"You're going to have to be faster than that, Fedorov," Jake taunted.

"So you know who I am."

"Your reputation precedes you. Although working for the Russian mob seems like a bit of a step down."

Fedorov moved Madison forward again. "Retirement didn't pay so well. This pays much better, but still, I can always use more. Where's the necklace?"

"Must be annoying to work with the Italians, though. They're not as detail oriented."

Fedorov let out a curse in Russian. "No organization. Very frustrating." The sound of the sirens was very loud now. Tires squealing and car doors slamming had added to the cacophony of mayhem.

Madison kept her breathing as even as she could. What was Jake up to? He was now pinned down in an office. Why would he do that? He had to have a plan of some kind.

Fedorov moved her forward again. He was making her go wide. In a few more steps, they would be across from the office, and then Fedorov would be able to shoot at Jake.

Madison tensed. If Fedorov moved her so he had a clear shot at Jake, the angle provided her an opportunity to do something. She had an idea from one of her self-defense classes. She just hoped it worked. Fedorov shoved her a little more to the right.

The door to the office was only open halfway. She could see Paloma's desk and the pink roses, but the rest of the room was blocked by the door. Where was Jake?

"It's time to come out," Fedorov snapped. "I will kill her if you don't tell me where the necklace is." He flicked the gun back so the muzzle rested on Madison's temple again. "One." Madison searched for Jake. "Two." There, behind the door. She could see shadows through the small space the hinges created. Then, the muzzle of Jake's gun. "Thr—"

"*Fermati dove sei!*"

Fedorov stopped counting.

Two *Polizia* officers burst into the hallway, guns pointed at Fedorov and *her*. The dark, deadly barrels seemed so large. Her breath caught in her throat and her heart stuttered to a stop.

Fedorov turned his head and then dropped the arm he had around Madison's neck. She immediately hustled away as he held up his gun by the butt. She raised her hands, unsure if they were friendly cops or on the Veridani's payroll.

Fedorov smiled. He spoke in Italian, but Madison understood the name Petrov.

The two officers looked at each other and then straightened up. They still had their guns out but they didn't seem as interested in Fedorov anymore.

Jake stepped out from the office. He also held his gun by the butt. The officers immediately pointed their guns at him. They yelled something in Italian, but Jake shook his head. The first one narrowed his eyes and then spoke in broken English, "Who are you? What are you doing here?"

Fedorov cleared his throat and spoke in rapid-fire Italian. The two officers ignored him and stared at Jake.

Jake waited until Fedorov was finished and then said, "He's actually Nikolay Fedorov, former GRU agent, not Petrov. I am Jacob Boxer. I was hired to protect Ms. Montgomery"—he pointed to Madison—"because Mr. Fedorov wants to kill her."

The two cops looked at each other again. They moved slowly forward, guns out but aimed downward.

Fedorov started speaking in Italian again, but the black-haired cop waved him off. "English. Your Italian is shit."

Fedorov frowned but switched to English. "Your boss, Captain DiCerbo, he knows me. I have been working with him to find these two. They stole the Veridani necklace."

When the dark-haired officer came closer, Madison could see his nametag. *A. Casini.* "You"—he pointed at Fedorov—"put your gun down on the carpet and move over to stand next to the wall."

"But—"

"Do it. I will check your story." Fedorov did as he was told and went to stand against the wall on the far side of Madison. "No. You stand here." He pointed to the wall closer to his partner. Fedorov looked pissed but went and stood where Casini had said.

The other officer approached with his gun pointed at Fedorov but still keeping an eye on Jake and Madison. His name tag read *P. Martini.* She would love to drink about a dozen of those right now.

Casini looked at Jake. "You are shot."

Jake nodded.

"Drop the gun on the carpet and turn around. Put your hands behind your back."

Madison wanted to reach out and strangle the cop as she watched Jake wince while moving his left hand behind his back. He seemed to be having trouble moving it at all. "He needs to go to a hospital." She started forward to help him, but Casini raised his gun and pointed it at her.

"You"—Casini pointed with his gun—"do the same. Turn around and put your hands behind your back."

"But we're the victims here. This man was—"

"I don't care." Casini stepped forward and handcuffed Jake, who grunted in pain, and then did the same to Madison. He turned them around. "Now walk down the hallway to the elevators. Don't try anything, or I will shoot you."

They started down the hallway. Jake's gait was a little slower than normal and his face was pale. Madison wanted to reach out to him, but she couldn't. She couldn't do anything. It was all so fucking unfair. She clamped her lips together to keep from screaming at the two cops. They went past Fedorov, who smirked at them. Madison had the intense urge to smash that leer off his face.

"You, follow them," Casini said, and Fedorov fell in behind them. They didn't handcuff Fedorov. They weren't treating him like a friend, nor were they treating him like a criminal. That answered that question. These cops weren't here to rescue Madison and Jake. They were working with the Veridanis and Fedorov.

What did that mean for her and Jake?

Casini stopped them when they got to the waiting area. He indicated to Martini to open the door ahead of them. Martini held it open, and they all trooped through. Then Martini opened the door to the stairwell. Madison tried to catch Jake's eye, but he was ignoring her. Why were they taking the stairs? Her stomach sunk. This just couldn't be good.

They went down the stairs single file. Jake stumbled a couple of times but made it to the bottom. Madison cursed under her breath. If only there was something she could do. Martini, who stayed in front of them the whole way down, opened the door at the bottom of the stairs. He waited until everyone had walked through and then opened the door to the back alley.

Two police cars waited, engines idling. Martini opened the back door of the first one and pointed. When Jake bent to get in, Martini pushed his head. He closed the door. "You go around." He pointed to the other side of the car. Madison walked around, and Casini opened the door for her to get in. She eased into the vehicle butt first and then swung her legs in. Not easy to do with her hands cuffed behind her back and wearing a short skirt.

Casini closed the door after her. She whirled around to face Jake. "Are you okay?"

Jake offered her a weak smile. "I've been better."

"Oh my God, what can I do to help you? How can I get us out of this?"

He shook his head. "Just stay calm. There will be an opportunity to do something but this isn't it. Keep your eyes open and watch for any signal I might give you, okay?"

She nodded.

His smile was reassuring. "It's going to be okay, Madison."

She wished she could believe him. Her heart felt as if it was being crushed to dust. The fact that Jake was hurt, was killing her more than the situation. She'd gotten him hurt. She would never be able to live with herself if he…didn't recover.

The two cops and Fedorov walked around to the front of the vehicle as several more officers approached. They all stood together in a group, chatting. Martini looked at the car and pointed with his thumb. The other guy nodded. More cops joined them. Fedorov said something, and they all laughed. Then Martini came around and got into the driver's seat.

"What do you think they're talking about?"

Jake just shook his head.

Casini and Fedorov walked by the car. Madison craned her neck to watch their progress. They got in the police vehicle behind theirs. She cursed softly. Fedorov sat in the front seat. This did not bode well for her and Jake.

Martini waved at the other officers who were now entering the building and then drove off.

Madison tried to hang on to her anger. This was an outrageous situation. She looked at Jake. Eyes closed, he was paler than he had been, and from the lines etched into his forehead, she figured he was in a lot of pain.

At the sight of him, her anger ebbed away, replaced with worry. Madison tried to stay calm, but she couldn't focus. Jake was in trouble, and he needed help. After everything he'd done for her, she was letting him down. When he squeezed his eyes tighter, as if battling a wave of pain, icy fingers gripped her heart. She tried to say his name, but no sound would come out. She nudged him. He opened his eyes and glanced her way. At her imploring look, he shook his head slightly.

Why wasn't he saying something? Why wasn't he demanding to go to the hospital? She looked out the window to try to figure out where they were going. They were heading away from Central Florence. This wasn't right. She stayed silent, but a few minutes later when they drove by the police station and then the hospital, the reality of their situation sank in.

This cop was taking them somewhere to die.

CHAPTER TWENTY-FIVE

The pain in Jake's shoulder was searing. He was tired, and his left shoulder to the tips of his fingers was numb from the bullet wound. All in all, he was in hard shape, but not as bad as he was making it appear. He was hoping Martini would let down his guard, maybe give him an opportunity to try something. So far, he'd had no chance, but maybe once the car stopped, it would be different.

He stole a quick glance at Madison. She was terrified, and he didn't blame her one bit. It was all his fucking fault she was in this mess. He should have said no when she insisted on coming. She would have been better off by herself in a coffee shop somewhere than at that office. Now the two of them were handcuffed in the back of a police car that was not heading to any police station.

He gritted his teeth. He would not let Madison be killed by these assholes. He would figure something out. She didn't deserve any of this. She just got caught up in something that was beyond her control because she was damn good at her job. Life just wasn't fair.

What he wouldn't give at this moment to have met her in a bar or at a ball game. To take her on a date. To build a real relationship with her. She was amazing and smart and funny and kind. Sexy as hell didn't cover it. Why did he have to meet the perfect woman in the exact wrong circumstances? No, life was not fair.

He glanced out the window as the cop car turned into a parking lot in a seedy part of Florence. There was some sort of warehouse in front of them. Martini rolled to a stop. He shut off the car and got out. He walked over to the warehouse and opened the small metal door at the corner.

Jake turned toward her. "I'm so sorry I didn't get you out of there in time."

"Jake," she choked out his name, "it's not your fault. It's my fault you're hurt. I can't believe this is happening." She sniffed. "I am so sorry you're involved in this."

"It's my job to protect you, and I failed."

He'd failed at so much with her. Maybe he really was done in this business. If they survived this, he'd have to find a new line of work, and it needed to be "they" because he wouldn't walk out of there if Madison didn't make it. He just couldn't live with himself. He'd make sure everyone who had a hand in her death would pay, or he would die trying.

"You didn't fail. You saved my life." Her eyes glittered with unshed tears.

He shook his head. "No. I stopped you from getting shot, but we're a long way from being out of danger." He had the intense urge to kiss her and tell her how much he cared about her, but what was the point? No, it was better to keep his mouth shut.

Martini emerged from the warehouse and strode around to Madison's side of the car. Jake's heart skipped a beat in his chest. If Martini took her out without Jake, there wasn't a damn thing he could do to save her.

The officer opened the door and was helping Madison out just as Casini and Fedorov pulled up next to them. The two men got out. They were laughing about something. Martini had Madison by the elbow. He handed her off to Casini and then came around and got Jake out of the car. Jake's gut relaxed ever so slightly. As long as he and Madison were together, there was a chance he could figure something out…that he could save her. Hell, he'd even let Hawk save the day if it meant Madison would be okay.

They all walked together over to the door, and Martini opened it. Casini walked Madison in and then Fedorov was next. Jake was still outside with Martini. If he timed it right, he might be able to hit Martini and take him down, but would that help Madison? He tensed.

"Don't," Martini said, looking him dead in the eye. Jake remained silent but let Martini lead him in the door.

It took a moment for Jake's eyes to adjust to the dim lighting in the warehouse. The few lights that were on cast shadows more than they illuminated anything. Madison, Casini, and Fedorov were standing in a semi-circle in the middle of the floor. Martini walked him over to join them. Then he and Casini stepped off to the side. Jake moved so he was between Madison and Fedorov.

"What are we waiting for?" Fedorov asked. "We need to get on with it. He knows where the necklace is. I want it, and then you can kill them both."

Neither cop moved nor said a word.

"Okay, give me my gun, and I will kill them, but let's get started. I have things to do."

"Mr. Fedorov," a voice echoed from the shadows, "please be patient."

The sound of footsteps on the concrete floor reached Jake's ears, and he turned slightly to the right. He positioned himself so he was in front of Madison. She started to move, but he growled, "Stay behind me."

Madison froze and then peered out from behind his left shoulder.

"Who the fuck are you?" Fedorov demanded. "I thought we covered this." He glared over at Casini. "I'm working with your boss, Captain DiCerbo. These are the people that stole the necklace. We need to find out where they've hidden it."

"I see," the voice said, getting louder. "Why should I give a fuck about some necklace?" The man walked into the light. He was tall, over six feet by a couple of inches and muscular without being fat. He was too far away for Jake to see eye color, but he noted the black hair and that there were no obvious scars or tattoos visible. He was wearing an expensive suit, gray with a white pinstripe and a stark white shirt.

Fedorov glared at the man. "Who the fuck are you?"

The man smiled. "Who I am is less important at the moment than who I am not." The man waved his left hand, and Casini and Martini stepped forward, bringing two men with them. One was medium height with medium dark brown hair that was curly. He wore it long in the Italian style. He was wearing a light-colored suit. The other was slightly shorter and a bit heavier in the middle. His hair was shorter and a lighter color.

Madison gasped behind him.

Fedorov stiffened.

"I'm not some small-time thug who answers to these men. Nor do I answer to Captain DiCerbo." He turned and faced the two men. "Giovanni, Marcello, why don't you tell me again how you don't know this man, Fedorov? I think he was just talking about your necklace."

The taller one with the longer hair answered, "Oh, right. We know him. He called himself Petrov. I didn't know him as Fedorov."

These were the Veridani brothers. Jake studied them. They were uncomfortable, scared even. Who was this guy?

"I see. Well, now you know his real name. Perhaps now you can tell me about the money you're laundering for the Russians?"

"We—that is, he—was just recommended to us." The tall one turned to his brother. "Wasn't he, Marcello? He is our head of security. We don't know anything about some other bosses."

"Sadly, I think that is true. You should have known. He works for the Russian mob. The same one you launder money for. I would imagine your friend Dimitry recommended him to you so he could keep an eye on you."

Marcello looked at Giovanni and swallowed. "We wouldn't know anything about that. We're a fashion house. We don't have anything to do with laundering money." Marcello raised his hands in the air in a helpless gesture.

"Marcello, I don't have time for your ignorant *cazzate*." Marcello flinched at the man's harsh tone. "You and I both know you've been laundering money for the Russians through your charitable organizations. I'm sure it started small and then blossomed into something beyond what you anticipated. I don't give a fuck."

Marcello snapped his jaw shut.

"My people are not pleased with you, Marcello, or you, Giovanni. You are cleaning Russian money when you should be cleaning Italian money. Where's your sense of civic duty?"

Giovanni said "We…that is—"

"Shut up. You will now start laundering money for my people. We will give you a small percentage for your troubles."

"But what about the Russians? We can't just stop. They won't let us," Marcello whined.

"I'll take care of the Russians."

Fedorov snorted and muttered something in Russian. "You think they will just go away? No. They will go to war before they will just disappear."

The man smiled. "Perhaps, but I am quite sure they would rather lose a few dollars than spend the rest of their lives in jail."

Fedorov chuckled. "You think they live here? You'll never reach them."

"I think I can have your boss Aleksandr arrested in his house in Spain or his place in Atlanta. I could also just have him killed along with his mistress in Monte Carlo. So many choices."

The smile fell off Fedorov's face. His eyes narrowed.

Jake had started to move backward just slightly. A little bit at a time. Madison understood and moved slowly, too. If they could get far enough back and they could make a run to the shadows, they might have a chance.

"Your boss and I have met a few times. I feel sure we can come to…an understanding. What is important for you to know is your services are no longer required."

Jake tensed. If the man or one of the cops shot Fedorov in front of them, then they would be killed for sure. They weren't far enough away to make a break for it. They would never make it. He searched the room, looking for something, anything, that might help them.

Slight movement in a shadowy corner snagged his attention. He peered through the murky light. A man moved ever so slightly, letting the light hit his face. Hawk! Then he eased back into the shadows again.

Jake turned to face the man directly. The man in the gray suit smiled slightly when their gazes locked. *Son of a bitch*. This had to be Enzo Valardi, Drake's former best friend and one of the most powerful mob bosses in Italy, or he used to be before he retired. Relief flooded his veins. Madison would be okay. It sucked that he couldn't be her superhero, but he was just damned glad she would get out of this alive. It was a nice bonus that he would live as well.

Valardi nodded to the two cops. "Gentleman, please remove Mr. Fedorov. His presence is no longer required."

Martini and Casini stepped forward. In seconds, they had Fedorov bound and gagged. They walked him out of the warehouse at gunpoint. Jake was happy to see they were taking no chances.

Valardi turned to the Veridani brothers. "My people are very upset with you. It will take them a long time to get over this betrayal. I would suggest you do your best to make amends. You don't want them to think your presence is also no longer required."

Both men nodded vigorously and started walking toward the door.

"Lest you should think about running, my man Carmine will take over as your head of security. He will keep an eye on you and everything else." Valardi paused. "Don't do anything stupid."

Jake was willing to bet that was the only warning they were going to get. The Veridani brothers left the warehouse at almost a run.

When the door closed, Jake turned back to face the man. "Enzo Valardi, I presume."

The man in the gray suit grinned and pulled out a key. He moved toward them.

Madison gasped. "Are you fucking serious?" She stared at Jake. "Did you know the whole time?"

Jake shook his head. "No, I had no clue until I saw Hawk over there."

"Thane is here?" She whirled around as Hawk stepped out of the gloom. "I fucking hate you all. I thought I was going to die. Worse, I thought Jake was going to die! Why didn't you say something, or at least give me a signal or something? Jesus Christ!"

"I'm sorry, Monty," Hawk said. "We thought it was better if you didn't know. It all had to appear real."

Enzo snorted as he unlocked Jake's cuffs. "It was real. There was nothing fake about any of it."

"Wait, you mean the Veridanis aren't going to prison for money laundering?" Madison rubbed her wrists after Enzo undid her cuffs.

"No. They will continue to launder money. They'll just do it for the Italian bosses versus the Russians."

Jake couldn't move his left arm at all. It hung limply by his side. He stumbled a bit.

"Jake!" Madison said as she immediately went to him and put an arm around his waist. "We have to get him to the hospital!"

Enzo nodded. "I have a car outside." Hawk moved Madison out of the way and draped Jake's right arm around his shoulder. He half-carried Jake out to the parking lot where an SUV with darkened windows was waiting. He helped settle Jake in the backseat and then got out.

"Hawk." Jake stopped him. "Thanks, man."

Hawk nodded. "You'd do the same."

Jake lifted his chin. "Valardi, I owe you one."

Enzo's grin was wicked and satisfied. "I'll remember that."

Madison climbed into the SUV next to Jake and slammed the door. "I don't know whether to hug those two or break their noses."

Pain ripped through Jake as he laughed. He groaned. "Please don't make me laugh. It makes my shoulder hurt." He grinned at her and then closed his eyes and lost consciousness.

CHAPTER TWENTY-SIX

Madison paced across the room for the umpteenth time. The doctor was in with Jake. After he passed out in the SUV, they'd driven to a farmhouse out in the Tuscan countryside. No matter how much she pleaded with the driver, he steadfastly refused to go to the hospital. He told Madison that she needn't worry, Jake would be taken care of, but that only frightened her more.

Enzo Valardi was an intimidating son of a bitch. She couldn't believe that the Veridanis weren't going to jail. That she wouldn't have to testify. That she and Jake were still alive. Was that a temporary thing? What if Valardi decided they were a risk to him and his associates?

Jesus, was she going to spend the rest of her life looking over her shoulder?

She was shocked that Thane had gone along with everything. Valardi implied that those policemen were going to kill Fedorov. It didn't bother her too much that Fedorov would be dead, but she didn't want to be a party to it.

She couldn't get over that Thane wasn't more upset about it. He was a lawyer. Wasn't he supposed to care? He was also an ex-Navy

SEAL. There was probably something in that, but it was too much for her to unpack at the moment and, quite frankly, Thane wasn't her concern. What he had on his conscience was his responsibility. Not hers.

Jake, on the other hand, was totally her responsibility. He'd taken a bullet for her. He'd put himself in mortal peril *for her*. The worst part was she loved him for it. Not just for that, but because of the way he made her feel about herself and everything else. He was kind and smart and he made her laugh. He was also tough and strong and made her feel safe in a way no other man had. So, how come they couldn't ride off into the sunset together like lovers did in the movies?

Because—she turned and stared out at the vineyards below—they were from two different worlds with difficult jobs and complicated lives. No matter how much she liked, or even loved him, her life was too difficult to nurture a relationship. The traveling she did, not to mention, she didn't do well with people in her space. She swallowed. The truth was she hated having anyone depend on her, and his entire job was having people depend on him. They were polar opposites, and in this case, no matter how much they were attracted to each other, it just wasn't sustainable long term.

Madison straightened her shoulders when she heard footsteps in the hallway. A little man approached her and smiled. He was short with a big pot belly and snow-white hair. If he had a beard, he'd be the perfect Santa Claus.

Madison asked him, "How is he, Doctor?"

"He'll be fine. He needs rest and plenty of fluids, but the wound is clean, and I gave him several pints of blood. I will come back and check on him tomorrow. He said he doesn't want pain medicine, but I left a bottle on the nightstand. Two pills, if he requires them. No more than that and at least six hours apart. You can go in and see him but please try to keep him quiet. He needs all the rest he can get for the next few days."

Madison nodded. "Okay, I'll do my best. Thank you." She frowned. Was she supposed to pay the man? "Um, do I—?"

The jolly little man smiled and touched her hand. "It's all taken care of, *signorina*. Don't you worry." He nodded at her and then took his leave.

Madison walked down the hallway to Jake's room. She didn't enter but leaned on the doorjamb. Jake lay back on the pillows with his eyes closed. His color had improved slightly, but he still looked pale to her. There were dark shadows underneath his eyes, and the lines in his forehead were deeper than when they'd first met a week ago. His left shoulder was swathed in bandages, but he appeared to be okay. The doctor had taken out the IV drip.

"Are you going to stand there and stare at me all day?"

Madison chuckled. "No, just for the next few minutes. Then I'm going to pour myself a scotch."

"Sounds good. Pour one for me, too."

"No." Madison moved into the room and sat down on a wooden chair beside the bed. "How are you feeling?"

"Like shit."

She smiled. "The doctor left some pain meds if you want them."

He opened his eyes. "I'm good. I hate pain meds. They make me feel worse. Did I hear Hawk's voice earlier?"

"Yes, he's here. He's on the phone but will come in and see you shortly. I think he's working out some details with Valardi on something. That guy is…scary as hell."

Jake smiled. "Yeah, I'm glad he's on our side."

"But is he, though? I mean he's not turning the Veridani brothers in or anything. They'll just be scamming people and laundering money for the Italians instead of the Russians."

"Actually," Thane said as he entered the room, "they won't be scamming anyone anymore. That's what I was talking to Enzo about. He thinks, and I agree, that not doing anything charitable was a stupid mistake. They were bound to get found out eventually. If you want to run a good money laundering scheme, you actually have the business do what it says it does."

"So what does that mean in this case?" Madison asked.

"It means that Enzo will get his people to clean up the Hope For Kids Foundation, and it will actually start doing the charity work they've been claiming they did."

Jake shifted on the bed slightly and winced. "But then how will they launder the money?"

Madison snorted. "There are so many ways to launder money, Jake. If you're smart and know the rules, you can do all kinds of creative things."

Thane nodded. "Plus, Valardi can still send more cash to the charity than they legitimately spend. It's the same setup, but the money that other people donate at the fundraisers will actually be used to help children."

Madison sighed. "I'm still not sure if that makes things better. The Veridanis are still in business although, unless they change their focus a bit, I'm not sure they'll last that long. Their designs are…not stellar, at least not to me."

Thane laughed. "Enzo said the same thing. He said their designs are shit, and he would be hiring some new talent to start taking the company in a new direction."

A small pulse of electricity ran across her skin. She could submit some designs and see what Valardi thought. She had a good shot, considering all she knew.

What the fuck was she thinking? Blackmailing a mobster to get a leg up in the design world was a fucking moronic idea. It had to be the lack of sleep and all the craziness getting to her, but it did bring up another point.

"Thane," she said, "did Valardi mention anything about me? I mean, I know what's going on. We all do. Is that going to be a problem for him? Is he…?"

"Going to want to frame you for theft or kill you over it?" Thane finished for her. "No. We have a deal. None of us say anything, and he leaves us alone. Drake assured him of our cooperation, and I agree. There's no upside for us coming forward now. There were never any charges against you, so the whole thing will be swept under the proverbial rug."

Madison nodded and let out a long breath. It was good news. Relief flooded her veins, releasing the knots in her shoulders. A thought struck her. "What about the necklace?"

Thane smiled. "I gave Enzo the fake they had made to frame you with, and he gave it to the Veridani brothers. It is now back on display in the offices. They made up a story about it being taken for cleaning and no one knew. It was all a misunderstanding."

"But the real one is still in Mugello in that vase." Madison willed the heat out of her cheeks, but it was hopeless once Thane and Jake started laughing.

"Ouch. It's good to laugh," Jake chuckled then winced, "but it makes my shoulder hurt."

"Funny." Madison glared at the two men.

Thane grinned at her. "Enzo told Marcello and Giovanni the loss of the necklace was the cost of doing business with the Russians instead of the Italians. So I say we just leave it where it is. We know where to find it, should the need arise. It's perfectly safe there."

"I agree." Jake smiled at Madison. "Even if someone finds it, there will have been hundreds of people through there since, so it can't be linked to us. Besides, what would we do with it? Give it back to the people who tried to frame you for stealing it?"

Madison cocked her head. "I guess you're right. It just seems so… wild to leave a necklace worth over five million euro in an old vase."

"Oh, I don't know," Thane said. "These types of things have been happening for centuries. Jewels, paintings, some of the world's most interesting treasures, have turned up in the oddest of places." He smiled. "Anyway, I have to make some calls."

He started to leave when Madison asked, "What's going to happen with the Russians? I mean, where's Fedorov, and will the Russians just let the Italians take over?"

Thane turned back and met her gaze. His expression was serious. "There are some questions that shouldn't be asked. None of that is our business. I have no interest in knowing the answer to any of those questions, and neither should you."

Madison nodded. Message received. It was none of her business, and if she wanted to stay alive, then don't ask the questions. A small shiver rippled across her body. Easy enough.

With a quick wave, Thane left the room.

She faced Jake. Leaning forward in her chair, she took his hand. "Thank you for saving my life." She wanted him to know just how much she appreciated all he did for her. 'Thank you' seemed so…inadequate.

"I'm not sure I did that. It was Hawk and Valardi—"

"No. It was you. You took a bullet for me. I will never, ever forget that."

"Madison, I made a lot of mistakes on this assignment. I think maybe…" He paused and shook his head slightly. "Anyway, I wanted to apologize for my actions. I took advantage of you when you were vulnerable." She started to protest but he raised his right hand to wave her off. His lips compressed before he continued. "I did. I should have had the strength to say no. To put your safety first above my…own needs, and I didn't. I have to live with that, but it's a tough nut to swallow. I've been doing this work a long time, and to fuck up so spectacularly is…rough."

"Jake, really it was all my fault. I—"

"No, it wasn't. You were my responsibility, and I dropped the ball. I broke the cardinal rule: never get involved with the client. It's there for a reason, and breaking it could have caused a lot of bad shit. Anyway, I wanted to apologize, and I want to ask you a favor. If you could go now, that would be…good."

"Go?" Madison's voice cracked a little on the word. Her stomach knotted. She'd planned on staying another day or two just to make sure Jake truly was okay. He was here because of her.

"Yes, Madison. I need you to leave if that's okay. I need to get some…distance from what happened. Seeing you won't let me do that."

The sudden, physical pain in her chest was proof a heart could shatter. Even though she'd come in here to do the same thing basically, his words were devastating to hear—he didn't want her here. She'd told herself their ultimate separation was for the best, but she still had a few more days to enjoy Jake's company. Now he was asking her to go. She swallowed a lump of tears that filled her throat.

"Of course." It came out as a whisper. She cleared her throat. "I'll go. I need to get back to New York anyway. I think Drake has another job for me. Hopefully, it's in the U.S. this time. I think I've had enough of Europe for a while." She smiled.

"Thanks, Madison." He gave her hand a quick squeeze and then closed his eyes and turned his head away.

CHAPTER TWENTY-SEVEN

Jake cursed as he pulled a navy T-shirt over his head. His shoulder hurt like a bitch. He'd gotten back to New York City the previous evening, and he was going in to see Mitch this morning. He sat down to pull on his shoes. He had never realized how much he used his left hand until it was out of commission.

He sat up and glanced around his apartment. He'd picked this place because it had a view of the Hudson River, not that he was here much to enjoy it. The apartment had an air of neglect. It was a nice size one-bedroom unit in a pre-war building, meaning it had thick walls and larger rooms than the new modern buildings going up all over the city.

Jake had no idea what this day would bring. Would he be fired? Had Madison filed a complaint? God knew, she should. He'd done a spectacularly bad job of taking care of her. She had every right to sue him and the firm for sexual harassment as well as failure to perform the duties he was hired to do. Which was ironic because he'd had no problem performing the thing he shouldn't have been doing.

He shook his head. No point in dwelling on the past. Madison was gone. Probably on her next assignment somewhere. He was sure she was wrapped up in her job and he didn't even cross her mind.

She, however, never seemed to leave his. He got up, grabbed his jacket, and left his apartment.

The future awaited.

"Six weeks! Are you fucking kidding me? What in the hell am I going to do for six weeks?" Jake fumed.

Mitch sat across the desk from his best friend and shook his head. "Heal. You said you were burnt out and needed a break. Now you're shot to boot. You need some serious downtime. Six weeks."

"Where am I going to go for a month and a half? I'll go crazy if I have to stay in my apartment that long."

"Go south," Mitch suggested. "Pick an island. Drink beer and lay in the sun. Find some woman to take pity on you and look after you."

The thought of six weeks on a beach with a willing female was only appealing if the woman was Madison, and that wasn't going to happen. "Mitch, can't we just discuss the future? You said you wanted to talk about it."

"No. We're not discussing anything now. Go. Relax. Enjoy. I have too much to do right now, anyway, to get into it. That's a much longer conversation and"—Mitch hesitated—"it's just not something I can get into right now." He glanced at his watch. "I've got another meeting. See you in six weeks."

Jake's gut knotted. He felt like he'd been sucker-punched. Mitch had just dismissed him. That had never happened before. He stood.

Mitch's face was blank.

"See you in six weeks," Jake mumbled and then found his way to the door.

He had decided to walk back to his apartment, but about halfway home, the heavens opened up, and by the time he got to his place, he was thoroughly soaked. This day had sucked. He was tired. His shoulder throbbed, and he still had no idea about his future. Now he had forty-two more days just like this one to look forward to before he sorted anything out.

Madison held up a dress to her frame and looked in the mirror. It was a deep green, and it made her eyes pop. The stylish A-line stopped above the knee. She swished it around a bit. "Nope, too flirty," she said to herself and then sighed. It was supposed to be flirty. She was going on a date. The whole point was to flirt, except she didn't want to. She didn't even want to go on the date. Her best friend, Meghan, was forcing her to go.

"It will be fun," she'd said. "It will help you get over this Jake character."

Except she didn't want to get over Jake. It had only been a month. She wasn't ready to move on yet.

She'd promised herself that she would make an effort to sort out her life once she got back to New York. Less travel for work. More time to spend developing her designs and working toward the career in fashion that she'd always wanted. If she learned one thing from her time in Florence, it was that life didn't happen in the past or in the future; life happened now, and if she didn't start doing what she wanted to today, she wouldn't ever achieve her goals.

She stared at the dress. *Why not?* She might as well wear it. Meghan was right. She really did need to move on from Jake. She was tired of thinking about him and even more exhausted from missing him. She needed to carve the loss out of her life. Mourn it and move on. She didn't have to marry this guy, Steve, or was it Will? She couldn't remember. She would text Meghan again and ask. A night out might do her a world of good.

Her phone rang. She glanced at the screen. *Why would they be calling?*

She hit the answer button. "Hello?"

CHAPTER TWENTY-EIGHT

Jake cursed as he opened the bulletproof glass doors to the Callahan Security's offices in New York. It was pouring again, and he was drenched. It had been sunny when he left his apartment, but it didn't seem like he could catch a break.

He smiled at the woman seated behind the front desk. "Hey, Abigail. How are you?"

"Hey, Jake. I'm good. Looks like you could use a towel."

"Yeah. I didn't think it was supposed to rain today." He shook water off his head and took off his navy suit jacket. His light blue shirt was wet on the front where the rain had hit his chest. His shoes were drenched, as were the bottom of his pants. If this had been a normal day, he would've run up to the gym on the fourth floor and grabbed some sweats out of his locker.

Today, however, was day forty-three. The day he and Mitch were going to discuss his future. He'd dressed in a suit to show he was taking this seriously. He hadn't felt this unsure of himself since he'd joined the Navy. His gut rolled and his shoulder throbbed.

He smiled at the receptionist. "I'll just grab some paper towels from the restroom. Is Mitch in his office?"

She nodded. "Yes, he's in."

He pushed the button for the elevator and looked around the lobby. It was small and intimate. There were two stools behind the tall desk with Abigail filling one of them. The desk had a gleaming wooden surface. The lighting was soft. The walls were a mixture of gray and beige. The artwork was a mash-up of modern and classic pieces, but all of them were originals. This had been his work home since he'd gotten out of the Navy. He wasn't prepared to be homeless now.

The elevator doors opened, and he said a small prayer and entered.

Five minutes later, he was sitting in the chair across the desk from Mitch. Gage was sitting next to him, and Logan was resting his butt on the corner of Mitch's desk. Having all of them in the room wouldn't normally bother Jake. It happened all the time, but this, this felt different.

"How's the shoulder?" Gage asked.

Jake nodded. "Not bad." It wouldn't help to lie. He'd used the staff doctor, and he had no doubts the doctor would report back to the brothers. It was part of the contract he'd signed when he'd joined Callahan Security. "It's still a bit stiff, but the doctor says it will be back to one-hundred percent in no time."

"Good to hear." Gage smiled. "That was a hell of a thing in Italy. Jesus. We certainly didn't see that coming when Drake called and asked us to look out for his accountant."

"Yeah, it was…unexpected." What the fuck was he supposed to say? Had Madison complained? *Oh, shit.* Had Drake said something?

Logan looked down at him. "We're just glad it worked out. You and Monty are safe. That's what matters."

Jake glanced around the room. All three men were staring at him. Finally, he couldn't take it anymore. "What? What the hell is going on? Are you firing me? Do I have some sort of disease I don't know about? You're all staring at me like I'm some sort of alien."

Mitch burst out laughing. "Sorry, buddy. We're just happy you're okay."

"And truth be told, maybe a little nervous ourselves," Logan said.

"Nervous? Why would you be nervous?" Jake was totally confused now.

Gage turned his chair to face Jake's. "Look, Jake, you've been here since the beginning, so you know what it's like. We've been expanding rapidly in all sorts of directions, sometimes faster than we'd like. That has caused some problems."

Logan sighed. "We haven't been as diligent in monitoring some of our employees as we should have been. Some assignments haven't gone as well as we'd hoped."

Jake clamped his jaw shut and squeezed the arms of his chair. This was it. He just had to sit there and let the axe fall on his career.

Mitch rolled a pencil back and forth on his desk. "We need to rectify the situation as quickly as possible." He locked gazes with Jake. "Starting with you."

Jake couldn't breathe. He had no idea what he was going to do without this place. It had given him a home and a reason to be. He would be lost without it. He opened his mouth, but just as quickly, he closed it again. He had nothing to say. No defense. He'd broken every rule with Madison and done a piss-poor job. He deserved to be fired.

"Jake," Logan said in a calm voice, "my brothers and I would like to offer you the position of CEO of our European Division."

"I understand. I'll clean out—" He stuttered to a halt, unable to get his brain around what Mitch had just said. "I—I'm sorry, come again?"

Mitch grinned. "I told you he wasn't expecting it. What my pain-in-the-butt brother is saying is we're in over our heads, and we need a chance to dig ourselves out, but we can't do it alone. We need someone to take on the European office while we get everything ironed out. We want you to be that guy. You know your shit, and you've been doing my paperwork since we were in the SEALs together. We know you can handle it."

Gage nodded. "Of course, you'll get all the salary and benefits that come with the position." He paused. "You will have to move to London, but we'll rent you a flat and give you a car to drive, or you can have a driver if you prefer. Driving on the left takes some getting used to."

"So, what do you say, brother?" Mitch asked as he threw a balled-up piece of paper at Jake's chest.

Logan shook his head. "It's a lot to process. Give him a chance to think about it." He turned to Jake. "If you could let us know by the end of the—"

"Are you fucking kidding me? Of course I'll take it." Jake's smile was so big his cheeks hurt. He couldn't have stopped grinning if his life depended on it. He was so damn happy he couldn't believe it. He'd thought he was out of a job for sure, and now he had a whole new life ahead of him. Him a CEO? Jesus. He didn't see that coming.

"When do you need me there?"

"A couple of weeks." Logan smiled. "We already have some people in place in the office that can help you with things. You'll meet them when you get there. You have an executive assistant who will walk you through things and help you get settled."

Jake just nodded. It was overwhelming, but he was so fucking happy.

Logan stood and offered his hand. Jake rose and shook it and then did the same with Gage and Mitch. Mitch then pulled off his tie. "Now that that's over with, let's go get a drink. We need to celebrate!"

Jake couldn't agree more.

CHAPTER TWENTY-NINE

Six Weeks Later

Jake stood at the window overlooking the Thames. He couldn't believe this was his new apartment. *Flat.* Mitch knew he liked looking at the Hudson so he'd made sure they'd rented one for Jake that had a view of London's famous waterway. *"Help with the homesickness,"* he'd said.

It was funny, Jake didn't feel homesick. Oh, there were lots of things that he'd have to adjust to. Who knew crossing the street would rank up there as one of the more difficult things in London? He kept looking the wrong way.

Still, the shine had gone off New York, and now he had a new place to explore. New people to meet and a new business to run.

Logan had flown over and introduced him to everyone a month ago. They were an interesting bunch, and he had to admit he was impressed by their resumés. He felt a little intimidated, if he were being totally honest, but everyone so far had been nice and easy to work with. He thought, given enough time, he could make them into a good team.

Callahan Europe wasn't like the New York office in that it wasn't as big and, although busy, not crazy. He'd already gone over their current client list and had spoken to every operator they had. He'd offered some tips on how to improve things on certain jobs and helped out when a few of them were down with a stomach bug. All in all, he was feeling it would work out nicely.

He took a sip of his bourbon and glanced at his watch. His new Chief Financial Officer was supposed to be here in a few minutes. That had been the one thing he'd been most nervous about. He could figure out the paperwork and make sure the office ran smoothly, but no way could he do numbers. They were beyond him. They just swam on the page in front of him.

Logan hadn't been very forthcoming about the new hire. All he said was that they came highly recommended. Jake hoped they would be easy to work with and not be assholes about his numbers issue. Mitch knew about Jake's problem, and he was sure Mitch had told his brothers, so he wasn't worried that the CFO was going to cause problems exactly, more he just didn't want to feel like an idiot around the numbers guy.

He shrugged. If the guy turned out to be an asshole, he could always fire his ass. That made him grin. He could fire people. Never before had he ever been in a position that he could boot some dickhead who drove him crazy. It was a good feeling.

The doorbell rang. It was slightly strange to be meeting at his apartment, but Logan had set it up so Jake went along with it. What was he going to say? No? Not bloody likely, as the Brits liked to say.

Jake walked through his living room out into the hallway and down to the front door. He opened the door and stopped dead.

Madison smiled. "Hi, Jake."

"Madison." It came out as a croak. He cleared his throat. "How are you?"

"I'm good. How are you?" she asked. When he just stared at her, she finally said, "Are you going to invite me in?"

"Um, yeah. Sorry, please come in." He stepped back and waved her in and then closed the door after her. He led the way down the wide hallway and then off to the right into the living room. "Can I pour you a drink?"

"That would be good." She nodded. "What an incredible view!"

"Yes, it is. It's one of the many things I like about this apartment." He went over to the bar area in the far corner of the room opposite the floor-to-ceiling windows. "Flat, I guess I should say."

Madison laughed. He loved the sound of her laugh. He'd almost forgotten how the tinkle of it made him smile. "Bourbon okay?" he asked. He'd switched to bourbon after the move. Scotch was made here. Bourbon was made back home. She nodded and he poured two fingers of bourbon into her glass and added some ice. He walked back over and gave her the glass.

"Cheers," she said and held up her glass. He saw it shake slightly. Good, he was glad he wasn't the only one nervous.

"Cheers," he repeated, and they clinked glasses. Each took a healthy sip of their drinks. Jake pointed to the couch, and Madison took a seat. "So, you're my new CFO."

"Yes." Her smile was more hesitant than before. "I mean, if you're okay with it." She set her drink down on the coaster on the table in front of her. "I brought my resumé, if you want to see it. I asked Logan not to tell you beforehand because I wanted a chance to explain, and I guess…pitch my services before you turned me down." She dug around in the bag that she'd brought with her.

Jake kept his face blank. Madison was always so forthright and direct. He loved that about her. She looked fucking fantastic. Her glossy long hair hung down over her shoulders. Her hazel eyes wore a look of concern, but the dark circles were gone and the fine lines around her mouth were light. Her forest green blouse clung in all the right places, and he'd already noticed that her black skirt hugged her delicious ass. And those boots. They made him smile. Those boots had landed her in his lap. He had no complaints about those.

But as a whole, working with her was going to be a problem. She was right to think he would have turned her down if he'd known she wanted the job. There was no way he could work with her day in and day out and not be with her. It would be a form of torture, and he was not that much of a masochist.

"Madison—"

"Here," she said, producing her resumé. "I have a lot of experience, and I know—"

"Madison," he growled, "stop. I'm sure you have the right qualifications. Logan would not have hired you if he didn't think you could do the job. That's not the issue." He stood up and put his hands in the pockets of his light gray suit. "I thought you were thinking of working in fashion. Becoming a designer. This job would be a far cry from that."

She hesitated. "Yes, but it's a step forward financially for me. Plus, I would be much closer to the center of the industry here in Europe."

He walked over to stand in front of the window. He ground his teeth. He had to tell the truth. "I can't work with you because of our previous…interactions." He turned to face her. He had to explain it face-to-face. That was only right.

"I can't, in good conscience, agree to you working with me when I would be constantly fighting my desire to have you. I still…want you, Madison. Badly. I miss you more than I thought possible. It would be torture to work next to you and not be part of your life outside of business." He sighed. "I just can't. I wish I was stronger but…I'm not."

"I see," she said and then stood up. She crossed her arms over her chest. "Here's the thing, Jake. I want you, too. I haven't stopped thinking about you either. I can't seem to…get over you. You haunt me, and I can't figure out a way to exorcise you from my life, so I think the best thing to do is to have you *in* my life." She looked up at him through her lashes.

Jake's heart stuttered. He couldn't believe what he was hearing. Was she serious? "Are you saying that you want to date me or work with me? I'm confused."

"I'm saying I want both, Jake. Within reason." Madison clasped her hands in front of her.

Here it comes. His gut knotted. He'd been overjoyed when she'd said she wanted to be back in his life, but he should have known there would be a catch. "Okay, what does that mean?" It had come out angrier than he'd meant but, dammit, she couldn't say she wanted him in one breath and then say maybe not in the next.

"It means I am not great at relationships, as I think I might have mentioned before, and due to my history with my mother, I tend to panic when someone starts to depend on me too much. So I was thinking if we take it slow, maybe we can make a go of it."

Jake tried very hard to keep the smile off his face. His spirits soared at her words. He took a step toward her. "So maybe we're together two or three nights a week." He took another step. "Maybe we have dinner, go see a movie. That type of thing."

She nodded and bit her lip as he took yet another step toward her. "And would this agreement include sex?" he asked. His voice was low and growly and raspy. Damn, if he wasn't getting hard just thinking about having her.

Madison dropped her arms to her sides. "Er, yes, that would be part of the deal."

Jake took another step so he was directly in front of her. "I see." He was about to kiss her when his last ounce of self-preservation kicked in. "But wait, you want to work with me, and you also want to be my girlfriend?" He gave her a hard look. "It would have to be my 'girlfriend' because I won't share you."

She nodded, and her lips parted ever so slightly.

"You want to be my girlfriend and my CFO?"

"Yes." It came out as a whisper.

He leaned back. "I'm not sure that's a good idea. I have a history of not doing my job where you're concerned." The words were so painful his chest hurt.

He wanted her so damn badly. Wanted to spend time with her. Wanted to hear her laugh and make her smile but he also loved his new job. It made him feel like he was finally good enough. He didn't want to give that up either. And the sexual harassment lawsuit this would open the company up to was huge. He couldn't do that to Mitch or his brothers. He just couldn't. He shook his head. "The human resources implications alone would be a nightmare."

"Um, about that." A guilty look crossed her face. "So Gage, Logan, and Mitch already know about us."

Jake froze. "Do they? How did that happen, and what exactly do they know?"

"Well, you see, Dani and I got together for drinks like we said we would, and well…she started asking questions, and I sort of had a meltdown after a few cocktails." She paused and pushed her hair behind her ear. "Okay, a lot of cocktails, and I confessed that we'd slept together and that I'm in love with you and miss you like crazy and she suggested I come here and see you but I pointed out that I needed a job in order to do that and with my current job the travel would just be too much. So she went to Gage and he went to Logan who then went to Mitch and then the three of them went to Drake." She sucked in a breath then rushed on. "And he assured them I could definitely do the job so they offered it to me with the caveat that you had to agree to it and we both had to sign paperwork to the effect that we're in a relationship outside of the company and we can't sue for any kind of sexual harassment. I have the papers in my bag."

Jake stuck out his hand. Madison blinked and then bent down and dug out the papers. She stood and handed the paperwork over to Jake. He took it and read the first page. He skimmed the second page and the third. He walked over, grabbed a pen off the table in the corner, and came back to stand in front of her. He put the last page against his leg and signed on the signature line. He handed the paperwork back to her. "I expect you to be at work bright and early tomorrow morning."

"Okay, but does that mean we're…?" Her voice died out.

"I also expect you to be in my bed tonight." He offered his hand.

Madison grinned and shook his hand. He pulled her hard, and she fell against his chest. He wrapped his arms around her and captured her mouth with a scorching kiss.

"I love you, too, Madison," he said.

She looped her arms around his neck. "I think we might have to renegotiate the deal. Two to three nights a week isn't going to be enough."

The End

Keep reading for a sneak peek at *Diverted*, Book 1 in the Coast Guard RECON Series

SNEAK PEEK: DIVERTED
COAST GUARD RECON BOOK 1

About The Book

Nick Taggert was injured on his last assignment for the Coast Guard. Now, too hurt to go back to his former position and not wounded enough to be benched, he's assigned as the new Coast Guard team leader in…Panama. They're there as part of a drug interdiction unit, but really, they're Team RECON. Recon as in reconstructed. Each of the four men is like him; a Humpty Dumpty. Except they were trying to put themselves back together so they could do what they loved best, kicking ass and taking names.

Dr. Carolina Alvarez had moved on from research and was working for Doctors Without Borders. A chance meeting with her old boss set her on a dangerous mission to deliver much-needed medicine to South America. Her failure would mean the sure extinction of a tribe clinging to their ancient ways.

Nick should have realized from the instant Carolina walked back into his life things would not go according to plan. But harbored resentment still clouded his vision. Now they were on the trail of the missing vaccine, and the assignment just turned deadly

DIVERTED: PROLOGUE

February 9th, 2021

Alejandro Garcia glanced at his watch and seethed. He abhorred tardiness, and the man was late. Stirring his coffee, he watched people stroll by the cafe window. He, unlike most of the world, hated Paris, especially in January. The cold invaded his bones, and gray skies hung heavy overhead. Even the Eiffel Tower looked dirty and dingy in the falling mist.

Garcia sighed. He found the French to be tedious. They thought too highly of themselves, and their lack of work ethic astounded him. The constant rioting about trivial things illustrated a society too pampered to be taken seriously. He had no idea why the French government tolerated such behavior.

He rechecked his timepiece and took a sip from his cup. However, they did serve excellent coffee, and for that, he was willing to forgive quite a bit.

A black car pulled up to the curb. The driver came around and opened the door. A tall distinguished-looking gentleman emerged. "Finally," Garcia mumbled as his ten o'clock appointment entered the café twenty minutes late.

Edward Langston approached the table, hand outstretched. "Sorry, I'm late. Ran into a traffic snarl. Protesters wouldn't let the car past."

Garcia stood and shook hands. "Of course. Please." He gestured toward the opposite chair. "May I get you something? Coffee perhaps?" It galled him to play host to this American, but it was a small price to pay for the benefits this man could provide to Garcia's country.

"I'm fine. Can't stay long." The men sat. "Look." Langston leaned forward. "Our agreement… I must say I have some misgivings."

Garcia ground his teeth. Langston couldn't back out now. Not when Garcia was so close to sealing his country's future on the world stage. "You don't want to run a live test of your experiment?"

"Of course, we want to run the test," Langston said. "Don't be stupid. I want to make sure you understand the risk you're taking. None of this can come out. Ever."

Garcia nodded. "Agreed. It would be bad for all of us and, yes, we understand the risk. Your mosquitoes will save millions of lives and change the world. We want to provide you with the opportunity to prove their efficacy. Many of our population are affected by mosquito-borne diseases; it is perfectly logical for you to test your theory in our country. As to the other part, that will remain a secret, I can assure you."

Langston hesitated before giving a curt nod. "We have a deal."

"When will the testing begin?"

Langston frowned. "Our people should be in place at the end of March, maybe slightly later. By the summer, we should know if it's working or not."

Garcia nodded again. "Good. The sooner, the better. No delays."

"Obviously," Langston snarled. "I'll be in touch when we're ready to go."

"Everything will be ready to proceed." Garcia forced a smile.

"Make sure it is. This is very important. To both sides."

Garcia's jaw ached. The American's attitude was insufferable. "It will be smooth on my end, I can assure you."

Langston studied him for a minute. "You're sure your boss is on board with this?"

"You need not worry, Mr. Langston. As I said, things will flow smoothly on my end." Garcia curled his hand around the coffee cup and squeezed. He would prefer if the cup were Langston's neck, but that was not in the cards. At least not yet. He reminded himself there must be sacrifice to achieve success. His day would come.

"Fine." Langston stood up, and Garcia rose with him. "I'll be in touch," Langston stated, then turned and exited the cafe. He got into his car and drove off.

Garcia returned to his seat and signaled the waiter, who brought another piping-hot coffee.

Americans. Another group Garcia hated. Not so different from the French. Always thinking they knew better and possessed the upper hand. Not this time. This time, Garcia had the advantage, and things were just as they should be.

DIVERTED: CHAPTER ONE

"Bring him over here, Muhammed!" Dr Carolina Alvarez pointed to the now empty table along the wall of the tent in the makeshift hospital. Two local men half carried half dragged the unconscious man between them over to Carolina and put him face down in front of her. The sound of sporadic gunfire erupted, but everyone in the tent ignored it.

"We found him washed up on the beach," stated Muhammed, the taller of the two. "We didn't want to just leave him there. It would not be right."

Carolina gave him a brief smile as Gabe, a nurse, came over and helped her move the injured soldier onto the table. The man was dressed in military fatigues so helping him could be risky for Muhammed and his son, but they were good people. They put politics and religion aside to help someone in need. Carolina had seen that a lot in Yemen. What the world was told about the Yemenese, and the truth of the matter wasn't even close. Of course, she'd found that was the way of it in most of the countries she'd worked in. Doctors Without Borders only went to places in need, and most of those countries had political problems.

"Thanks for rescuing him, Muhammed. Do you know where he

got shot?" Muhammed and his son Ahmed both shook their heads. The son was the spitting image of the father. It was like seeing double.

"He's not shot." Ahmed turned and mumbled something to his father in Arabic and then said, "Stabbed. In the back." It was hard to hear him over the din of voices in the tent.

Carolina helped Gabe turned the man onto his side. "Take his vitals," she said as she leaned over to see the injured man's back.

Muhammed cleared his throat. "We go now."

Carolina nodded. "*Shukran*, Muhammed," she said, trying to thank him in his own language but he was gone. Probably good he wasn't there to hear her butcher it.

There was a lot of blood soaking into the man's shirt. She peeled it back to reveal a long, deep gash that went right across the man's back from his right shoulder to his left hip. "Jesus. He was hacked, not stabbed." She peered closer at the wound. It was ugly and it was going to take a lot of work to fix. She cursed silently. A slash like this needed a plastic surgeon in a real hospital not a general surgeon in a makeshift hospital tent. She'd do what she could, but it wasn't going to be pretty. "Colin, I'm going to need your help!" Carolina didn't even look up as she yelled for the other doctor. "Gabe, how are his vitals?"

"They suck," he stated. "His pulse is weak and his pressure is low. His breathing is shallow."

"Hang a unit of blood and then grab the portable x-ray. I need to see if his ribs are broken."

Gabe quickly hooked the man up to the IV and then skirted the table and moved to the other end of the room.

"Colin?" Carolina called again as she noticed a birthmark on the man's right shoulder. It looked sort of like a four-leaf clover. Another flurry of gunfire sounded, drowning out Colin's answer. Just then the flap of the tent was pushed open wider, and a new group of injured were brought in.

"You're on your own," Colin called. "I'll take the new ones."

"Shit," Carolina mumbled. "Let's hope your birthmark is a sign you're lucky." *You're going to need it.*

Gabe came back with the portable x-ray and set it up. He quickly took pictures of the man's torso. After a brief pause, he consulted the tablet on the machine's stand. "Look like four broken ribs."

"That's not good. Okay, let's get his wound cleaned and stitch it up. But first we need to see if any of his organs were damaged either by the hacking or from the broken ribs." She leaned closer. "It looks like it missed his spine completely. This guy is lucky as hell. Half an inch more, and his spine would have been severed."

She heard a grunt and straightened, looking down at her patient's face. The lines on the exposed side of his face were etched into his skin and his eyes were open. They were a very distinctive shade of blue. Like the sky on a cold day in winter. "Hey, can you tell me your name?"

He remained silent, staring at her.

"Do you know where you are?"

He watched her but said nothing.

"Okay, well then, whoever you are. We're going to take care of you. I'm going to give you something for the pain, and then I'm going to stitch you up. You were very lucky."

He raised an eyebrow. "Lucky. Sure." He closed his eyes again.

A NOTE OF THANKS

YOU READ MY BOOK. You read the whole thing! I cannot thank you enough for sticking with me. If this is the first book of mine you've read, welcome aboard. I certainly hope it won't be the last! If you are already a fan then I can only say, thank you so much for your continued support! Either way, you have made my day, my week, my year! You have transported me from writer to *author*. I feel so special! You have made my dreams come true. Genuinely, truly, you are a fairy god-parent. So thank-you!

Now I'm hoping you love this new-found power of making dreams come true and, like a truly dedicated reader, you'll check out my other series, Coast Guard Recon and the Brotherhood Protectors World. You can find links to these books on my website, www.lorimatthews-books.com.

If you would like to try your hand at being a superhero, you can always help make me a bestselling author by leaving a review for **Catch and Release** on Amazon, (My Book) or Review On Goodreads or Review On BookBub. Reviews sell books and they make authors super happy. Did I say thank you already? Just in case I forgot, thank you soooo much.

And now that you are reveling in your superhero status, I would love it if you would stay in touch with me. I love my readers and I love doing giveaways and offering previews and extra content of my upcoming books. Come join the fun. You can follow me here:

Newsletter: Signup Form (constantcontactpages.com)
Website: www.lorimatthewsbooks.com
Facebook: https://www.facebook.com/LoriMatthewsBooks
Facebook: Romantic Thriller Readers (Author Lori Matthews) https://www.facebook.com/groups/killerromancereaders
Amazon Author Page: https://www.amazon.com/author/lorimatthews
Goodreads: https://www.goodreads.com/author/show/7733959.Lori_Matthews
Bookbub: https://www.bookbub.com/profile/lori-matthews
Instagram: https://www.instagram.com/lorimatthewsbooks/
Twitter: https://twitter.com/_LoriMatthews_

READ THESE OTHER EXCITING TITLES BY LORI MATTHEWS

Callahan Security
Break and Enter
Smash And Grab
Hit And Run
Evade and Capture
Catch and Release
Cease and Desist (Coming Soon)
Coast Guard Recon
Diverted
Incinerated
Conflicted
Subverted
Terminated
Brotherhood Protectors World
Justified Misfortune
Justified Burden
Free with Newsletter Sign Up
Falling For The Witness
Visit Https://www.lorimatthewsbooks.com for details on how to purchase these novels or sign up for my newsletter.

ABOUT LORI MATTHEWS

I grew up in a house filled with books and readers. Some of my fondest memories are of reading in the same room with my mother and sisters, arguing about whose turn it was to make tea. No one wanted to put their book down!

I was introduced to romance because of my mom's habit of leaving books all over the house. One day I picked one up. I still remember the cover. It was a Harlequin by Janet Daily. Little did I know at the time that it would set the stage for my future. I went on to discover mystery novels. Agatha Christie was my favorite. And then suspense with Wilber Smith and Ian Fleming.

I loved the thought of combining my favorite genres, and during high school, I attempted to write my first romantic suspense novel. I wrote the first four chapters and then exams happened and that was the end of that. I desperately hope that book died a quiet death somewhere in a computer recycling facility.

A few years later, (okay, quite a few) after two degrees, a husband and two kids, I attended a workshop in Tuscany that lit that spark for writing again. I have been pounding the keyboard ever since here in New Jersey, where I live with my children—who are thrilled with my writing as it means they get to eat more pizza—and my very supportive husband.

Please visit my webpage at https://lorimatthewsbooks.com to keep up on my news.